XOXO
LITTLE BUTTERFLY

I0769632

XOXO
LITTLE BUTTERFLY

🦋 🦋 🦋

N.J. ADEL

To naughty little butterflies who like to be
chased through the woods by 6'4" masked
men…
Are you still seeing that therapist?

Who are you kidding?

If you were seeing one, you'd give them a mask
and tell them to chase you through the woods
themselves to "cure" your "worst fear"
Just read on, bestie

CHAPTER 1

Birdie

Something isn't quite right.

My eyes snap open, and my heart is about to explode. Two nights in a row, I'm yanked out of my sleep with a terrible feeling shooting my anxiety through the roof. Yesterday, it was because I thought I missed Butterfly Man's note. Tonight…I don't know.

Although I should feel safer I have Jacob in my corner along with Tristan and his team, and more in control after the moves I've made this morning, I can't shake the feeling something bad is going to happen, like the sudden death of your favorite character in a book.

What are you up to, Butterfly Man?

Without getting up—I don't want Tristan to barge in again—I reach for my phone on the nightstand to check the time. 1:36 a.m. Great. I only got two hours of sleep. I guess stress and fear do that to you.

Emotions are little, tricky things. As a woman who, at a very young age, has been taught not to show her emotions—or there will be heavy consequences—for self-preservation purposes, I've learned to keep them locked. With time, however, there was no closet big enough to contain them, no lock strong enough to hold them back. That's why I write. I let my feelings out in my stories, a safe haven where they roam free without fear of being caught.

Opening the nightstand top drawer, I glance at the many journals and notepads hogging most of the space. I need an outlet for the emotions that are tearing me apart. Tempted, I brush my fingers over the engraved leather cover of the journal on top.

Swiftly, I draw my hand back and shut the drawer. If I start writing, I won't stop, and I need to get some sleep. So I open the second drawer and settle for the next best thing to blow off some steam. The rose.

Unpopular opinion, but wands, dildos, even bullets aren't my best friends. The idea of inserting anything that runs on batteries inside my vagina is terrifying, and if I'm being honest, nothing works better than my own fingers while my all-time favorite written smut scenes play together in my head. The rose, though, has changed my perspective about sex toys. Whoever invented it must be a woman as she clearly understands female body anatomy and the annoyance a cock-shaped toy—anything man-related in general—could bring.

Glancing up at the security camera, I hesitate to start. What's Monarca's protocol on intimate privacy? I don't think it's detailed in the contract, and I've never bothered to ask. Sexual pleasure in any form has been at the bottom of my priority list since my performance for Butterfly Man. The last thing I want is another self-pleasure scene caught on camera.

Should I put a towel on the camera and text that I need a moment? *Could you be more obvious, Birdie?* I blow out a frustrated breath. "I just need to get some sleep."

My eyes dart between the camera and the drawer. "Fuck it." I slip the rose under the covers. It's a covert toy—hopefully the men don't know what it's for—and the room is dark. If I stay very very quiet, no one will even notice.

The team in the control room, maybe, but you know Tristan is also watching, and he will notice.

I don't care. It won't be the first time he sees me come. My need for some shut-eye is bigger than my shame.

And if he comes in? Right in the middle of it? Or

❦ 3 ❦

just when you're at the edge and desperate for release? Will you have the clarity to tell him to leave? Will he have the decency to listen?

Images of shirtless Tristan barging in while I'm spread open, a sex toy between my thighs, play in my head. My whole body throbs with forbidden desires. I close my eyes, and I see it. The hunger that will spurt in his intense gaze, the swelling in his pants that will grow with every undulation of my body as I chase my pleasure. Every contort of my face, every gasp, an invitation, a call to everything primal in him to take over. To punish. To claim.

I bolt out of the bed and lock the door.

"Okay. He can't come in. Let's do this. Nice and quick." I slide under the covers, pulling them over my head, and give my back to the camera. Setting the rose on my favorite mode, I pull down my panties.

As soon as the vibration hits my wetness, my dirty imagination does its thing. Vivid visuals of my antiheroes come alive, in my room, in my bed, touching and tasting every inch of me, doing, together, naughty wicked things to my body, each in their way.

Then it sneaks up on me. A face I haven't written yet, fully masked with a neon butterfly for a mouth, peeking in from the dark like a flash of lightning that disrupts the night.

My heart skips a beat as my eyes snap open.

The rose humming its vibrations along with my accelerated breathing are the only sounds in the room, but, for a second there, in sync, another breath joins mine.

I pause the toy and sit upright. In the darkness, my gaze bounces from one wall to the next. "Are you there?" I whisper.

When silence answers, I swallow and switch on the light on the nightstand. Bracing for the worst, I hold my breath and look around like a maniac. Except no one is there. It's just me, alone, with made-up monsters to fuck me to sleep.

"It's all in my head. You're not here. You can't be." *But I can feel you getting closer, watching me, as if you were here, in the same room with me.*

I switch off the light and bury myself under the covers. With the rose back in position, behind my eyelids, I banish my familiar dirty friends and stare at the neon butterfly. A beautiful, terrible trap I'm falling into.

My fingers tremble as I restart the toy, the vibrations seem to intensify at the perverse fantasy. The terrifying glow pulses, a symbol of my madness, a hypnotic reminder of the danger that both frightens and entices me.

I imagine his breath on my neck, phantom fingers trailing across my skin. My own touch becomes his, and I shake at the thrill it gives me. The line between fantasy and reality blurs.

Butterfly Man isn't a fictional villain written to entice. He's a stalker obsessed with me to the point of killing, and I'm soaking the sheets with my arousal picturing him in a scary mask claiming me.

"This is wrong," I whisper to myself between gasps, even as my nipples harden painfully against the satin of my gown, and my legs spread wider in desperate need. The thought of him watching my fingers between my thighs, drinking in my vulnerability and darkness, comes into play, and it sends a shiver down my spine. Is it revulsion at the violation or the desire for more?

How many times has he replayed that scene? How many times has he touched himself to it? What sounds did he make when he came? Did he groan or growl? Did he break with my name on his lips? If he did, which one?

The neon butterfly smirks at me, mocking me with its silent glow. Then the mask vanishes, but the smirk stays, one I'm so irritably familiar with. Tristan's.

No. My eyes twitch as I shake the intrusive flickers of his face off my head. *I won't go there.* I reprimand myself as if masturbating to a killer is acceptable but to my bodyguard is an unforgivable sin.

Frustration huffs out of my lips. If I crave

a villain, why do I not stick to the harmless ink-on-paper kind? If I desire a hero, why do I not rely on fiction to deliver one who isn't morally gray?

But it's not about the choice between villains and heroes. The truth is, I'm tired of fantasies. What I crave is something real. Butterfly Man is real. Tristan is real.

Jacob is real, too. Why is he not an option? He's good, handsome, sexy, gentleman on the street, freak in the sheets and has proved he'd do anything—

"Don't stop." A strained whisper rips the silence as shadows congeal and take form beside me.

A gasp rips out of my throat as my heartbeat bursts my chest. Eyes wide, I jolt to open the lights, but forceful weight pins me to the mattress. Arms flailing, I open my mouth to scream.

My voice clashes against a firm grip unheard. The scent of leather fills my nostrils, and my wrists are squeezed together above my head. I kick as hard as I can, but my strength is nothing against the weight rendering me immobile.

My eyes squint to adjust to the dark in hopes of making out any details about him. A shadow around his head. A hoodie perhaps. His face and figure are a silhouette of black. I can't see the glint of his eyes or the outline of his features. There's only a flicker of a color where his breaths come out. He must be wearing a mask. Butterfly Man's mask. Exactly how I've pictured him, except the butterfly isn't glowing.

"No, darling. No kicking, no screaming, none of that," the voice rasps, low and gruff and menacing, but, a part of me notices, it doesn't threaten me, not outright anyway. "You'll be a good girl for me and stay quiet. No need to tell anyone our little secret. I'm not here to hurt you. I never will. You know that. But I won't hesitate to hurt anyone who stands in the way between us, like those bodyguards…"

Panic floods my system as the reality of the situation crashes over me. He's here. Butterfly man has found a way to break into my house again. That breath I've heard… He's been here in my bedroom all this time, watching me, and now, he's pinning me down to my bed in the middle of the night, threatening to kill anyone I ask for help. Shuddering, I try to lie very still.

"Good. Now, if I take my hand off your mouth, do you promise not to scream?"

How can I make that promise? I should scream. I should fight.

His fingers tighten around my jaw, stabbing and smothering. Then a click echoes above my head, and cold metal scrapes against my flesh.

🦋 8 🦋

It's a gun. He has a gun in the hand holding my wrists. "Do you?"

Frantically, I nod. It's best to play along for now, to pacify him. When the protagonist is more clever than strong, this is how they outwit the antagonist. I turn into an easily squashable little mouse to get Butterfly Man to show off his power. Then I find a chink in his armor, a flaw to exploit, or a need I make him believe I'll fulfill.

All I need is time.

Soon enough Tristan will spot Butterfly Man on the cameras. My bodyguard will assess the risks and come with enough men and firepower to save me without getting caught in the crossfire. No one should die tonight. Neither Tristan and his men nor my stalker.

Not yet.

"Good girl." He releases my face but keeps his gloved hand near my throat.

My breath comes in short, sharp gasps. They collide with the calm and steady exhales seeping out of him. "There are cameras in the room. They can see you, and they'll come in any second now."

"No, they can't see us, darling. All that's playing on their monitors is you alone in this bed, sound asleep."

Cold sweat trickles down my back. "You hacked it?"

"And your knight isn't the one standing outside your door either. He's out, leaving your *protection* in the hands of his team. So don't worry, darling. No one will interrupt our time together tonight."

Oh God. Tristan isn't here, and the rest of my bodyguards think I'm sleeping safely in my room. The only way to get help is to scream, and someone will end up dead.

"Even if they could see me, they couldn't stop me," he whispers, the bed sinking on either side of me, and the weight on top of me shifts but not enough for me to move. I think about wriggling my way out of bed anyway. Blake's gun is in my dresser drawer. If I get to it, I—

Swiftly, as if my stalker could read my mind, he cages my thighs in between his knees, killing my plan. "No one can stop me from having you, Reagan."

I curse the way my name sounds so sinful and sacred all at once on his tongue. His words are marred by the darkness his soul embraces so willingly, dangerous and toxically alluring. His voice, a deep, velvety timbre, wraps around my heart and squeezes ever so gently.

"Reagan," he repeats, as if savoring the sound, the air between us thickening. "You've been a very, very naughty girl." He switches the gun from the hand holding my wrists to his free one. "A date with another man when I move heaven and earth, delivering the souls that have wronged you to their hell? And this bullshit you had him say to the whole country? Do you know what happens to naughty girls like you?"

"You're angry," I breathe.

"Yes. I'm not a prank or a joke." The gun muzzle presses at my temple and tracks its way across my forehead. "I'm not an illusion you conjured from this beautiful brain."

I freeze. The rough metal sends violent shudders down my spine. I'm one wrong move, one wrong word away from getting myself killed.

He traces my jawline with his weapon and then presses it to my chin. "I'm the man you're destined to be with for the rest of your life, and I am very, very real."

The ignorant mind, with its infinite afflictions, passions, and evils, is rooted in the three poisons. Greed, anger, and delusion. "I know you're real. I've always known."

He leans closer, his breath, warm and quick, against my cheek. "Then why the games, darling?"

I've provoked him out of his hiding for a reason. My plan has worked, but the outcome is unexpected. I made my move, and this is his. Not exactly how I've hoped he channels his anger. "I think you know why."

Silence stretches between us for a thrashing heartbeat. I picture him smirking under that mask in response, a cruel awareness of the desires he unravels deep within me.

"I do, my naughty, impatient queen. But I need to hear you say it."

My throat constricts as fear and a perverse excitement war inside me. "I want you to finish what you started."

Moving the gun off my face, he brushes the pad of his leathered thumb over my lips, and another quiver runs through me. "Oh, my darling, you have no idea how long I've waited to hear those words, coming out of your beautiful lips, while *I* am here, looking straight at your face." A hushed chuckle escapes his chest. "I knew you'd understand. Like Enzio and Bianca, we're two sides of one dark soul, and I know exactly what you want."

"Do you?"

"Blake," he says, the name dripping with venom. "You want him gone as much as I do. Like the pervert, like the thief."

A plain confession that leaves no room for doubt. He killed them. He killed Aaron and Saldana.

My heart races, torn between exhilaration and terror. I've crossed a line, one I can never uncross. But isn't this what I've wanted all along? "When?"

He laughs under his breath again. "Patience, darling. I promise you I'll make him pay for what he's done, just like the others, the ones you know about and the ones you haven't known about yet."

What? Does he mean Gia? Are there more? Unrevealed murders he's committed in my name already or upcoming kills? I gulp. "I don't want anyone else dead. Just him."

"You have to trust me, my queen. I have a plan, and you'll thank me for it when it's all done. I promise you Blake will be gone soon." His fingers feather over my face, and then the gun traces a cold path down my neck, further down the line between my breasts, a chilling reminder of the danger I'm in. "Sooner if you let *me* finish what *you* started."

"What?" I shiver involuntarily, the weight of his words crushing me. Part of me wants to scream and end this madness. But another part, the part that dances with monsters and lays with them in the dark, the part I'm no longer ashamed to acknowledge, drips wet at the unforgivable.

Slowly, the gun slides with his hand down my abdomen, then, as it reaches my inner thighs, he tries to spread my legs apart. "You heard me, darling."

"No." I press my thighs as tight as I can,

hyperaware my panties are below my knees. I'm completely naked under my gown. If he reaches under it… "Stop. This has gone too far. You can't…" A sob rips out of my throat. "Are you going to rape me?"

His hand stills on my leg. "Rape you? How could you say such a terrible word? I'm breaking my back to earn your love, and you think I'm just gonna… If that's something I'm capable of, if that's what I want from you, why go to such lengths to show you I'm worthy of you?" His tone turns gentle, even sweet. "You're much more than a body to me, my darling butterfly. You're my queen."

"But you're touching me without my consent."

Silence—the complete silence of a predator—slices the air surrounding us again. My temples pulse wildly. He said he was never going to hurt me, but how can I trust a murderer who has broken into my house, armed, and cast implicit threats of violence? Is he going to stop or have I angered him some more? Will he force himself on me? Kidnap me?

Kill me?

"You don't want me to touch you?" His voice wavers with heartbreak and disbelief. The hurt is palpable, laced with a plea for reconsideration and a rawness to his tone that comes from having your deepest hopes shattered.

Despite the fear of the impending atrocity—he has a gun between my thighs—I can't bring myself to lie or give voice to the truth; I crave his affection as much as I dread it.

"Then who is it you want?" His voice takes a harsher turn. "Who was touching you in your head tonight? Who was making you moan like a dirty slut?"

You. How can I want him so badly when every instinct screams he will be my demise?

"I've always thought it's the characters that pleasure you when you need a release. I mean, them I can forgive. They make me jealous, but I can't kill them. I can't even hate them because they're part of you." The heat from his body radiates closer, and then his mask touches my ear. "And I worship every piece of you." His breath falls on the hollow of my neck before it's buried in my collarbone. "You. All of you." He takes sharp inhales along the side of my neck, like an animal sniffing his mate. Then his nose, beneath the softness of his mask, glides up and down my shoulder. "Your darkness, your light, every shred of your soul."

I shut my eyes, my lips trembling. The intensity of his twisted emotions, his simplest touch… Everything he is ignites an unholy fire in me that forges rather than destroys. An abyss that sees right through me, ready to embrace me when I fall.

"But it was someone else tasting your pussy tonight, wasn't it?" Abruptly, he lifts his face and tightens his grip around my wrist, his knees closing in on my hips. "I can't have that. You are mine, Reagan. No one touches what's mine. Not even in your head. Do you hear me?"

"You're crazy."

"Maybe. Yes. I cross the lines of sanity for you, but when you let someone else touch what's mine, watch me cross the lines of insanity. Who is it?"

"No one," I lie.

"Who is it?" he hisses. "The cop? The man with the motorcycle? Both of them together at the same time?" He presses the gun to my vagina. "Tell me."

"It wasn't them. I swear." I've never been more terrified, and I've never throbbed harder.

"No more games. Tell me the fucking truth."

I can't. I can't just tell my stalker how wet I've become imagining him in my bed in his creepy mask fucking me into oblivion. How curious I am to find out how many times he's come watching me touch myself. How close, when he's holding a gun to my pussy, I am to orgasm.

A gasp breaks on his lips. Then his breath hitches. "Oh."

The room closes in on me. The arms of the

abyss open wide. A chasm of no return. My stalker has figured it out. He knows he's been my darkest fantasy. The secret I can't hide in a grave.

Slowly, he takes my hands and places them on his chest, and his heart dances against my palms. "Then why lie and say you don't want me to touch you when I'm here, ready to take care of you, darling?"

"Because it's wrong and sick." It's everything I've feared, everything I've secretly desired. "Even if you're real, in my head you're still a fantasy I control. But this…"

He caresses the back of my hands, his grip freeing my wrists. "This is what?"

The moment I've been waiting for.

I gather all my strength and speed and push myself back, yanking my hands out of his hold and kneeing him in the groin. Swiftly, I wriggle my feet out of my underwear and roll out of the bed, his groaning curses following me, and dash toward the dresser.

My fingers claw at the drawer and tear it open so hard it nearly comes off its tracks. I plunge my hand inside. The darkness thickens around me, mocking my fingers as they scrabble uselessly against wood and fabric to find Blake's gun.

"No, no, no." Panic rises in my throat. The gun is not there.

"Looking for this?" Butterfly Man's voice cuts through the darkness. "Didn't think I'd come unprepared, did you?"

I whirl around. He's already on his feet, towering over me, a dark silhouette against the faint moonlight. My eyes strain in the gloom to see what he's holding. My stomach drops as realization hits. The gun Butterfly Man has is Blake's. My stalker has been holding me at gunpoint using my husband's weapon all this time.

Backing up, I slam into the dresser. My mind races, cataloging everything within reach. Lamp. Books. Picture frame. But nothing that can match what he's got. "If you take another step, I'll scream."

"What is this all about, darling? You want me, and I want nothing more than to make you happy. But then you call our love wrong and sick, and then this. I don't understand. Do you like to be chased, my love? Is this what's happening here? I'm more than happy to oblige, but tonight we don't have the time."

"Just get out of here."

He chuckles nastily. "No."

My muscles coil, ready to spring. But he's stronger, faster, darker. His big arms squeeze me from behind, a snake capturing its prey. "Go ahead. Scream, little butterfly."

A knock on the door echoes in my bones. "Mrs. Abel. I mean, Birdie," Brandon's hushed voice calls. "Are you okay?"

Hope pulses through me. It's not Marcus outside, it's Brandon. It's *Gatsby*. A sign God hasn't forsaken me. This is it. My chance to scream for help without alerting Butterfly Man. I don't have to scream. All I need to do is say, "I'm fine. Just trying to sleep, Gatsby," and Brandon will know I'm in danger. He will get enough help to take Butterfly Man down.

The gun clicks as my stalker chuckles next to my ear. "As if on cue. The way I see it, you have two choices how this night is gonna end, darling. You either tell him you're okay and come back to bed so I can give you the pleasure you seek like a good girl or you tell him to come in where he's gonna get a bullet in his head."

As much as I dislike Brandon, he's only an innocent boy. He's too young to die. *If you use your signal word, he won't because he won't engage alone. Marcus, Riley, Dixon and more, if needed, will be with him, too. You hired those men to protect you. Let them do their job.*

"Birdie, ma'am?" The doorknob moves several times. "Please unlock the door or I'll have to break it to make sure you're safe," Brandon says uncomfortably.

"What's it gonna be, my love?" my stalker whispers, sending a chill down my spine.

I stare at the door. Images of Brandon's

face with a hole in his forehead trickling blood jump in my mind, and a sob clogs my throat. Then Butterfly Man's face, naked but featureless, lies pale and bloody on my bedroom carpet freezes on display.

"I'm fine." I try to force every ounce of composure I have into my voice. "Just trying to sleep…Brandon." My shoulders slump in defeat as I swallow the tears threatening to give me away and feign irritation. "Do I need permission for some privacy in my own bedroom?"

The doorknob stills. "Oh, I… Sorry. Of course not. I'm so sorry to wake you, ma'am. Have a good night."

"That's my good girl." Butterfly Man plants a kiss on my neck and carries me back to bed. He lies next to me and folds an arm around my waist like an invited lover, not a sick man forcing me into submission with a gun. "I knew you'd make the right choice."

When his hand slides under my gown and between my thighs, I don't fight. With a mix of dread and exhilaration, with a twisted sense of freedom, I realize I can't resist the pull of him leaning into the abyss, surrendering to the inevitable.

Later, I'd tell myself I did it to save a young man from dying, but deep down, my stalker and I would know I did it to save him.

Because I want him to kill for me.
And because I want him.

CHAPTER 2
Butterfly Man

Touching her is the most beautiful and most terrifying thing I've ever done.

I marvel at her softness, the warmth that spreads from her flesh through my body, igniting something primal and desperate. I've lived so long in the cold, convincing myself I was beyond warmth. Only she sets my soul ablaze. A lifetime of longing, doubt and carefully constructed walls melts away as my fingers trail along her skin, slow, tentative, as if I might shatter her with the slightest pressure. But it's me coming apart, unraveling at the seams.

Fingers trembling, I reach out to the forbidden, hovering just above. I've wanted this—fuck, I've needed this—yet now that she's within reach, her pussy glistening in the dark, spilling secrets on the delicate skin of her inner thighs, the fear gnaws at me, a beast with no compassion tearing at the edges of my resolve.

Reagan consumes me, a gravity that pulls at the darkest parts of my soul. I can't stop the thoughts, the images that attack me without warning—what I could do to her, to her body, if I let go.

My heartbeat, a wild thing hammering against my ribs, threatens to burst through and lay every fucked-up fantasy and urge she ignites bare. They writhe, whispering that I'll only corrupt her, taint her light with my shadows until there's nothing left but the dark. I don't want her to see them, to see me like this, fractured and jagged. It makes me sick, makes me want to pull away, but I can't. I don't deserve her, but I just can't stop.

I'm poison, and she's the antidote. Still, I'm tethered to her, caught in the web we've spun with no escape.

The distance between us is agony, like the last breath before the plunge. My hand moves before I can think. I part her lips and trail my middle finger along her slit.

She's so wet. God, she's so fucking wet, and it's from fantasizing about me. *MY REAGAN IS WET FOR ME.*

The world crumbles around me. There's

nothing but her heat seeping through to my fingertip. I should say something, anything, but the words choke in my throat. My breath comes in ragged gasps. The only thing I see and hear and smell and feel is Reagan. I want to immerse myself in her, drown in her, and forget everything else. Do I dare hope it's possible? Do I dare believe it's real?

No, it must be one of my fantasies. In reality, she wouldn't accept me, let alone *need* me.

I pull back, withdrawing my hand, and inhale her scent off my finger. My eyes roll behind my mask in bliss. It's not a fantasy. I am here with her, the sweet familiar scent of her arousal I know by heart filling my nostrils. It's real. As real as the living, breathing monster in me, hungry and relentless, that will destroy us both if I let it.

But how? If this were only my imagination, she wouldn't be opening herself to me. She wouldn't be dripping wet under my touch. So I look into her eyes, searching for revulsion, waiting for her to recoil, for the moment she realizes her mistake. Instead, I find a reflection of my own longing, my own fear.

"Why did you stop?" she whispers.

Making sure you're not a dream. But it's too cheesy to say. "Sorry, my queen." I spread her lips open again and dip one finger inside her.

With a hiss, she leans into my touch, just

slightly, but it's enough to undo me. Something inside me snaps, a thread wound too tight for too long.

In one brief, vivid flash in my head, I pull her closer, until she can't breathe, until her soft hiss is smothered against my chest. Then I tighten my hand around her wrists, the playful touch morphing into dark possession. My fingers, once trembling with restraint, now dig into her skin, a need to leave red, angry, unforgettable marks on her flesh that scream, MINE.

The panic in her gaze as she begs me to stop, as I don't let go, the moment when her trust I've barely gained shatters into a thousand pieces tears at me and excites me at the same time. My breath, hot against her neck, my lips biting her ear, I whisper things that should never be spoken. Cruel words meant to wound, to break her spirit, and she flinches, tears welling up in those eyes that once looked at me with something like love.

The sound of her tears springs my cock to life as she struggles, her fear palpable, trying to get away, and I don't let her. I watch her flutter her wings, a little butterfly caged in a jar, trapped beneath me, powerless, just like I've always felt.

Her face contorts in pain as my grip moves from her wrists to her throat. Her sexy rasps in that voice that brings me to my knees plead. I still don't stop. I can't. I've been drowning alone for so long. Time to pull her with me, let her drown, too.

The bruises bloom on her skin, a grotesque testament to the monster I can't contain. Her mouth is wide open, desperate for breath, but what I do is fill it with my cock. I only pull it out to spill my cum and watch it drip on her lips.

And then, the final image attacks, sudden and visceral—Reagan lying still, silent, eyes empty, because I've gone too far. Life drains from her, a cold, broken thing left in my wake. Horror twists my stomach, but the vision doesn't fade. It lingers, taunting me, showing me exactly what I could do if I ever gave in to these urges.

These thoughts, these fantasies—they're not real. But they could be. When she hisses and writhes and bucks, needing more of my touch, it's so easy to just let go, to surrender to the violence that simmers just beneath the surface, clawing at the edges of my sanity, begging to be unleashed.

My mind screams at me to pull back, to save us both from what comes next. But my need for her sweeps away any semblance of control. Instead of dragging myself out of here before it's too late, I slide another finger inside her.

She moans and lifts her hips. I curse at God and her. "I hate you."

"You hate me?" she rasps.

"Yes," I slide my fingers out to the tips and then slide them back in, "for making me feel this way." For making me believe in heaven again when I've long accepted my place in hell.

"What way?"

Weak. Desperate. Obsessed. In pieces. Tormented because I don't want to hurt you. I mean, I do, but... I won't let myself hurt you.

"Why are you doing this?" she asks. "Touching me like that, does it make you feel powerful?"

"Powerful?" I press the gun between her breasts, and a gasp stutters on her lips. "I'm holding the gun, you're spread wide, and yet all I'm doing is getting you to orgasm." Can't she see who has all the power here? "I came here to punish you for what you did, and look at me... My life would have been a lot easier if I'd just killed you years ago and ended all of this pain."

Her eyes sink toward the gun. "You promised you wouldn't hurt me."

"Then please don't twist our first date into something we both know it's not. I didn't force you to take my touch. You want me as much as I want you, Reagan. If you still don't believe it, here." I rub her wetness over her mouth. "Lick the mess you're making all over my hand then tell me it isn't yours."

Her breasts rise and fall rapidly. "I don't want to."

I trail the gun down to her pussy and enjoy the way she shivers. I lay it flat on her mound before I slap her pussy with it. She gasps wildly, and I slide the muzzle against her clit. "You were saying?"

Terror washes over her face, but her eyes twinkle before they give me that look I know by heart. That roll and flutter that signal she's in her horny-little-bitch mode.

"Do as I say, Reagan."

Twitching, she opens her mouth and lets my fingers in. Her tongue twirls around her taste and licks it off me. I swallow my groans, drinking in the view. One day, it'll be my cock she wraps her lips around to taste herself.

"You're such a good girl when you do as you're told." I drag my fingers back to her pussy when she's done and remove the gun. "Did you have enough proof or do I have to make you lick the gun, too? Spoiler alert, it's even slicker than my fingers."

"Fine. I won't deny it. I won't lie and say my body has betrayed me because it's bullshit. I've fantasized about you, and the fear that comes with you. I crave your touch. It feels intoxicating, exciting, even familiar, as if it makes sense, as if you've touched me a hundred times before. Now, it's your turn. Tell me how you feel."

Her gaze searches my face for something—maybe reassurance, maybe the truth. I don't know how to give my truth to her without drawing blood. What I feel isn't simple. It's everything at once, a torrent of emotions and twisted desires crashing together in chaos.

Touching her is like holding fire in my hands. It burns and yet illuminates what will be her worst nightmare. There are parts of me that want to possess her completely, to claim her in ways that terrify me. Parts that no longer know where the line is—if it even exists.

"Now you don't speak." Disappointment laces her whisper.

She doesn't understand. How could she? I've spent years keeping the monster hidden, locked away where it can't touch her. But now, standing here, so close to her, I realize it's always known I can't hold it forever, lurking just beneath the surface, waiting for the moment I'd finally crack. I can't stay away. No matter how hard I try, I keep coming back to her, like a moth circling the flame.

I want to lose myself in her until there's nothing left but the two of us, intertwined in a way that could either save me or destroy us both.

"Then let me see your face and glimpse

what you feel," she demands. "I don't care if you're Beast or Phantom or a hideous mythical creature. I just want to see *you*. It's the least I deserve, to see what I'm up against."

"You deserve the world, and I'd bring it down for you. I wish I could touch you in the light the way you let me in the dark, but I can't. I can't let you see me. Not now."

"Why?"

Silence stretches between us again, thick and suffocating.

Hurtful confusion darkens her eyes. "I'll answer for you. It's because you're not a stranger emerging from the shadows. Because I've seen your face before countless times, but you think I didn't really see you. So you wear this mask, hoping this time I will."

I've put on this mask, thinking it's impenetrable. Suddenly, it feels paper-thin. How could she see through it so easily? She's right, of course. I've hidden behind this facade, terrified of being rejected once she sees the real me. But now, faced with her understanding, I'm even more afraid.

What if I let her in and she still walks away? What if the broken, yearning creature beneath the mask is too much for anyone to love?

Not ready to find out, I press my thumb to her clit and circle it. My fingers flutter inside her, mimicking the exact rhythm of her sex toy. She purrs and moans, telling me I've got it right.

"Will you talk to me?" she huffs. "I don't like the silence."

"Want me to talk dirty to you? Does it turn you on?"

"A little. I want to hear you say the things you want to do to me."

"Trust me. You don't."

"But I do. You've just put a gun inside my pussy, and I creamed all over it."

Would she cream if I told her I fantasized about using it to make her cry and bleed? Guess not.

I sigh, distracting myself by memorizing every path inside her, the right amount of pressure on her clit that makes the pleasure almost unbearable, the speed that forces her to bite her lips on a hiss.

"Please," she begs.

Fuck me. I can't say no to her when she begs like that. "Well," I swallow as I take in the swell of her breasts, the nipples protruding like pebbles in the dark, "I wish I could feel your nipples harden between my lips. I wish I could taste you when you were dry and then learn the difference as you became wet on my tongue. I wish I could kiss you, Reagan."

"Do it," she rasps. "You can blindfold me to lift off your mask and do it."

My cock jerks. *She* is giving me ideas? I feel one of her nipples with my thumb and fill my palm with her plump flesh. She's so fucking pretty. I want to sleep and cry and play and die on these beautiful tits. "It's crossed my mind, darling, but I'm afraid even that isn't a liberty I can take."

"Why not? I want you to."

God, she's killing me. "Same reason I didn't take my glove off before touching you. I can't leave a trail. Saliva is DNA."

"You told me to trust you, but you can't do the same?"

I insert a third finger and watch her squirm. "Trust, like love, is earned. Isn't that what you wrote in Twisted Obsession, Birdie, *little bird*?"

"Don't…call m-e th-at."

"Okay, darling. Okay, Reagan."

"Say it again. My name, say it again just like that."

I oblige, my voice hoarse with every latent need and desire I've kept all these years as I whisper against her ear, "Reagan."

"Tell me what you did."

"What I did?"

"When you watched me touch myself the first time."

"You really like dirty talking, you horny little slut, don't you?"

"Did you touch yourself?"

My cock strains against the zipper of my pants as my mind drifts to the moment she's referring to, even though it's not the first time I've watched her work on herself. But she doesn't need to know that. "Yes. I couldn't help myself. You were a vision."

She moans harder, her pussy throbbing around my fingers. "Did you come?"

"Right with you. My body and yours are synchronized beyond our understanding. We were made for each other. We were born to be together, Reagan."

Her pants fill the room. My shoulder rocks as I work faster. She's clenching, swallowing my fingers with insatiable hunger. "Did you mark me on the screen with your cum?"

A sigh shakes out of my throat. "Not the first time I watched...but later…yes."

She's practically riding my hand now. Her orgasm is so close I can feel it. "I want to touch you."

I'm too lost, watching her about to come, barely holding myself from coming in my pants, when she reaches a hand to my cock.

Flinching, I almost fire the gun. "No." I grab her hand and squeeze it so hard she yelps. "I'm sick of your tricks."

Her breath snags, and she whimpers. "What tricks? I just want to touch you."

"No. You try to get me to show you my

face and leave DNA on you, and when that doesn't work, you do this. You think you can identify me by my cock because you believe you know who I am or, at least, suspect." I snort bitterly. "And you talk about trust…"

"You're wrong," she sniffles.

Is she crying? Reagan doesn't cry. Not like that. "My beautiful liar, enough. None of that. Aren't you tired? You don't need to lie anymore. Not here. Not with me." I ease up on her hand. "You don't need your camouflage around me. When I'm here, you show your true colors, little butterfly."

"Okay," she says softly, no more fake tears in her voice. "But I wasn't lying when I said I wanted to touch you."

"Well, you haven't earned that yet."

Her brow arches. "*I* earn the right to touch *you*?"

"Like I'm earning your love, yes."

She stares at me like I grew a second head. "Has it ever occurred to you that even after all the murders you're committing for me I still won't love you?"

"You will."

"No, I won't."

Is it an attempt to hurt me like I've hurt her pride or is it the truth? My jaw ticks. "I don't care. I'll still make you mine. As much as I want you to love me, I don't care if you spend a lifetime hating me as long as you're mine." I press the gun to her temple. "Do you hear me, little butterfly? No one else will have you. You. Will. Be. Mine." I shrug helplessly, blowing out a defeated breath. "As I'm yours."

She shakes her head, unfazed by the weapon pressed against her temple. "I'm done with this game. Get out. I don't want you here anymore, Butterfly Man."

With a chuckle, I pin her down and squeeze her wrists together above her head again. "Don't you learn at all, naughty girl? I'm done taking it easy on you. *I* tell you what to do, and you listen or you'll be punished." I shove the gun in the back of my pants. It doesn't scare her anymore. Then I slide my fingers inside her pussy again. "You have twenty seconds to come or I'll kill one of your guards anyway."

"But I—"

"Nineteen. Eighteen."

"Please. That's why I wanted to touch you. It'll make me come faster."

"You think I want nothing more than to fuck you until you can't remember your name? But if I lose control, and trust me, I will if my cock feels your touch or so much as catches a glimpse of your pussy, there will be nothing left of you when I'm done." I circle my fingers and rub her clit, gaining the right pace. "Twelve. Eleven."

Her breath catches. "Remember when I said in my head you were a fantasy I control? That's the only way I can come this fast. I'm begging you."

She's not lying. Her heart racing against my chest tells me this much. That's progress. As much as she wants to obey me so I'll kill Blake for her faster and maybe save the random soul I've threatened to take, I want to see the face she makes when *I* make her come.

My eyes travel to her wrists in my grip. "If it's control you need," I take her hand down to her pussy and wrap her fingers around mine, "there. You lead. It's your narrative, my brilliant storyteller. Control it. Own it. Write our story as you deem right."

She nods and guides me inside her, setting the rules, wielding the path, and we both surrender. Eyes pinned on the butterfly on the mask, she moves her hips to chase that orgasm, and I marvel at her expression, the pain, the rush, the sound of her pants, carving them into memory. And I allow myself to imagine a future where moments like this aren't so rare.

"Seven," I count, and she works her hips faster. "Six. Five. Four. Three. Two. O—"

A wild moan flees her lips as she clenches and explodes all over my glove.

I stare at her in awe as she comes down from the climax. "Six times. Your pussy clenches six times in release."

She blinks, catching her breath. "You counted?"

"I counted. I learned. I filed every inch of your face when I made you see stars and you made me see God. And the sounds you made will sing in my head day and night until the day I die."

"That's…"

"Cheesy? Sick? Plain psycho?"

"I was going to say—"

Footsteps, followed by heavy knocking, interrupt. Both our heads jerk toward the door.

"Ma'am, I'm so sorry to wake you again, but I hear noises coming from your room that aren't consistent with the feed we have for it. I have to come in," one of her bodyguards says.

Fuck. I really want to know what she was going to say. "Looks like I don't have much time to continue our conversation."

"You have to go," she whispers to me, "now."

I tangle my fingers in the back of her hair and press her to my chest. "I'll see you again very soon, darling." Then I drag myself away and dart to the terrace. Casting one last look at her before I leave, I say, "When the man with the motorcycle returns, prepare for some good news. I've left him something precious where he's at."

CHAPTER 3

Tristan

I jump out of the car and run to Marcus. "Where is she?"

"Locked herself up in her bedroom after she lashed out at Brandon. She said not to be bothered until your return."

"Did you find anything?"

He marches with me past the other details swarming in front of Birdie's house. "I only arrived twenty minutes ago, but I questioned the men and checked both the surveillance and the security system."

"And?" Impatiently, I pass the hallway toward the control room.

"No one saw him. There is no sign of forced entry anywhere, and surveillance shows nothing. The team swept the house and the perimeter twice and found no trace of any unidentified male or female. Riley is working to find out if the system has been hacked, but so far, no breach is detected."

"That's not possible unless there's a magical portal in her room that lets him in and out unseen."

"Or he wasn't there at all."

My hand halts above the doorknob. "What?"

He looks around him warily and lowers his voice. "None of the shit she's saying makes any sense. Like why was her door locked? Why didn't she signal Brandon when she had the chance? And let's say the bastard found a breach to sneak in past all the details guarding the house, how the hell did he run out of a two-story-high window without a sound or a trace?"

I squint at him, unappreciative of the skepticism. "I don't know the answers to any of these, but if she says he was here, then he was."

"Listen, I know you respect and admire this client so much. I still remember back at camp, whenever you had any free time, you huddled down with one of her books like they were your only solace in hell. But the woman spins *stories* on the spot so fast it's scary.

"You weren't there when Detective Douche first came here to interrogate her. The way she spun everything in her favor… And look at him now. She has him wrapped around her finger, doing her bidding. How could you trust someone like that to be telling the truth, someone who lies for a living, and for other purposes?"

A need to defend Birdie rumbles in me. No one talks about her like that. No one. "You're crossing a line, Marcus. We're here to protect her and that means we trust her like she trusts us. Besides, why on earth would she lie about something like that?"

"Who knows, but Birdie Abel is the definition of what readers like you call an unreliable narrator. You'll understand when you see the footage from her room."

Jaw clenching, I rip the door open. Riley is sitting behind the monitors, lines between his eyebrows, his fingers working fast on the keyboard. I stand next to his chair, following the progress. "Tell me you found the breach."

Riley shakes his head. "All cameras are in place and working. No downtime or discrepancies. I've investigated all the footage we have. No signs of any intruders. Both surveillance and security systems are intact."

"Look harder."

"Yes, sir."

I massage the pounding in my temples. "Play the feed from the bedroom first."

Riley presses a couple of buttons, and Birdie's room footage at 1:40 a.m. streams from different angles.

Marcus points at the screen. "Look. You can see there's no one in the room but her, and the windows are closed. She stirs in bed, gets *something* out of the drawer, stirs some more and then bolts to lock the door."

Riley chuckles.

My jaw aches from clenching so hard as I glare at him. "Something funny?"

Humor slips out of his face when he sees the look on mine. "I mean she…locked the door…and…used something from her drawer in bed…" His stare returns to the screen. "No, sir."

A mix of anger and possessiveness flares hot and wild through me at the thought of him—or any man—imagining Birdie in an intimate situation. Part of me wants to forbid anyone from even thinking about her that way, while another part is tortured by the images now burned into my brain.

As I watch her sliding under the covers, her breath low and catching, all I can think about is Birdie, alone in that room, and how desperately I want to be there with her instead of watching from afar, consumed by emotions I have no right to feel.

And killing the two men watching what should be only mine to see.

I can't think like that. My feelings for her are clouding my judgment, making it impossible to focus on the actual security threat we're supposed to be addressing. "Speed that part up already and turn off the audio," I order.

Marcus cocks a brow at me. I fix him, too, with a glare I hope conveys just how close to the edge I am. "What?"

Marcus shrugs, but it shows in his gaze: my professional mask is slipping, my inappropriate emotions written all over my face—jealousy, protectiveness, and a hunger I can't contain.

"There." Marcus points at the screen again, and Riley resumes playing the footage at regular speed. "She turns on the lights all of a sudden. She looks around supposedly in panic and says…"

Riley presses a button, and the audio is back on. Birdie's voice comes in a whisper. "Are you there?"

"When she finds nothing," Marcus continues, "she mumbles something to herself, turns off the lights and goes back to what she was doing."

Heat engulfs my body when the sound of her panting fills the room again. I turn down the volume myself. "Then what?"

"Nothing," Marcus answers.

"Nothing? What do you mean nothing?"

"Watch for yourself. For the next fourteen

minutes, it's nothing but her huffs and puffs under the sheets until Gatsby interrupts. Wonder why she was taking so long."

Riley presses his fist over his mouth, covering another chuckle. My fist clenches and flies to his throat. He almost falls off the chair, his coughs wild, his face beetroot red. Choke on that, motherfucker.

"Tristan!" Marcus pushes me away from rattling Riley. "What the fuck?"

"Let's see how hard you're gonna fucking laugh now." I yank myself out of Marcus's grip. "If you want to keep your jobs and your dicks attached to you, I suggest you start acting like professionals instead of clueless buffoons and give me goddamn answers."

"The answer is right in front of you, Tristan. If you don't trust your eyes and ears, why don't you ask Gatsby himself? She said the stalker was holding her in the middle of the room when Gatsby knocked the first time, but we hear her answer Gatsby while she's in bed."

"Then we've been fucking hacked." I jab a finger at the monitors. "The real feed has been replaced with this bullshit."

"That's what she said, too. The stalker *told* her all we could see was her sleeping. But is that what you see? She locked the door. She turned on the lights. She turned them back off and spoke to Gatsby." Marcus fast forwards the footage. "Listen."

"I'm fine." Birdie's voice streams in while she's still under the covers. "Just trying to sleep…Brandon. Do I need permission for some privacy in my own bedroom?"

Marcus places his hands on his hips. "According to Gatsby, that's word for word what she told him. How could the stalker add live audio to bogus streaming while he's busy doing God knows what to her? Let's say that's even possible, how can we find no trace of a breach?"

"Unless you want to guard a parking lot in Antarctica, that's what you're going to find out!" I storm out of the control room and head upstairs.

Brandon, as pale as the dead, paces the hallway in front of Birdie's room. He freezes when he spots me. "I'm so sorry, sir."

"You did your job," I say before he shits his pants. "You followed your gut, paid attention to details and found out something was off. It's the assholes in charge of surveillance that fucked up."

"But I feel equally responsible. I was literally standing at her door. I just… I couldn't hear another person's voice in the room."

"Walk me through what happened."

His account matches the others. I'm tired of listening to the same story over and over again with zero answers to my questions, but I can't ignore the facts staring me in the face.

No stranger has been in this house tonight.

With a heavy sigh, I knock on Birdie's door. "Hey, it's me. Please let me in."

Soft footsteps scurry behind the door. The lock snaps open, and hope flashes on her tear-stained face. "Tristan, thank God you're here."

My heart clenches at the sight. I step in and close the door behind me, giving us privacy. "Of course. I'm so sorry. But I'm here now. You're safe."

She nods reluctantly, wrapping her arms around her waist in a protective circle. I wish I could hug her, give her the comfort and security she needs, but she's made it clear I'm not written to fit that role in her book. "How are you now?"

She curls up on the bed, small and vulnerable. Her eyes, red and puffy, barely hold mine, and she shrugs.

"Do you want to talk to me about what happened?"

Her lip curls under teeth, and her trembling fingers hover over her mouth. "No."

"Okay. Just know that I'm here, ready to listen anytime."

"Thank you."

"Birdie…we have to call the police."

"No." Panic floods her eyes. "No."

"I understand your position and fears, but in situations like this, they can help. They have extensive databases. The DNA tests they will run—"

"They won't find any. He made sure of it. The only thing I'll get from calling the cops is credibility loss that will lead to a scandal, possible jail time, and provoking Butterfly Man in the wrong way."

"You have a point." We've been hiding and falsifying evidence. We've lied repeatedly to the police and the press. "But he hurt you, Birdie." I'll never forgive myself for it. Another sin written in a long list but somehow weighs more than all of them combined. "You need a doctor to examine you."

"I'll be fine. Did you find anything?"

I don't know if I should push any further. This is a sensitive situation for any woman, and I'm only a man. I don't want to let this go, but any word I say may lack perspective or come out inconsiderate. The last thing I want is to make things worse.

I sit on the edge of the bed. "I've thoroughly reviewed all the footage and checked the security systems."

"He replaced the footage, Tristan. He explicitly said the only thing you'd be seeing was me sleeping in bed."

"Even if that's the case, there will be a trace

to the breach, a hacking mark of sorts, a back-door entry."

"Even if that's the case?"

Taking a deep breath, I steel myself for what I have to do next. "I need to show you something." I pull out my phone and queue up the bedroom footage.

As we watch, I point out the facts as objectively and gently as I can, the closed windows, the locked door, the lack of any other presence in the room and what she said to Brandon while she was lying in bed.

Anger builds in her eyes. "This is bullshit. I don't give a crap about what your broken system is showing. I know he was here. I felt him, talked to him. Even Brandon heard him."

"He heard *you*. Only *you*."

"What are you trying to tell me, Tristan?"

"For an intruder to enter undetected, they would have had to bypass not just our technology, but also somehow fight our guards without leaving any trace. Our electronic security systems show no breaches, and all the guards have been at their posts all night in one piece. There's no evidence of any intruders, Birdie."

"You think I'm making this up?" she snaps, pushing the phone away, and jumps out of the bed.

"No. I know you believe this is what happened, but… You've been under a lot of stress, and you haven't been sleeping well. We must consider all possibilities. Is there any chance—"

"No!" she cuts me off. "Don't you dare suggest it was a dream or my imagination. I felt his breath on my skin, his hands on me, his fucking gun between my legs. I can still feel his fingers inside me."

Her words hit me like a physical blow. I can't wait to feel the son of a bitch's heart pop in my hand. I take a step toward her, but she moves away from me. My shoulders slump. "I'm sorry. I'm so sorry. I'm just trying to understand—"

"No, you don't." Fresh tears spill down her cheeks that she wipes out fast. "He said he'd been watching us for weeks. How is that possible if your security is so impenetrable?"

A chill runs down my spine. We have a much bigger problem on our hands than I've thought if what she's saying is real. "I don't know," I admit, hating the words as they leave my mouth. "But I promise you, I'm going to find out. We're going to go over every inch of this place, review every second of footage from the past weeks. If there's any way he could have gotten information about our security, we'll find it."

"More promises when you don't even believe me… How naive do you think I am?"

"I believe you, Birdie. I do. But give me

something to work with here. Any detail that can lead me to find him."

She closes her eyes and presses her palms to her temples. "He was wearing all black, and he had the butterfly mask on his face. His scent didn't stand out. The leather from the gloves was overpowering. He's tall, strong, unhinged." Her eyes open as she shakes her head at me. "But in a way, he's…gentle, even familiar."

My heart skips a beat. "Familiar? Do you recognize anything about him?"

"Not really. Nothing I can place."

"What about his voice? He talked to you."

"It was gruff, but I don't think it's natural. He was altering it on purpose. You know, like Bruce Wayne and Batman." She looks away with a scoff. "I know how ridiculous I sound right now, but it's the truth."

None of this helps. Based on the evidence and facts, Butterfly Man could easily be nothing but a fragment of Birdie's overactive imagination. I walk over to her. I need her to look me in the eye when she answers my next question. "Why didn't you say your safe word to Brandon? You called him by his first name when you could have easily said Gatsby. Why didn't you signal him to come in and take Butterfly Man down?"

Something flickers in her gaze, a mix of fear and anger and…something she's trying so hard to hold back. "Because Butterfly Man threatened to kill Brandon if he came in. I couldn't risk it. I couldn't bear the thought of someone innocent getting hurt because of me."

The idea that she put herself through something so drastic and dangerous to protect one of us… It's almost more than I can bear.

It's almost too good to be true.

"That's exactly what we're here for. We're trained to handle these situations."

She shakes her head, looking away as if she's remembering the events all over again. "You don't understand. Butterfly Man knew things, Tristan. Things about the security here, about you. He knew you weren't here, and I thought he chose that time to break in because he could take Brandon down if he had to. Maybe if it was you at my door, I wouldn't hesitate. I knew you could handle it, but Brandon… He's just too young." Her gaze locks on mine. "Where were you?"

I don't appreciate the blame in her voice. "You should never put yourself at risk like that. Every man on the security team is more than capable of protecting you. I wouldn't leave here if that wasn't true."

"Yeah? Well, I didn't feel that way when I ran to get Blake's gun to fight Butterfly Man myself only to realize he was fucking me with it all along."

My blood pounds my skull at the image that will sear my brain forever. Growling like a wounded beast, I punch the nearest thing next to me.

"Tristan!"

Fuck. I shouldn't snap in front of her. I should never snap in front of her. My fist shakes as I stare at it. It's fine, but the dresser isn't so lucky.

She glares at me. "Instead of punching holes in my furniture, answer my question. Where were you?"

"Gia's place."

"Why you? You always send another guard to hers."

My eyes squint at one of the dresser drawers that has fallen open. "After what the detective told the press, I didn't want to take any chances, so I sent Marcus to Abel's and went to Gia's myself." I glance back at her. "Guess what I've found there."

Surprise etches on her face. But nothing I found in the assistant's apartment can be as surprising as what's nestled in that drawer.

Blake Abel's gun.

CHAPTER 4

Birdie

The room spins. Every shadow hides danger, every sound an intruder. "I'm not crazy."

"Nobody is saying you are." Tristan cuts through my spiraling thoughts. His face is a mix of concern, unasked questions and unspoken doubts.

My mind reels. "The gun wasn't there. He had it. He used it on me." The metal against my skin has left a cold trail so visceral it's almost visible. The raspy breaths in my ear. The feeling of his fingers… I didn't imagine all of that. The fear, the pain, the excitement, it was all real.

"I need to get out of here," I say abruptly, moving toward the door. I can't bear to be in this room any longer, surrounded by reminders of what I've gone through—or what I think I've experienced.

Tristan steps in front of me, blocking my path. "We need to talk about this. We need to figure out what's going on."

"What's going on is that you don't believe me. None of you do." My breath races with frustration and fear. "And I don't blame you. Everything I said has happened. He altered it to appear like it didn't. But I know what I experienced, Tristan. It wasn't a dream or a hallucination. He was here, in this room, and he... he..."

I can't finish the sentence. The memory of Butterfly Man's touch makes me feel sick and dirty. The memory of what I let him do to me… I want to scrub my skin raw, to erase every trace of him from my body and my mind. "Get out of my way."

"No. I can't let you leave like that. Look at me. Please," he urges.

I glance up at him, searching his face for any sign of the trust and belief I so desperately need.

He leans in imperceptibly. His hands, resting at his sides, twitch with the desire to reach out, but he lets only his gaze convey what his hands cannot. "If the entire universe conspired to doubt your truth, my heart would defy them all, forever anchored in unwavering faith in you."

The Nightingale's Whispers, chapter fifty-six.

"I believe you, even if you don't think I do," he says softly. "You have no idea how much it hurts me to know that you've been in danger and I wasn't there to save you. You have no idea how I feel that you're in so much pain and there's nothing I can do to take it away. Please, Birdie, I just want to understand so I can do something. Help me understand."

I rack my brain, revisiting the tormenting incident step by step. "He must have put it back. Before he left, he must have put the gun back in the dresser. It was dark, and I was too distracted and worried about…Brandon…to notice."

"You said he," he squeezes his eyes shut for a second, "inserted it inside you."

The image flashes bright and hot in my head. My insides twist. "Yes."

Confusion and concern rise to his expression again. He's looking at me like I'm a puzzle to be solved. "But the gun looks pretty clean to me, Birdie." He goes to the dresser and examines the gun. Then he shows it to me. "No signs of any…fluids on it."

I stare at the dull weapon that mocks everything I have to say. It looks exactly as it's always been since Tristan confiscated it from Blake. If I was fucked with it, it would, at least, have a trace of my wetness on it.

"The stalker might have had the time to put it back but not the time to clean it. Besides, DNA on the gun could be evidence you insist he's made sure not to leave," Tristan says.

"I…" My shoulder lifts in resignation. "He didn't use this gun on me then. That doesn't mean it didn't happen at all. He lied. He must have had another gun, and he just hid Blake's. Then he returned it before he left."

A tired sigh leaves Tristan's chest, as if he's saying, "Are you listening to yourself?" He has every right to question me and my sanity. Am I losing it? Have the stress and lack of sleep pushed me over the edge? Have I imagined Butterfly Man doing unspeakable things to me in my bedroom?

Doubt plants its roots in my mind. I mean, the whole scene seems to be cut out of one of my books. And I was in my head, picturing him, before it happened.

No. I didn't imagine it. Butterfly Man was here. I point at Tristan, my eyes wide. "He said, and I quote, 'When the man with the motorcycle returns, prepare for some good news. I've left him something precious where he's at'."

"What?"

"Did you not say you found something at Gia's? He knew exactly where you were going, and he left you a note there, didn't he? How could I have known that if I'd imagined it?"

His jaw clenches. His eyes, a storm of un-
certainty as they flicker between doubt and affection.

I lift my chin. "Unless I'm lying to make
you believe me. Say it. Don't be shy."

"You're just not making any sense. How
could he know where I was? He's watching,
okay, but how could he watch me and be here
with you at the same time? I'm not bugged. I
thoroughly check daily. We all do."

"What about your bike? You found a track-
er in my car."

"My bike is still at the garage in Boston. I've
arranged for it to arrive on the island tomorrow. I took one of our cars tonight, which are
all secure, Birdie."

"Then, like you, I don't know how Butterfly
Man did it. All I know is that he is real, and he
was in my room tonight, whether you believe
me or not."

CHAPTER 5

Birdie

Tristan scans the car he drove to Gia's place in front of me. "See? It's clean."

My exhale, a misty plume, dances briefly in front of my face before it dissipates like a fleeting dream. Cold nips at my cheeks and nose. I hug myself tightly, the thickness of my coat useless against the island air at this time of the night, against the doubt swirling in my head. If you can't trust your mind, what else is left?

Tristan opens the passenger door for me. "It's cold. Why don't you get inside? The box I found at your assistant's house is in there."

"Was she there?" I ask. "Any sign she's been to her place since the last time she was here?"

"No, but the door was open. That's how I

got in."

"What about Blake? Did Marcus find him?"

Tristan shakes his head. "Abel wasn't at his office then, neither was his car."

We climb in, and he reaches for the backseat. Then he puts a box on the center console between us. It has a butterfly drawing on the top.

I swallow. "Did you open it?"

"Not yet. I thought we'd do it together. But before we do, is there anything you need to tell me about what happened tonight, anything you forgot to mention, anything at all?"

His questioning stabs at me, but part of me knows I deserve it. I haven't been one hundred percent honest with him about tonight. There are things I hide, things I'll always be hiding.

I clasp my fingers in my lap, staring at them absently. "Everything we deduced about him is true. He's someone I met a long time ago, and he knows who I am. There's something he's said, a confession of sorts."

"The murders?"

"Yes. He called them the pervert and the thief. Then he promised he'd make Blake pay for what he did, just like the others, the ones I knew about and the ones I hadn't yet."

"Others? Is that what we're gonna find in the box?"

Silence thickens around us, but I can feel his

gaze boring into me. I drag my eyes toward his. "I think so, unless I made this whole thing up."

He lets out a restless sigh. "Open it."

My eyes zero in on the box. The butterfly drawing on top seems to flutter, a trick of the light or my frayed nerves. I take a deep breath, preparing myself for what I may find inside.

"Here goes nothing." I lift the lid slowly, as if expecting something to leap out at me. Instead, I'm greeted by a neat stack of newspaper clippings. My heart races as I pick up the first one.

Principal of Troubled Youth School Dies in Suspected DUI Accident

My gaze widens at the photo under the headline. "That's our school principal."

Tristan snatches the piece of paper from my hand and examines it. "Oh God."

"There's more." I reach for the next clipping, my fingers steady, as if they belong to someone else, someone more composed, someone who isn't unraveling by the second.

He shifts, his impatience palpable. I pull the next piece of paper out, and my breath catches.

Fatal Car Crash Claims Life of Prominent Therapist

Bile rises in my throat. Another familiar face stares back at me from the photo. "That's... that's…"

"The school therapist." His jaw tightens, the

tension radiating off him. "The two men who didn't believe you. The people who wronged you."

"The ones I hadn't known about yet. See? I'm not crazy or a liar. He was there, and he told me all about them."

"He killed them, too, and made it look like an accident."

"But how did he know about what they'd done?"

"The same way he knew about Aaron. He's been stalking you for years."

"Aaron was following me everywhere. He harassed me in public. It's easy for a stalker to figure Aaron out, but the principal and the therapist, all our interactions were in the school, and no one knew about the way they'd treated me. I told you they'd covered everything up."

His eyes sparkle. "Birdie, this could be a massive clue. Think about it. The only way someone would know about Aaron, the principal and the therapist together is that they were there when it happened. They've witnessed everything. What if your stalker is someone who has worked at the school with you?"

My breath comes out shallow. The pieces slowly come together. It makes a lot of sense for Butterfly Man to be someone from the school. "But I don't remember anyone who could be…" My voice cracks under the weight of the revelation. "No one who stood out."

"It wouldn't have to be someone who stood out. Think about it. Could be a janitor, a teacher, anyone who had access to the school. Someone in the background."

"Not a stranger emerging from the shadows but a face I've seen before countless times. A man who thinks I didn't really see him, so he wears this mask, hoping this time I will."

He nods solemnly. "Exactly."

"Who could it be?" My head spins. "I can't place him, Tristan."

"I'll get a list of every person who worked at the school back then, and we'll go through it one by one. I'm sure something will refresh your memory and help you identify him."

"Maybe there are more clues in here." I peer inside the box. There are more clippings about more accidents. The lawyer who covered the school's tracks. Aaron's parents. It's too much blood, more than I've ever wanted, more than I'm prepared to accept.

"Why would he do this?" I rasp. "Look at the dates of all these accidents, Tristan. They all happened in the span of a week. Last week. So why now?"

Tristan leans closer, his voice dropping to a near whisper. "You've been provoking him for quite some time. He's showing you he hasn't forgotten about his promise. This is his idea of proving he's the only one worthy of protecting and loving you because no one else would go to such lengths for you."

A chill runs through me. "I didn't want them dead."

"Of course you wanted them to die."

"No. No, Tristan. How could you say that?"

"Birdie, there's no one else here but me. I understand you in ways no one else can, and I'll never judge you. With me, you can drop the act. You wanted him to kill them. You wanted someone to make them pay in ways you couldn't. You wanted revenge. You still do."

He lowers his head to my level, leaning in, his stare searching mine. "Isn't that why you didn't say your safe word to Brandon? You weren't scared for his young life. You were afraid your stalker would get caught or killed before he kept his promise till the end."

His breath fans my cheek, hot and shallow. The proximity is overwhelming, his body a looming force just shy of touching mine. I don't flinch. I won't give him the satisfaction.

You think you see right through me? Perhaps you do understand me in ways others can't, but you don't see half of the darkness that swells to fill every corner in me, the chaos, the pain. Definitely not the pain.

"You keep saying you never judge me, but first you don't believe a word I say, then you question my sanity. Now that there's evidence I didn't imagine the whole night, you question my integrity?"

A smirk stretches the scar above his lip. "It wasn't a question, Birdie."

It's a truth he believes is damning. Birdie Abel is a lying, manipulative, morally grey character. What does that say about him? About all of them? How they stick to their moral high ground while swimming in a world filled with villains in crisp suits, uniforms, leather jackets and carefully crafted smiles that bleed lies…

He shifts closer, tension vibrating in the inches separating us. "I just wish you were honest with me."

There's no honesty here—only strategy. A plot. A story to be written, and I'm the one who must write it.

I wet my lips, deliberately slow. His gaze tracks the movement, and something flickers in it, a shift in him, the crack in his resolve. The tension between us tightens like a string pulled taut, ready to snap.

"How do you like to be written, Tristan? A hero, a villain, an antihero or a side character that ends up a casualty, a victim? Which one do you choose to be? Because you can't be all of them. You can't be the war hero, the protector with an impeccable moral compass, and the man who promised to lie and kill for the forbidden woman he's been fucking his fist to since he knew how."

He swallows hard, the muscle in his jaw ticking as he fights whatever hunger is raging inside of him. The kind he's spent years burying under that mask of righteousness. The urge to close the gap, to kiss me, to push me away—it's all there. But he stays still, letting the moment stretch on, letting the tension coil tighter.

"Why are you still here, stuck in this…game with me?" I tilt my head just enough that our lips are almost brushing. "I'll tell you why. Because you like it. The lies, the blood, the thrill of not knowing what I'll do next. You like it when I'm bad."

"You think I like it?" His voice is rough, barely restrained. "What I like is control. And you… Goddamn you."

"What am I, Tristan? A chaos you've yet to tame but no matter what you can't?" I lean in just enough for our lips to graze, the barest hint of a touch. "Someone you, too, hate for making you feel like this?"

There's a beat where the world narrows to just this moment, just us, the flames between our mouths and the pitch-black secrets swirling with every breath.

And then he pulls back, seething. "There's another piece of paper in the box. Check it. Maybe it's a clue."

CHAPTER 6

Birdie

The last card Butterfly Man has dealt burns a hole in the bottom of the box.

It's not a newspaper clipping but a photograph.

A stark white lighthouse looms against the sky, its beam cutting through the darkness. Edgartown Lighthouse.

I hold the picture. "What is this supposed to mean? He knows my favorite lighthouse in MA? We've already established that when he left that envelope the other day."

Tristan's demeanor shifts subtly. To most, he'd appear calm, but I've learned to read the signs. The slight tightening around his eyes, the imperceptible tension in his shoulders—he's on high alert. His hand shoots out. His eyes, sharp and focused, zero in on the back of the photo. "Jesus. Behind it. Look."

I flip the photo, and my heart dips. Scrawled in what looks like blood are two chilling words: *FIND ME*.

"Oh my God. Is this blood? Real blood?"

He takes the picture from me and brings it to his nose. "Yes."

"Butterfly Man was in one piece when he broke in tonight. He left that box before he came to visit, which means this could be the blood of his next victim. Gia. Blake. We must go to the lighthouse." I nod emphatically. "Now."

His gaze darts around the car and back to the photo as he seems to assess potential threats. His hand moves absently to his side, where he keeps his concealed weapon. "No. This is a classic ambush setup to lure us out, to unsettle us and push us into making a mistake."

"Tristan, I have to see it for myself. If they're dead, I need to see it."

"And if they're not? What if he's left them for dead at the lighthouse, and you arrive at what will be a crime scene? What are you gonna tell the police? Your detective won't be able to save you then, Birdie."

It's not the first time Butterfly Man has tried to make me look like a suspect. Blackmail is his backup plan to claim me; be mine or rot in prison. He knows I won't be able to resist, and

I'll rush to see if he's kept his promise. A trap like Tristan says.

"What do you suggest we do? I can't just sit there."

"That's exactly what you need to do. Go to bed for fuck's sake."

"Are you fucking kidding me right now? If you think for one second that I can sleep or go back to that room where I've been violated by a creep *twice*…"

He winces. "You don't have to say anything to make me feel more guilty than I already feel. You hired me to keep you safe, to stop him from violating you, and it happened again under my watch, and for that I can't even begin to show you how sorry I am. But like I own up to my shit, you should own up to yours. All of this could have ended tonight if you'd chosen to stop him."

Rage jolts inside me. "So now it's my fault you failed to keep your fucking promises?"

"I didn't say that, but I know what you're doing." He stares right through me. "You never wanted me to catch or stop him. What you really want is the people who hurt you dead, at any cost."

"I'm tired of this shit. Running in circles, wasting time when there could be a body out there—"

"Do you even want him gone after he kills

your husband for you?"

"What kind of question is that?"

"Answer me, Birdie. Do you want that murderer to die or not?"

I open my mouth, but the words catch in my throat. Do I want Butterfly Man, the murderous psycho who has used me for his sick pleasures, who has put blood on my hands, who has infiltrated my life and is on the verge of ruining it, dead? The answer should be simple, shouldn't it?

But nothing is that simple. That unhinged killer is the only one who truly sees me, who understands what I need. He's doing what I couldn't. When everyone else has failed me, he's brought me the justice I've been robbed.

Tristan's eyes narrow. "That's what I thought."

"You don't understand," I whisper.

"Oh, I do, Birdie. Trust me."

I have no time for this. "Then take me to the lighthouse."

"No!" He waves a hand angrily at the box. "There are only two things we can do right now. You just sit here while I get rid of this shit or we call the cops and we deal with the consequences before the situation escalates beyond containment. I'm not gonna let you destroy yourself over that bastard."

"I won't, I swear. We're just going to drive there and take a walk. No one will suspect anything. I go there all the time, and everybody knows it."

"At four in the morning?"

"I'm having trouble sleeping, and I thought the beach air might help, or I want to watch the sunrise because it'll inspire me… I don't know, if it comes down to being questioned, I'll come up with something."

"Like you always do."

"Yes, like I always do. Because everything is a story, and I'm the storyteller. Now, please, take us there, Tristan. He left me that clue because he wants me to see whatever is there, and I don't wish to disobey him. Not after what he's done to me tonight."

"Why can't you see that this is too dangerous?"

"Not as dangerous as provoking him again. Do you not want to know whom he might have killed? To find out if it's all over?"

"It's not over, and you know it. This is a trap."

"Perhaps, but what if we don't go and he punishes us by leaving something there that could incriminate us?"

His head jerks at me, and concern flashes across his face. "Fuck."

"Yes, fuck, so please start the goddamn

car."

His nostrils flare as he lifts his wrist to his mouth. "Marcus, Brandon, do you copy?"

A faint crackle comes from his earpiece before he says, "We're heading to Edgartown Lighthouse. I need you two to follow us but keep your distance. Stay out of sight unless I give the signal. Understood?"

Another crackle.

"The rest of you, stay on high alert," he continues. "Secure the house. If anyone, and I mean anyone so much as approaches the perimeter, engage to kill. Clear?"

My heart skips a beat. "What?"

"I repeat, engage to kill." His eyes dare me as he turns the key in the ignition, the engine roaring to life. "You do things your way, and I'll do things mine."

My stomach ties into one knot after another. I text Spencer the second we move, a casual request to let me inside the lighthouse if possible. The timing and sending location could be used as evidence; I was nowhere near the lighthouse—the crime scene.

The drive to the lighthouse is eerily quiet. The roads are empty, the world oblivious to the flames licking us unsatisfied until nothing is left but ash.

As we round the final bend, the lighthouse comes into view, stark white against the inky sky. Flashes of red and blue surround the parking lot.

"Fuck," Tristan mutters, slowing the car to a crawl. "That complicates things."

"The police are already there. It *is* a crime scene."

"And we have incriminating evidence right here in the car."

My eyes widen at the box. "What are we going to do?"

"Give me the clippings and the photo."

Swiftly, I open the lid and fish them out. He takes the car lighter out and burns the evidence. Then he throws it out of the window. "Now, it's just an empty box. You can't get arrested for having one of those. Not unless they test it for blood and DNA, which I don't think they will right now, not yet."

I swallow hard. "Thank you, I guess."

We pull into the parking lot. Police cars and an ambulance crowd the small area. Yellow tape surrounds the perimeter. The lighthouse an accusing finger. The familiar setting now cut out of a nightmare. Tristan kills the engine, his eyes scanning the scene as two officers approach the car. My heart pounds so hard I can barely hear over its rhythm. Part of me wants to flee, but it's too late. There's no turning back. I must find out what Butterfly Man has done.

"Stay in the car and don't say anything," Tristan mutters, his hand hovering near his gun.

The gesture, meant to reassure, only amplifies my anxiety. "What are you going to do?"

His jaw tightens as he holds my gaze. "Protect you."

An officer knocks on the car window, and Tristan half opens it, getting the license and registration documents ready. "Good day, Officer. Tristan Morra, Monarca Security. This is Mrs. Birdie Abel, and I'm her security detail. Is everything all right?"

The officer cranes his head and inspects us suspiciously. The chilling ocean breeze carries the scent of salt and something sinister. Is it the metallic tang of blood? The cloying sweetness of death? My imagination runs wild, conjuring images of what awaits us beyond the yellow tape. He takes the papers from Tristan and examines them. "The lighthouse is closed. You need to turn back."

"I see. May I know what happened?"

The officer twists his lips as he hands Tristan the license back. "Murder."

Who died? Is it Gia? Just Gia? I can't turn back before I know everything. Just as I rack my brain to find an excuse to stay, a familiar figure emerges from the crowd of officers.

Jacob.

A cold sweat breaks out down my neck as

he spots us and makes his way over. My carefully constructed world of lies and half-truths suddenly feels as fragile as a house of cards in a storm.

What does Jacob know? What has he found? And most terrifyingly—what will I have to do to keep my secrets safe?

He exchanges a few hushed words with the officer, who nods and steps away. My fingers dig into my palms, leaving crescent-shaped indentations when Jacob leans down to the car window.

"Birdie?" He glances between me and Tristan, his voice a mix of surprise and suspicion. "What are you doing here? Did someone call you already?"

"C-call me?" I clear my throat. "Why?"

"To identify the body." Jacob frowns suspiciously. "But that should be done at the morgue."

My stomach drops. "Body? Whose body, Jacob?"

"We believe the murder victim is Gia Connelly, your assistant."

It shouldn't come as a shock. I knew Gia was going to die. When I came here, I expected to find her dead. Part of me even wanted it. But why when I hear Jacob's words, the definitive finality in them, does it feel like the world has tilted on its axis?

Gia might have lied to me, failed to support me when I needed her the most and slept with my husband, but I blame Blake for it. Sweet, efficient Gia wasn't malicious. She was naive and fell for his charm just like I did. She didn't deserve to die like this, another casualty in this twisted game.

Or am I the naive one here? The delusional girl desperate for any shreds of love in any form, who still believes there are good people in this world whose intentions aren't exploiting her for themselves?

A scream builds in my throat, but I swallow it down. I can't break now. "What?" I choke out.

"I'm sorry, Birdie. I thought you knew. When her sister didn't answer, I thought they called you. You're listed as the victim's emergency contact."

"How...how did it happen?" *Please don't say she crashed her car after loading her blood with drugs.*

Jacob hesitates, his eyes flicking to Tristan. "She was shot."

"Shot?" I don't need to feign surprise. I didn't expect that at all. "Here?"

"I can't say that for sure yet, but most likely not. No one heard a gunshot, and the preliminary body examination indicates an earlier time of death. She was killed elsewhere, and then her body was dumped here." He narrows his eyes at us. "What are you doing here this time of the day if no one called you about the murder?"

I swallow. "I…had trouble sleeping again, so I thought to come here, watch the sunrise, get some ocean air. It helps me sleep…and write."

"Could you not get the same from your terrace or the sunrise and ocean air here are different?"

The air rushes out of my lungs. I open my mouth to speak, but Tristan rolls his gaze at Jacob. "They are for her. This is her favorite spot on the island. Don't you know that from the *investigations*? The whole town does, so you must have already been tipped off."

"I must have forgotten." Jacob starts a staring competition against Tristan. "But thanks for the pointer on my next date, Morra."

Tristan's fist clenches on his thigh. "What are *you* doing here, Detective? This is Edgartown. Last time I checked you're with Oak Bluff Police or did you transfer? Again?"

Yeah, why is Jacob on Gia's case?

Neither Jacob nor Tristan blinks. "I was called in because of Saldana's case," Jacob says finally without breaking the menacing eye contact, his voice low. "There are…similarities in the crime scenes that can't be ignored."

Similarities. My mind races. What has Butterfly Man done? What clues has he left behind this time?

"There might be a connection between Connelly's murder and Saldana's," Jacob adds.

My blood runs cold. "Connection? But Saldana wasn't murdered; she committed suicide. It's official. You told me and the whole country that."

Jacob studies my reaction. "Then you can imagine the spot that puts me in. I don't like it either, but the investigation has reopened. Let's hope Saldana's manner of death is the only thing I got wrong."

Tristan tenses beside me as I struggle to keep my face neutral. "What do you mean, Jacob?"

"It means I'm going to need both of you to come down to the station. We have a lot to discuss."

"So I'm a suspect again?"

"Right now, everyone is a suspect."

CHAPTER 7

Tristan

"What are you gonna do, Birdie?" I keep my eye on the road, heading to the station.

She purses her lips at the sky. The sun peeks over the horizon, painting the sky in hues of pink and gold. A new day or the beginning of the end? "We don't have a choice. We have to talk to the police or we'll look guilty."

"Are you sure about this? We're walking into dangerous territory. You're not under arrest. You don't have to go. Let them come to you. That will give you a chance to, at least, talk to your lawyer first. Besides, at home, I can be with you when they ask their questions but not at the station."

"They want to question you, too, Tristan,

and I bet there are more reporters blocking my driveway by now. It's all about the optics. It's best if we go willingly instead of being dragged out of the house in cuffs in front of them."

"But what are we gonna tell the police? We need to get our stories straight."

"There's only one story to tell. We don't know anything about the murders, and they can't be connected. Saldana killed herself out of guilt. Gia was unexpectedly and tragically shot."

"You serious? That's what we're gonna say?"

"Of course. What else?"

"The truth for once."

She chuckles a humorless laugh. "The only truth you can count on is that I'm being tested. This whole scene, whatever leads left purposely to tie the two murders together, is nothing but a punishment, and the only way to make it stop is to pass the test and prove my loyalty."

"You can't let your stalker control your life like that. This is getting out of hand. We have to come clean and let the police handle it before it's too late."

"It's already too late, don't you think? We passed the point of no return many chapters ago. You want to tell the police the truth, here's one. Neither of us could have killed Gia or Saldana."

"But how can we prove it? We don't even know when Gia was killed to confirm an alibi."

"Lucky for us, we can be each other's alibi any time we wish because we have an *immune* security system with cameras to prove it."

Is she asking me to manipulate the security footage to fake an alibi if I need to? Like the stalker did? There's nothing Birdie Abel would stop at to prove her loyalty to him, to make him trust her enough to kill her husband for her.

But, in a way, she's looking after me, too. I'm the one who bought the burner and faked Gia's texts. I'm the one who burned the evidence in the box.

The realization sits heavy in my chest, a weight I can't shake off. I've crossed lines I never thought I would, all for her. And, regardless of the risks, I'd do it again in a heartbeat.

"Judging by your silence, I'm sure you've done the math by now," she says. "Butterfly Man may not be testing only me."

My fists clench around the steering wheel as the pieces fall into place. Unlike her, I'm the one who leaves the house alone and might need an alibi. She couldn't have killed those women, but I could have. "He could be trying to eliminate me from your story by framing *me* for the murders."

"Exactly. It's his fail-safe backup plan. He

knows I'll always have your back, Tristan, even if, to do so, I must protect him, too."

The words echo in my mind, stirring up feelings I've tried so hard to bury. I chance a glance at her, and the look in her eyes nearly undoes me. There's fear there, yes, but also determination. And something else. Something that mirrors the ache in my own chest.

"Jesus Christ, Birdie. Don't do this to me." I shake my head in anger, stopping the car.

She turns to me, her eyes blazing with an intensity that both terrifies and captivates me. "Do what?"

"Say anything, do anything, to get what you want. You don't have to do this with me because I'd do anything for you without asking for anything in return," I confess, the words tumbling out before I can stop them. "Lie, cheat, manipulate evidence, even kill. So don't fucking lie to me."

"I'm not lying, Tristan. I have no reason to. I mean every word."

The car suddenly feels too small, too confining. Her scent, the heat radiating off her body, it's intoxicating and suffocating all at once.

She leans in closer. "Butterfly Man won't hurt me, not like that, and you know it, but he will hurt you. I'm looking after *you*."

"Why?"

Her face softens, dropping the mask of strength and cruel indifference she hides behind, and a hint of a smile crosses her lips as she drops her gaze. "Because we're survivors, Tristan." Then she stretches her hand and rests it palm up on the center console. An invitation. A seal of fate. "We are meant to survive this, together. *Almost like destiny.*"

"Birdie," I start, eyes pinned to her anticipating palm, not sure what I'm going to say—I love you. I hate you. I wish I'd never met you. I'm destined to love no one but you—but needing to say something.

"I know, Tristan," she says softly. "I know."

I squeeze my eyes shut, shuddering, and lace my fingers into hers. Her touch sends electricity coursing through my body. In that moment, everything crystallizes. The danger we're in, the lines we've crossed, the feelings we can't acknowledge—it all comes into sharp focus. And it hits me with gut-wrenching certainty.

I'm in love with Birdie Abel as much as I've always been in love with Reagan Fletcher. It isn't just dangerous or toxic—it's a death sentence. And God help me, I'm ready to serve it.

I meet her gaze one last time, printing a kiss on her palm, before I start the car and drive. We pull up to the police station about to walk into a lion's den of our own making, with only our wits and our lies to protect us. I kill the engine, but neither of us moves to get out. In the silence, I can hear her breathing, rapid and heavy. Or maybe it's my own.

"Last chance. It's not too late to back down," I say.

Her throat bobs with a gulp before she takes a deep breath. "It's going to be o—"

The radio screeches with an unclear signal over static.

She frowns at it. "What is this?"

"Nothing." I turn it off. "It must have picked a random frequency. We're outside the police station. It's not unusual for our radio to pick their comms."

A line between her eyebrows deepens, and I can almost hear the gears turning in her brilliant, terrifying mind. "Can they do the same?"

I blink, following the direction she's going with the question.

"You said earlier you and the team weren't bugged, and you checked yourselves and the vehicles thoroughly. But what about the radio?"

"Our comms are secure and encrypted, Birdie."

She points a thumb behind her at the station building. "So are theirs, but your radio picked them up."

I nod pensively. "The only thing that could be breached without a trace... With the right equipment capable of picking up the specific frequency, *someone* could be eavesdropping."

"Oh God. *He* heard you and Marcus were leaving the house and planned his move. You see? I'm not crazy, Tristan. Every word I said is true. Butter—"

I put my index finger on my lips and blink three times. I've turned the radio off, but we can't be too careful. "Guess who has easy access to such equipment."

Her head whips toward the building and then back in my direction. She slumps down in her seat. "No, Tristan. No way."

"You still think it's a good idea to walk in there?"

CHAPTER 8

Birdie

I sit across from Jacob in the sterile interrogation room. The cold metal of the chair seeps through my clothes, a reminder of where I am and what is at stake.

Who am I looking at? The good man who promises a future of love and respect? The detective who has lost his trust in me and considers me a suspect again? The psychopathic killer hiding in plain sight whose hand I came all over last night?

The questions swirl in my mind, each one more terrifying than the last. Is Jacob Torrance *the* Butterfly Man like Tristan believes, playing some sick game with me? Or does he genuinely suspect me of murdering Saldana and Gia? I can't read him. His face, a cold mask as steely as his eyes, gives nothing away.

His gaze is as sharp as ever, yet devoid of any of the warmth he's shown me in the past few days.

I'm a butterfly pinned under glass, unable to break free, observed from every angle, and he's the catcher.

"Mrs. Abel," he starts formally, intimacy scrubbed clean, and the name feels awkward coming from him, staring at a thin file in his hand. "When was the last time you saw your assistant?"

The day Saldana died. "March 5th."

"She hasn't been coming to work since?"

"She texted she was sick."

"At what time?"

"I don't know exactly…sometime in the evening. I can check my phone for the exact timing."

He brings out a pen and a notepad from the pocket of his suit jacket and starts writing. "Evening of March 5th?"

"No. March 6th."

"So she missed a full day of work without notice. Is this normal for her?"

I shake my head. "She never missed a day at work."

"And how was your reaction to that sudden change in behavior?"

"I found it odd," I lie. We had a fight that night. I totally expected she wouldn't come to work the next day, perhaps not ever. "I texted and called her that morning, but she didn't answer. Then at night, she texted she was sick… and she'd lost her phone. That was why she didn't call in sick earlier."

He pauses to read my face. "Did you make any contact with her after March 6th?"

"Of course. We were texting daily until a few days ago. I got worried so I asked my bodyguards to go check on her. They never found her home, though."

He scribbles something on his notepad. "When she left your house on March 5th, was she upset about anything?"

Should I tell him about the shock in her eyes when she finally found out the truth about my husband, the man she loved and tried to steal from his wife, her boss and best friend, or the fight we had when she tried to spill my secrets to Tristan without my permission? "Saldana's suicide. It shook us all."

"Did it?" He can barely hide the scoff.

"Yes, Detective. Saldana stole from me, and I wanted her to pay the price, but not like that." I wanted her to live through the shame, to watch her career fall apart in front of her eyes and feel the burn. But she was given an easy way out.

"Where were you on March 11th between seven p.m. and one a.m. on March 12th?"

"Is this a trick question? You knew exactly where I was that night."

He glances at the camera nestled in the corner. "Please answer the question for the record."

With a half-smile, I lean back in the chair. "Seven p.m. I was at home getting ready for a meeting with a *friend*. Eight p.m. he came to pick me up. We had dinner at The Alchemist. Then I went home around midnight and went to bed. I'm happy to give you his number to confirm."

He rolls his eyes. "Can we check your security cameras as well to confirm your whereabouts at the hours you weren't having dinner with your *friend*?"

"Of course. My bodyguards can give you their statements, too." I lean forward, examining his expression like he's dissecting mine. "That timeframe, is that when Gia…?" If that was the time Butterfly Man killed her, Jacob couldn't be him. He was with me all the time.

Unless he killed her right before or after our date.

Hello, I'm Jacob Torrance. I shoot people dead and then go buy flowers for the woman I like, go out with her, talk sexy books and eat vegan ice cream for dessert. And I'm the stupid woman who is falling for it.

"Why were you going to Edgartown's lighthouse in the middle of the night, right where we discovered the body of your assistant?"

"I already answered that question. I had trouble sleeping and decided to go there. It's one of my favorite spots. I go there all the time. You can ask Spencer, the lightkeeper. I even texted him to see if he could do me a favor and let me in. The view from the gallery is the best, and we go way back, since my wedding photoshoot."

"Why do you need bodyguards, Mrs. Abel?" he asks.

To protect me from you, I guess. "I'm a celebrity. Better safe than sorry."

He puckers his lips on a grunt. "When was the last time you saw your husband, Mrs. Abel?"

Why is he asking me about Blake? "The morning of March 5th. Why?"

"He's an ex-cop, right?"

"Retired early, yes," I answer warily.

"Why? Why did he retire?"

My fingers instinctively move to my mouth, but I clench my fist under the table before they give me away. "My career was taking off, and he decided to retire to become my manager. Can I ask why all these questions about Blake and what he has to do with Gia or Saldana?"

"Has your husband had any affairs during the course of your relationship?"

I cock a brow. Where does this come from?

No one knows about Gia and Blake except me, Tristan and the team, and Butterfly Man. What does Jacob really know? And how? Could he really be my stalker? "I've had doubts. Only doubts."

"I see, and how is your current relationship with your husband, Mrs. Abel?"

My jaw clenches. "We're getting a divorce."

"Because of suspicions of his infidelity?"

"Because Blake Abel is a violent man, Detective."

Jacob's eyes gleam as if he's just discovered a precious secret, as if he hadn't already known. "How is he violent, Mrs. Abel?"

An angry sigh leaves my chest. "Last year, we had a fight, and he pushed me down the stairs. The police wouldn't help, so he got away with it. I asked him for a divorce. He refused to give me one, said he'd go to therapy and work on his issues. Unfortunately, the medication he was prescribed was too strong. He's developed a substance abuse issue that has gotten out of hand, so I've filed for divorce myself."

"How did he take it?"

"Not nicely."

"Do you or your husband own a gun?"

The question catches me off guard. Of all the things I expect him to ask, this isn't it. He said Gia was shot. Does he suspect the murder weapon is a gun Blake or I own? I blink, trying to hide my surprise. "I don't own any guns, but Blake does." And it is nestled in my dresser. Butterfly Man has made sure of it.

Do the police think *that* is the murder weapon? My mind races. Blake hasn't been near me in over a week. If someone used his gun, it wasn't him.

Butterfly Man killed Gia with Blake's gun and put it back in my dresser. If the police find it, along with the photos that prove Blake and Gia's infidelity, and add it all up to the fight Gia and I had the last night I saw her, I'd be their number one suspect.

"What kind?" Jacob asks.

I stare at him, my pulse quickening. He's bluffing—he has to be. In order for Butterfly Man to have used the gun to kill Gia, he must have entered the house to take the gun before yesterday. How is this possible?

But Jacob's poker face is flawless. Is he using privileged information to shake me because he is Butterfly Man or has he found real evidence as a detective doing his job? "A Glock. I don't know the exact model, but he's always had the same gun since he was on the force. He was allowed to buy it after retirement. Can you please tell me what this is all about?"

He sighs, pulls a paper out of the file and slides it my way. "Ballistics report came. It identifies the weapon the killer used on the victim. It's a Glock 23."

I shrug at the paper. "I'm not an expert, but aren't Glocks the most popular guns in the country?" For officers and civilians. Blake has one. Tristan, too. It was the backup gun he gave me the night my stalker was following me down the street. I'm sure there are more Glocks with the rest of the team as well as with other officers. "The killer could be anyone."

"Actually, the weapon is modified. *Police* modified. Precisely, with a *Miami*-compliant barrel. Wasn't Blake Abel with Miami PD before he retired?"

CHAPTER 9

Tristan

"What did you think of Ms. Connelly, Mr. Morra?" Detective Douchebag starts questioning me.

I recall the last time I saw her and the conversation we had. "Unfortunately, I didn't get a chance to know her that well, but she seemed like a kind lady." Until I realized she betrayed Birdie, sleeping with her husband under her roof.

"Was Ms. Connelly and Mrs. Abel on good terms? Did they like each other?"

"They've been working together for so many years, so I guess, yes."

"Have you ever felt that Ms. Connelly was jealous of Mrs. Abel?"

My gaze narrows. "Everybody is jealous

of my client. Everybody wants a piece of what she has." *Like you.*

He takes his time studying my face. "In your opinion, which piece did Ms. Connelly want?"

I shrug.

"Her money? Her fame?" He leans his head forward. "Her husband?"

"You think Abel was having an affair with Ms. Connelly behind my client's back?"

"You tell me."

"I'll tell you what I know." I clasp my hands and rest my elbows on the table. "Any man who cheats on Birdie Abel is a dickhead."

He waits for me to say more, but I just smile. Infidelity and murder go hand in hand. If he thinks for one second he can spin off my words into a motive to use against Birdie, he's in for a mighty disappointment.

"When was the last time you saw Ms. Connelly?"

"The day Katie Saldana was announced dead. Ms. Connelly was at the house until late at night."

"Does she stay late at Mrs. Abel's house often?"

"I think so. Mrs. Abel told me her assistant sometimes stayed over in the guestroom downstairs." Where she fucked her husband.

"If they were that close, on a harsh day like that, don't you think Ms. Connelly would have stayed over, especially if she was there at a late hour already?"

That was probably Gia's intention, but she was upset Birdie yelled at her and left. I'm not stupid to give him that much, though. Birdie had a fight with Gia. Police can twist *that* into motive, too. "Maybe, but we turned the guestroom into the control room when we took the job, and all other rooms were occupied by the team."

He smirks. "Convenient."

Wipe that shit off your ugly face or I'll wipe it for you. "Excuse me?"

"Where were you on March 11th between seven p.m. and one a.m. on March 12th?"

My nostrils flare. "With Mrs. Abel, doing my job, protecting her while she's out having dinner with *you* at The Alchemist."

The motherfucker smirks again. "What time did you reach her house after dinner?"

"A little before midnight. I didn't leave the house until the next evening. You're welcome to check the security footage to confirm."

"How do you describe Blake Abel as a person, Mr. Morra?"

A piece of shit that doesn't deserve Birdie, just like you. But what's Abel got to do with Gia's death when I'm one hundred percent positive her killer is in this room? "He's my client's husband."

"And?"

"It's hard to form an opinion about a man you've only met once," I lie.

"When did you meet him?"

Eight years ago. "My first day on the job at my client's house."

"Was he still living with Mrs. Abel back then?"

"No. He'd stopped by. Was shocked she hired us without his approval. He got angry and tried to fire us. When she stood up for herself, he…" My fists ball as I remember the feeling of his face bruising under my punches.

"He what?"

"Became a threat to my client I had to neutralize."

"He attacked her?"

I nod. "It's all on camera. Again, you're welcome to check the footage. Why the sudden interest in my client's husband?"

"Please just answer the questions, Mr. Morra. Was Mr. Abel carrying that day he attacked your client?"

You little piece of shit. When I prove you're the stalker bastard, I'm gonna enjoy watching you take your last breath. Let's see who will have the power then.

"Mr. Morra?"

I nod again. "I confiscated the weapon after he tried to attack her."

"Where is it now?"

I think you know exactly where it is. I see what you're doing here, scumbag. You want to pin your murder on Abel and be the fucking hero in Birdie's eyes. Not on my watch, you prick. "I returned it to him after the team escorted him out of the premises."

He stares at me for a while. I stare back without a blink.

He clicks his pen and turns a page on his notepad. "What kind of gun did he carry?"

"A Glock 23."

CHAPTER 10

Birdie

ristan ushers me out of the station. We exchange a glance, my heart rumbling in its cage. What the hell is going on? What evidence have the police found that connects Saldana's murder to Gia's? Why do they insinuate Blake killed my assistant? With a gun I have?

What story are you writing, Butterfly Man? Because it certainly isn't mine. He controls the narrative again, and I can't figure out the twist or even when it's going to hit.

"Birdie," Jacob's voice echoes behind my back as Tristan opens the car door for me.

"Get in the car," Tristan orders and stands behind me, blocking the way, before I turn. "Are there any more questions you need to ask my client, Detective?"

"I'm talking to her, not you," Jacob says, his voice laced with animosity. "Get out of my way."

When Tristan doesn't budge, I move aside and incline my head just enough to see Jacob. "I think we're done here, Detective. Unless you'd like to interview me again, with my lawyer present."

"Birdie, please," Jacob's gaze wanders between Tristan and me, "I can't reveal sensitive information about the case, but please trust me. I don't think you're safe, and I can't help you unless you stop making up stories and start telling me the truth."

Truth or story doesn't matter. As long as you end up where you need to be, all is fair. "I've already told you everything I know."

"No, Birdie. You lied to me," he whispers gruffly. "The stalker, he's not a made-up story or a prank. Your nemesis and your assistant were murdered. Your husband is tangled in their stories. All three are connected, and you hold the missing pieces to this mystery."

What exactly do you know, Jacob? And how? How long before all the lies we've spun twist around our necks? I glance at Tristan and climb inside the car. "Good luck solving your crime, Detective."

"You're making a huge mistake. Let me protect you before it's too late."

Protect me? He gives quite the performance with his persistence. Pure intentions or a mask for the red flags I've been blind to all this time? I stare at Jacob, Tristan shutting the door. "I have all the protection I need. Thank you for your concern, though."

Tristan drives us away from the station. I start humming to ease my nerves.

"Hey, are you okay?"

"I will be. Sorry about the humming. I know it's annoying, but it—"

"Stimulates the vagus nerve, which helps regulate emotions and lower heart rates. They teach us this technique in the military. Where did you learn it?"

"Something I picked up from research, I guess." I swallow, my eyes pinned to the radio. "Is it safe to talk?"

"Yes. I've shut down all comms."

"The police think Gia was shot by Blake's gun. The one I have in my dresser. If they search the house, I'm—"

"It's being taken care of. I won't let anything happen to you."

"What do you mean it's being taken care of?"

"When you said we were going to the police, I had a feeling… My protective instincts flared, and I told Brandon to keep the gun in a safe place, out of the house."

Relief courses through me, not only because Tristan is so intuitive and protective he'd do anything for my safety, but also because he entrusted Brandon with the task. Right now, Brandon is the only one on the team I can fully trust; he was outside my door when Butterfly Man was in the room with me. "Thank you, Tristan. I don't know what I'd do without you."

His lips press into a thin line as his gaze narrows at the horizon. Then the intensity in his eyes bores into me. "You'll always have me, Birdie."

A chill runs through me. I don't know why that sounds more sinister than tender. "Wait," I look down the road, "this isn't the way to the house. Where are we going?"

He doesn't answer, the lines of his jaw sharp and unyielding. His grip tightens on the steering wheel, and he slams the gas pedal.

"Tristan?" I try again.

His gaze flickers toward me, unreadable, before returning to the road. Then the car veers off, tires crunching gravel as we pull onto a secluded path shrouded by trees. The sky darkens and casts eerie shadows on his face, carving his features into something almost unrecognizable.

My instincts scream at me to act, to do something, anything. I get my phone out, but

Tristan grabs it before I can unlock the screen.

"What the hell are you doing?! Give me my phone back! Now!" My voice rises, panic bubbling underneath.

He turns my phone off and pockets it. "No phones." Then he taps something in his sleeve. "I've just jammed the cell service so no one can track us."

"What? I don't understand. Tristan, you're scaring me."

"You need to trust me, Birdie." His tone is soft but steely, like a velvet-wrapped dagger. "You said you trusted me, didn't you?"

I did, but now I wonder if it's the worst mistake I've ever made. "Tristan? Where are you taking me?"

CHAPTER 11

Tristan

There is fear in her eyes. Birdie is afraid of me, the man who has done nothing but save her over and over again. It's almost amusing, and in a way, exciting. They should write about that in psychology books, fear as an aphrodisiac. How the tremble in her lip, the way her pupils dilate like she's prey caught in a snare, can ignite something primal in a man like me.

It's mesmerizing, really, watching her mind race, trying to calculate her next move while knowing there isn't one. Not for her. Every exit, every escape route, has already been sealed. I made sure of it when I chose this place.

She doesn't realize yet that her fear is misplaced. That I'm not the monster she thinks I am—but I could be. Oh, I could be. Isn't that the delicious part? The possibility. The potential.

What would it take to shatter that stubborn will of hers? To make her stop trying to wrest control of the story and accept her role in mine? Would it be pain? Betrayal? Or something simpler, more intimate, like a whisper in her ear, a hand at her throat?

I stop the car at the end of a winding dirt road wide enough for a single vehicle. Darkness engulfs us, save for the faint glow of the dashboard.

Birdie's chest heaves. "Tristan, why did you stop the car? Where are we?"

"Get out and you'll see."

Blood drains from her face as she hesitates to grip the door handle. "What's going on? Why are you—"

"Birdie." My voice cuts through the tension, quiet but commanding. "Out. Now."

Her hand trembles when it pushes the door open. I step out, circling the car to meet her. The cold air slices through me. I watch her wrap her arms around herself and take in the cabin hidden behind a natural curtain of towering pines and oaks.

"What are you doing, Tristan?" She forces herself to look me in the eye. "What is this place?"

A thrill courses through me. I step closer, too close, and she takes a half-step back, her breath catching as if she's realized too late that retreat only makes the predator hungrier.

"Birdie," I murmur, letting her name hang between us like a trap waiting to spring. "You think I've done all of this for you to fear me?"

Her silence is deafening, her defiance crumbling under the weight of her terror. She won't answer, not because she doesn't know, but because she does.

She takes another look behind the trees. The property is surrounded by dense thickets, creating a fortress of greenery that muffles sound and obscures the house from view. The cabin itself is rustic but sturdy, built of dark cedar shingles that blend seamlessly into the forested backdrop. Its sloped roof is partially covered in moss, and the windows are shielded by heavy blackout curtains, ensuring no light escapes at night.

Around the cabin is a modest clearing, encircled by wild berry bushes and ferns. A narrow footpath leads to a hidden beach cove just a short hike away, where jagged rocks shield the shoreline from prying eyes and the ocean waves crash loudly enough to mask any conversation or—some might think—acts of violence.

The perfect place to vanish from the world—or to hide from someone hunting you.

"It's a safehouse." I rented it when I took the job. Common procedure. "After what happened last night, there is no way you're going back to your house, not until I catch the bastard."

Her shoulders relax, and a long sigh seeps out of her lips. "I hate you right now. Why did you not say something? What's with the scare, asshole?"

"Do you really scare that easily?" I smirk. "Or do you really not trust me?"

She arches a brow and drags her gaze toward the cabin. "I'm freezing."

I put my hand on the small of her back to usher her in. "After you, my lady."

Inside, the safehouse is spartan but functional. The main living area is dominated by a large stone fireplace, its hearth stocked with chopped wood. There are a leather couch, a sturdy oak table, and a pair of wooden chairs. A small kitchen with all the necessary appliances is stocked with non-perishable supplies.

A trapdoor in the pantry leads to a small, concealed basement—a small space that serves as an emergency hideout—equipped with a cot, bottled water, canned food and a radio.

There are two bedrooms, each with a reinforced door and a closet hiding a gun safe and emergency supplies.

"The air smells of salt and pine. The only sounds are the distant waves and the occasional rustle of leaves." Birdie looks at me. "Here, isolation is absolute. Is it where my haven lies or my demise?"

"No one knows about this place. There is no cell service so you can't be tracked either, and I'll never let you out of my sight." I close the distance between us and meet her gaze. "No one can find you here, Birdie."

"Should I be relieved or more scared?"

"I installed the CCTV system myself. It covers every inch and has multiple levels of security to stop any hacking attempts for each camera individually and—"

"That's not what I meant."

I swallow, catching the undercurrent in her voice. Swirling in the blue of her eyes is something beyond fear now, something that makes my pulse quicken in an entirely different way.

"You're not as scared of a psycho stalker as much as you're scared of this?" I gesture at the space between us, and I realize we're standing too close to each other but never close enough. I can't take my gaze off her lips. Birdie's breath hitches, but she doesn't retreat. I'm one breath away from inhaling hers.

I've been fighting for so long, but, in her presence, I'm only a man, and she's an electric and undeniable storm here to break me. With a gulp, I bend my head down to her mouth, ready to surrender.

Her lips part. "You said you'd protect me."

"I am protecting you."

"From everything, but no longer from myself, no longer from you."

Fuck. Fuck. FUCK. "When will I ever learn? I can't win this game, not with you." My eyes squeeze, and I grit my teeth on a shaky breath. Pulling back, I claw at my chest as if I could rip my heart out and end all this suffering once and for all.

"Tristan—"

"Stop. I beg you to fucking stop." Both my hands run through my hair, pulling at the ends, and I turn away from her. "I'll go check in with the team and tell them to come over to take their posts here."

"No. No guards."

I face her. "Excuse me?"

She folds her arms across her chest. "I… don't want anyone else here."

"Why, so you can toy around with me a little more, watch me burn to satisfy whatever sadistic urges you have every time you give me hope and then brush me off?"

Her expression pales and then darkens in a split-second, as if I've just stabbed her in the back. "You really think this is what I'm doing?"

You really think I'm falling for your crocodile tears you won't even shed? "If I'm wrong, enlighten me."

Her mouth opens and then closes. She presses her lips and shakes her head before she says, "It doesn't matter. Anyway, I didn't mean no guards because I wanted you here alone for whatever fucked up reason you thought I had. I don't want other guards, period."

"Well, I wish I could stay up twenty-four seven and guard you by myself indefinitely, but I hate to break it to you that I need more manpower and weapons to fully protect you, Mrs. Abel."

"Then bring Brandon, only Brandon."

The one guard on the team she hates the most? I'm about to ask why, but then it all registers in my brain. Brandon is the only one she can trust because he was there, talking to her, when Butterfly Man was in her bedroom.

She puts her hands in front of her to pacify me. "I know you don't want to hear this, but it's—"

"You're right, I don't. Wake up and smell the coffee. Your stalker is Torrance, Birdie."

She cocks a brow in defiance. "Or one of the guards."

"For God's sake, not again. Did you hear him at the lighthouse? He asked if you couldn't get the same sunrise and ocean air from your terrace, not house, not office, not front yard, not room, *terrace*. There are only two terraces in the house, Birdie. One in your bedroom and one in mine. The only one that has an ocean view is yours. As far as I know, he's never been to your room or upstairs at all, how the fuck did he know that?"

Her gaze slants around the corners, and then she shakes her head pensively. She understands where this is leading. She just doesn't want to believe it.

I throw my hands in the air. "How could you be so blind?"

"How could you? You said it yourself, no one came in or out of my house. The most viable explanation is that it's someone who is already inside and isn't expected to leave."

"Unbelievable," I scoff.

"Is it? Put your emotions aside for one minute and tell me if it's not possible."

"How about you do the same and admit that Torrance is also a viable possibility?"

"I do, Tristan. I'm here, aren't I? I let you drag me down to the middle of nowhere, and I'm staying without a single argument because it is possible that Jacob is Butterfly Man and so is any of your men."

I force myself to consider her theory through the haze of anger and jealousy. Of Torrance. Which is exactly why she thinks I'm not being objective. "Fine. I'll bite." I lean against the wall, crossing my arms. "Who do you think it is? Marcus, who was out looking for your husband at the time of the breach? Or Dixon and Riley, who are both from Minnesota and have never set foot in Florida except when each of them got married, and I treated them and their wives to a weekend in Miami as their wedding gift?"

She blinks rapidly, pursing her lips. "What about the last member of the team? I can't even remember his name, the one who is always in charge of guarding the back gate?"

"Morrison?" I chuckle.

"Yes, him. Come to think of it, I don't believe he's said two words to me since you put him on the job. I never see him around, like he's always in stealth mode. It's like he doesn't exist. He certainly fits the character bible for a stalker."

"You think Morrison is Butterfly Man?"

"The guy is a creep. He has access to the house and the system. He knows all your moves, when you're out and when I'm alone and vulnerable. He's always in the back, which means he could have been listening to our sensitive conversations at the blind spot, and he keeps a low profile so that when he strikes, no one suspects him. Where is he from?"

"Arkansas…but he did serve at Homestead

Air Reserve Base, near the southern end of the Florida peninsula, about twenty-five miles south of Miami."

Her jaw drops. "Are you kidding me? And not once have you thought it was him? I can't believe this shit. He's been right under our noses all this time and—"

"Morrison can't be your stalker, Birdie."

"Because he, too, is married with four kids in Oklahoma? Give me a break."

"For fuck's sake, he's gay, okay? Like that Spencer guy, Morrison is gay. He can't be obsessed with someone like *you*."

She blinks again. "Unless he pretends to be to keep suspicions away."

"Puta madre, you'll just say anything to protect your stupid boyfriend." *I'm gonna kill the tall fucker myself.*

"I'm not trying to protect anyone but myself, Tristan. I'm tired of running in circles. You have your theory, and I have mine. Then let's prove it. One way or another."

I cross my arms. "How?"

"Butterfly Man will go crazy if he doesn't have access to me or know where I am, which will lead him to do something gruesome enough to force me out. I won't let him control the narrative anymore. The only way we take charge is by setting a trap." Her eyes gleam with determination. "Two traps, actually."

I push off the wall. "What kind of trap?"

"We leak two different pieces of information. Tell your team I'm being moved to another safe house of yours in a different city. Tell Torrance I'm renting a cabin on the other side of the island to take a break from all of this. See who shows up where."

"That's..." I pause, considering. It's not a bad plan, except for one thing. "Too dangerous. We'd be splitting our resources, leaving you vulnerable."

"Not if I'm somewhere else entirely." She steps closer, her voice dropping. "Here. Where no one can find me."

Fuck. This plan actually...can work. But no. "No. I don't like this, Birdie."

A ghost of a smile touches her lips. "You don't have to like it. You just have to help me prove you wrong."

The challenge in her voice stings my pride. I run a hand through my hair, already regretting what I'm about to say. "Fine. Three days. We'll set up both scenarios, but you stay here with me and Brandon at all times. We do this my way, do you hear me?"

"Sir, yes, sir."

I ignore the sarcasm. "And if anything feels off, if I see anything—anything—that suggests this is going south..."

"You'll protect me. That's what you do, isn't

it?"

"Damn you, Birdie Abel." I sigh. "If you're wrong about this…"

"I'll owe you one hell of an apology."

My strides aren't fast enough. I reach her and lift my hand next to her cheek, but I don't touch her. "Not enough."

She steps forward, placing her foot between my feet, her body grazing mine. "What else do you want?"

You. "Stop playing games. You already know what I want."

"I want to hear you say it."

My tongue darts to lick her breath that has just fanned my face. Then my upper lip curls under my teeth to contain the hammering of my heart—and hopefully the swelling in my pants. "When I prove to you Torrance is Butterfly Man, I'll get rid of him, and then…you will be mine."

"Someone has just grown a pair. A brazen one, too." A tilt of her lips unfolds slowly, equal parts charm and warning, promising both pleasure and pain. A gesture that somehow manages to be both playful and menacing. There's something cruel in it, sharp as a blade and twice as dangerous. Paired with the sardonic arch of her brow and that gleam in her blue eyes, it becomes her most effective weapon— one that disarms before you even realize you're under attack. A smile that says she knows something I don't, and she's enjoying every second of my ignorance.

A predator's smile, a hint of the monster lurking beneath the beautiful camouflage. "You're forgetting a tiny little thing, aren't you?"

"Never forgotten. I'll get rid of your husband, too, Birdie. You have my word."

She grunts. "But if you're wrong?"

"What do you want?"

The smile turns into a smirk. "You'll put all of this behind, and we'll go our separate ways. You will forget all about me, Tristan, and never look back."

The muscles in my jaw clench so hard I can hear my teeth creaking, but I force that twisted smile anyway, one that feels like glass shards cutting into my cheeks. "You mean let you be with Torrance while I fucking watch and do nothing."

She doesn't answer, but the silence says it all. She's asking me to let her go. To watch her walk away with him. To pretend that every moment, every touch, every shared breath between us meant nothing.

My mind spins, replaying images I don't want to see: the way he fucking looks at her, at her body, her smile directed at him, her laughs at his whispers…. Rage builds in my gut. My hands shake as I shove them into my pockets to hide the evidence. I want to break something. Everything.

The pressure builds behind my eyes, in my chest, threatening to explode. Each breath feels like inhaling broken glass, and still, she stands there, looking at me with those eyes that only make it worse. Because I can see it—the pity. The fucking pity.

I want to laugh. Or cry. Or howl. Instead, I stand here, drowning in this toxic cocktail of love and hate and jealousy that's eating me alive, as she asks me to let her choose someone else in peace while pretending I'm not dying inside.

Words bubble up my throat—bitter, angry words that taste like copper and ash. I swallow them back, but they sit there, burning. She has no idea how much I'm holding back, how much it takes to stand here and not grab her, shake her, fuck her until she's pieces, to make her see what she's doing to me. The urge to destroy something beautiful pulses through me with each heartbeat, matching the rhythm of these thoughts I can't control: Mine. Should be mine. Only mine.

But I stay still, while everything inside me screams and rages and begs to be let loose. Because that's what she wants, for me to be reasonable, controlled, understanding. To be the bigger person while she rips my heart out with her gentle hands and kind words about "moving on" and "what's fucking best."

The worst part? Even now, even like this, I still love her. And that makes me hate myself most of all.

"I will…not be wrong, Birdie."

CHAPTER 12

Birdie

Sleep has found me again. The soothing sounds of nature and waves, along with the sense of freedom no one knows where I am, have silenced the havoc and allowed me some peace at last. In these precious moments before consciousness fully claims me, I float in the space between nightmares and reality, where I can pretend I'm just another soul seeking solitude on this island.

Then I wake up, and the weight of facts crashes over me, each truth a rock pressing against my chest until breathing becomes an act of defiance.

I curl up by the window, my laptop on my thighs—Brandon brought it and some clothes with him yesterday—a cursor blinking on a blank page.

He's splitting wood outside, shirtless in March, I might add. Tristan is in the kitchen. He's chopping garlic and herbs with military precision.

For a romance author, this is a deluge of inspiration. Based on this scene alone, my mind plots four and a half books with thirteen steamy chapters I won't even write. For a woman, in a secluded cabin with two muscular bodyguards all to herself, it's a pleasant distraction, a fantasy coming true and a dangerous temptation.

For me, a woman and an author, however, it's a nuisance. Because one of them looks like he needs a fake ID to drink, whose eight-pack can't distract me enough from the face that reminds me of my worst mistake, and the other is…well, Tristan.

And somewhere out there, the stalker's deadly obsession that has driven me into hiding, is lurking, taking over my life, potentially orchestrating more murders I can be framed for if I don't comply with his psychotic demand—becoming Butterfly Man's fucktoy forever.

My fingers vent on the keyboard.

I have a stalker. He is someone I knew eight years ago when I was teaching at the school in Miami and has been stalking me since. He is here now on Martha's

*Vineyard. He is tech-savvy and has expensive equip-
ment that can hack encrypted comms and complicated
security systems.*

The words feel clinical on the page, a writer's attempt to distance herself from tragedy, to
turn personal terror into plot points that can be
controlled, managed, edited into submission.

He kills for me.

Four words that I've written and rewritten,
as if changing their order might change their
meaning. As if the act of writing them down
might reveal some hidden truths I've missed, a
way to wake up from this nightmare I've been
living.

Aaron is dead.

My fingers tremble as I write his name,
knowing that somewhere on my computer lies
a fragment of the truth of what happened between us.

*His parents, the principal, the therapist
and the lawyer are also dead.*

Each name represents a thread in this tapes-
try of horror, a pattern, all of them connected
to that time, to that school, to those choices
I made, thinking I could outrun their conse-

quences.

Saldana is dead.

Gia is dead.

The names blur on the page. Each death another step closer to me, another piece of my past erased by someone who thinks he's writing our future in blood.

The only one left on the list is Blake. The final gift before Butterfly Man comes to collect his prize.

My stomach churns at the nickname I've given him in my head—another writer's trick to make the monster manageable, to give shape to the shapeless fear that stalks my nights.

Tristan thinks my stalker is Jacob. I think it's one of my bodyguards. Morrison fits the profile. But how is he connected to my school? I've never seen him before in my life.

Words on a page, suspects lined up like characters in a story, but this isn't fiction I can control. This is my life unraveling in real-time, and every theory feels simultaneously possible and impossible.

The police think Blake is connected to the murders. His gun is a murder weapon.

Blake… My husband told the press about my stalker, exposing one of my many secrets. Vengeance for the divorce or war, the first battle of many to come if I don't retreat?

My writer's mind spins possibilities, each scenario more devastating than the last. I see the headlines that haven't been written yet, feel the judgment of readers who don't yet know my shame.

What if he's ready to expose more? What if he tells the world about Aaron? The video I have on Blake can put him in prison. The secrets he has on me can end my career and ruin any future I try to have.

I write these questions knowing there are no good answers, only choices between different forms of destruction. Whose stakes are higher, the man who has lost everything or the woman that has everything to lose? The author in me appreciates the symmetry of this dilemma, when the woman in me drowns in its implications.

My fingers hover over the keyboard, wanting to write more, needing to write more, as if putting it all down might somehow force this chaos to make sense. But some truths resist narrative structure, some fears can't be contained by paragraphs, and some choices can't be edited once they're made.

I slam the computer shut and distract myself with a more tolerable rage. Brandon shouldn't be freezing his ass out. He's just a kid.

"He needs to finish that woodpile," Tristan says without taking his eyes off the knife.

That man reads me too well, and his peripheral is too good; sometimes I suspect he has eyes in the back of his head. "You should be the one chopping wood, not him. It's freezing out there."

"And you care because? I thought you hated Brandon."

"I don't *hate* Brandon." I just don't like to look at him for reasons that have absolutely nothing to do with his person. "He's just a kid, really, trying too hard to prove himself useful." A maternal instinct replaces my initial unease when I catch him axe another log in the cold. "Tell him to get inside and you do it. I'll take care of food. You're not as great in the kitchen as they say anyway."

Tristan rolls his eyes. "Brandon isn't a kid. He's a soldier like the rest of us. He can handle it." Light catches his perfect hair when he glances my way. Mischief glows over his curving smirk. "But if you want to get me out of my shirt, you don't need an excuse. You can just ask."

Even in mischief, his voice carries commanding confidence. Everything about him radiates competence and control. It's begging to be ruffled up. I'm itching to see what happens when all that careful restraint finally snaps. He was this close to shattering last night. How much will it take today?

I take my time getting off my seat and sauntering toward him. "How does it work?"

"Taking off my shirt? Easy, I pull it over my head and then slide the arms out."

Someone had a clown for breakfast. I squeeze in the tiny kitchen and slouch, my back to the counter. My eyes roam his body until his shoulders tense. I bend my head, coaxing my way into his space, demanding he looks at me. When his hand stills on the knife, and his gaze holds mine in warning, I strike. "*Sex*, Tristan. How does it work for you? What happens after you take off your clothes, and you're alone with a woman you're so desperate to *fuck*?"

His infamous smirk reappears, as if he's unfazed, as if he's still in control, but the way his pupils dilate and the slight tremor in his fist he hides in his pocket tell on him. "Fucking? You want me to educate you on fucking, Mrs. Abel?

I thought you were the expert. Everything I've learned, I've learned from you." He shrinks the distance between our faces, his eyes on my lips, and his tongue darts and licks his. "But I'm happy to show you how much of a good student I've been."

We both know he's read my books—every steamy scene, every passionate encounter, every dark fantasy that screams THERAPY. The thought of him studying them, learning from them...

My heart echoes over the sound of the axe splitting wood outside. Vivid images of the forbidden man, when the wolf beneath the guard dog comes to play, race in my head, but I hold my ground. "I doubt you can. For someone who doesn't like to be touched, it must be... challenging."

His jaw works, a muscle jumping beneath the skin, and his fingers twitch toward his hip where his gun usually sits. An unconscious tell—reaching for a weapon that isn't there when he feels cornered. Not by physical threats, but by words that cut too close to home.

"Not if I'm in control." There's a roughness to his voice that hasn't been there before. The confidence in his voice sounds forced now, like he's reading from a script of how he thinks this scene should play out rather than letting himself feel it. "Women love that, don't they? A man in charge."

The kitchen feels even smaller as he uses the height difference to his advantage, looming over me with predatory intent. "Isn't it every woman's dream to be tied up to a strong man's bed while he chokes and spanks and pulls her hair as he fucks her senseless every way he wants? A good girl to a very bad boy."

Every letter is a match on gasoline, and for a moment all I can think about is rope against my skin and those capable hands putting me exactly where he wants me. But there's something mechanical in the way he describes it, like he's reciting what he thinks he should say. The fantasy he assumes I want, pulled straight from the pages of my books.

"Maybe." I lean in, close enough to feel the heat radiating off him, but careful not to touch. "Is that what you think *I* want?" My voice comes out huskier than intended. "Or is that what *you* need, complete control so you never have to let anyone close enough to really touch you?"

His breath catches, and I swoop down before he recovers. "But what if she's a little sassy, a little bratty, and decides to act on her impulses?" I swirl a hand in the tiny space between our bodies. "A touch you don't command," my breath collides close, too close, on his lips, "a kiss you don't initiate." I drag my stare from his mouth to his eyes, and I see it, the exact moment his careful facade cracks, the last inch of the tactical territory he'd die before he'd surrender falls. "Are you going to run like a scared little boy again?"

A gasp rips out of my throat as his fist chokes me. He squeezes, a warning, a promise, a surrender all at once. The counter edge digs into my lower back as he crowds me against it. Then he yanks me up and places me on top of it, my back to the wall. He's so close I can count his eyelashes, see the ring of gold around his blown pupils, smell the raw desperation in the way he holds me, a man who's been starving himself finally faced with a feast.

Feel the sharp tip of the kitchen knife on my chest.

"I warned you." He spreads my legs with his weight, his body finally, finally closing that careful distance he's maintained from day one, his cock, stiff as a rock against me. "I fucking warned you."

When you knock on hell's door, who do you think will open?

His thumb traces my pulse point. Can he feel how fast my heart is racing under his palm? How wet and hot my pussy is? Does he know that for all my brave words, he's not the only one terrified of what happens next. "I won't run. Not this time." He slides the knife down the line between my breasts. "But you should."

The wolf is out now. The devil. No. I thought I saw his devil that day in the shower, but this… This is what he's promised. Hell's doors have opened wide like he warned, and all the demons are out to play.

The knife's path down my chest leaves fire in its wake, but it's nothing compared to the inferno in his eyes, the throbbing of his erection against my flesh, the gushes of arousal soaking my panties. His warning should terrify me. The barely contained violence, the fear, the threat, the way he's pinning me like prey should send me running. Instead, each thundering heartbeat under his palm screams *closer*.

"Should I?" My voice comes out breathless, and I arch into the blade. "You forget, Tristan. I wrote the devil. So many devils and demons they've become all I know, all I crave." My legs tighten around his hips, and his hard cock is practically digging a hole in my stomach. "I've been imagining what this devil tastes like for weeks."

A growl erupts from him. His fingers tighten against my throat. One demand. That's all it would take to shatter him completely. Just three words to unleash whatever darkness he's been caging inside.

"Kiss me, Tristan." My lips part, the invitation hovering between us like a lit fuse. "I know you want to."

His answer is a chuckle so dark, almost cruel. The knife traces up my neck, gentler than the hand around my throat leaving only to fist my hair and yank my head back until my pulse strains against the blade.

"Want to?" His voice is gravel and sin. His breath fans hot across my exposed skin. "I've wanted to devour you since the first time I laid eyes on you." He rolls his hips, grinding his cock against me in a slow, torturous rhythm that makes the knife quiver against my skin. "But you don't get to make demands. Not any-more."

The flat of the blade slides along my jaw as his teeth graze my ear—not quite a bite, just a taste of what he's holding back. "You crossed this line. You pushed until I broke." His grip in my hair tightens, sending sparks down my spine. "So if you want my kiss, you're going to have to beg for it. Let me hear how badly you want to taste this devil."

An attempt to dominate the situation, to put himself back in charge. There's a tremor in his hands that betrays him. The knife dances against my skin. Need wars with his last grasp for control. I feel it, how close he is to coming undone.

"Beg me to kiss you, Birdie. Fucking beg

me to kiss you, Reagan."

"Please." My body arches into the blade with the pleading whimper. "Please kiss me, Tristan. I need it. Need you. *Please.* I beg you."

The knife clatters to the counter. Victory blazes in his eyes as he leans in, his lips just a breath away from mine. But before they connect, I move faster than he expects. My hand finds the knife, and in one fluid motion, I press the tip against his groin and pierce my teeth into the soft flesh of his lower lip.

His entire body goes rigid. The grip in my hair loosens as shock replaces triumph on his face.

Rolling my hips against him while the knife keeps him frozen in place, I let go of his lip, but not until the taste of blood fills our mouths. "You thought you had me, didn't you? Thought you could make me your good little girl?" I trace the knife higher, letting it drag along the bulge in his pants. "But you forgot something important," I purr, "I create the monsters. I don't submit to them."

"You," his breaths, tinged with blood, rumble, "will pay for this."

"Is that a promise?" I lean forward until my lips brush his ear. "When will you learn, Tristan? In this game, I'll always win."

An awkward cough echoes over our breaths. I glance over Tristan's shoulders. Brandon is standing, eyes unsettled where to land. "I…I'm sorry."

I smile at the boy. "Sorry for what? Tristan was showing me a couple of self-defense moves. After *that* night, he thought I needed it."

"Yes, Mrs. Abel, I mean…Birdie, ma'am."

Sliding off the counter, I can't resist throwing another smirk at Tristan, and then I walk over to Brandon. "Where are you from?"

"Texas."

Texas and the military, it explains a lot. "And how old are you?"

"Twenty-one."

My brow cocks at Tristan, who is still facing the wall. It won't be a nice look if Brandon sees his boss so messed up with a hard-on the size of *Texas*. "And he sends *you* out in the freezing cold to chop wood. It's a shame that a grown-a—" I swallow the bad word around the boy, "—man huddles in the kitchen and lets the youngest member of his team do all the hard labor for him."

"With all due respect, ma'am, I'm a soldier and a fully trained security detail. I'm capable of doing any task my boss assigns me."

"I'm sorry, Brandon. I didn't mean that in any offensive way to you. I have no doubt you're more than capable, and that's why you're off wood chopping duty. Instead, *you* will train me. Maybe I'll learn something I don't already know."

Brandon, flustered, shoots a look between me and Tristan, who, at last, stares back in our direction.

"Oh, don't look at him. He's your boss, but I'm *his*." I flash a full smile at my fuming body-guard. "By the way, Tristan, I need the internet."

"What for?"

"What everyone uses it for, silly. Social media, of course."

CHAPTER 13

Tristan

irdie doesn't do social media. What the hell is she up to now? What new mastermind plan has taunting me to the point of shattering inspired? It seems my destruction has become her diabolical muse these days.

"Gatsby, hit the shower," I grumble, turning to face her. The kitchen is still charged with tension. She's turned provoking me into an art form, each challenge designed to push me closer to the edge while keeping me guessing about her true motives.

"Sir," he says, his feet too eager to escape the awkwardness.

"Gatsby," Birdie crosses her arms over her chest, mischievous defiance in her gaze, "I thought that was *my* safeword, not yours."

The things I'd do to that mouth… The things I'd do to show her she should have never messed with someone like me… *Time will come, Birdie. Time will come, Reagan.*

"The whole point of coming here is staying off the grid so that no one tracks you or knows where you are, and you suddenly wanna post to your story?"

"You said there's no cell service here, but you reached Brandon to order him to come here, contacted the rest of the team to get our traps in motion and Boston to get working on that list of everyone who worked at the school in Miami. It means you do have secure comms that can't be traced to this place, and it can't be the radio in that bunker, right?"

I watch her carefully, an attempt to decipher what new game she's playing now. She must be already three steps ahead in whatever plan she's formulating. "Yes, I'm using Monarca's own network with proxy servers and satellite comms that will trace back to freaking Kyrgyzstan."

"Where?"

"Exactly." A hint of a smile tugs at my mouth despite my better judgment. She has a way of making me forget myself, of turning every interaction into a dance between protector and provocateur.

She shrugs with practiced nonchalance. "So

there is no problem for me to use the internet."

My patience wears thin. Every instinct screams she's planning something dangerous, something that could compromise everything I've done to keep her safe. "Birdie, what the fuck are you up to?"

"Language, Mr. Morra."

I let out a dark chuckle, remembering how she wielded that kitchen knife against my dick. Always pushing, always testing limits. But with Birdie, the real danger isn't physical. It's in the way she sees through every defense, every carefully constructed barrier. The way she matches my intensity and turns my own tactics against me. "I'm not gonna ask again. If you want the internet, you'd better come clean and tell me the truth."

"I already told you."

The cabin grows smaller, too small for the collision course we're on. Before she can throw another smart lie, I reach her in two strides. My hand shoots out, gripping her jaw, thumb pressing against the spot where I held the knife. Her breath hitches—the first sign of *real* submission I've seen from her all day.

"You think because you got the upper hand once, you run this show?" I lean in close, my voice a low growl against her ear. "Let me remind you of something, *Reagan*." I emphasize her real name, savoring her shiver against me.

"That little stunt with the knife? I let you have that moment. Could have disarmed you before you even touched the blade."

My other hand finds her hip, pinning her against the counter. "So here's how this works. You tell me exactly what you're planning or you don't get anywhere near that internet connection. And if you try to play another one of your naughty games..." I drag my thumb across her lower lip, reminding her who's really in control. "Well, let's just say I won't be so generous next time."

Her pulse quickens under my palm, that delicious mix of defiance and desire. But this time, I need her to understand. "Your safety isn't a game I'm willing to lose, and for that to happen, you must know who is in charge. Me, Birdie. What I say goes. No objections, no manipulation, no fucking lies. Do I make myself clear?"

"Yes." The word comes out breathy, almost vulnerable. But there's something in her eyes—a glint of mischief that makes my gut clench with warning. She leans into my grip, her lips brushing against my thumb. "Crystal clear, *sir*."

Submission laced with mockery, and yet it goes straight to my cock. My fingers tighten on her jaw. "Sing, little bird. What's your plan with the internet?"

The mask of compliance slips just enough to reveal the calculating mind behind it. "I need to check something." Her tongue darts out, a quick swipe against my thumb that sends electricity down my spine. "About Blake."

She knows exactly how to play this—how to mix truth with temptation until I can't tell where one ends and the other begins. I force myself to focus past the distraction of her mouth, past the heat of her body against mine. Blake. Of course this comes back to him. "What about him?"

"The night Butterfly Man broke into my bedroom, you sent Marcus to Blake's office, but he didn't find him. Based on Jacob's interrogations, I don't think the police have Blake in custody either." Her voice takes a serious turn. "His response to the divorce was to leak one of my secrets. I need to see if he's made any public statements since the press conference. Especially now that the police suspect he killed Gia, he'll be thirsty for blood. If he's planning to expose more of my secrets, I need to know."

My grip softens. "Or maybe he's dead like Gia."

"You have no idea how much I hope so, but what Butterfly Man said to me begs to differ. My stalker is punishing and testing me, not rewarding me. He's leaving Blake for last but only if I submit to his twisted love." Real vulnerability flickers in her eyes. "Blake is alive, and he has the means to destroy me."

She's right. Every person related to the Aaron West scandal is dead. The only one still breathing that knows that secret is Abel. We need to know what he's doing, what he might reveal next and how to prepare for it before it's too late.

"And…" She hesitates.

Damn it. "And what, Birdie?"

"I've been asking myself…what if you and I are both wrong?"

"Wrong about what?"

"Who the real Butterfly Man is."

Not that shit again. "I'm not wrong, Birdie."

"You don't know that. Everyone is a suspect. It could be Jacob, it could be Morrison… or someone else entirely."

"For God's sake, we can't keep running in circles. Give that writer's mind that's always spinning stories a break. You're always seeing plot twists where there should only be clear lines and boundaries. Jacob Torrance is Butterfly Man."

"No. Because Jacob has never worked or been to our school, and honestly…I don't think Morrison has either."

Leaning back, I drop my hands. I'm the one who has made the connection that the stalker is someone from the school. "Morrison finished high school in Arkansas. He joined the military right after. He never attended nor worked at any school in Florida."

"And Jacob is too old to be a student at my time as a teacher. He doesn't have any children either. And he certainly didn't work there. I'd have remembered him."

"Your memory is hardly proof, Birdie. I mean, you don't remember me. And we don't know much about Torrance before he trans-ferred here, so…"

She steps away from the counter, but her eyes never leave mine. "When a woman admits she might be wrong, a smart man knows better than to play dumb to prove himself right."

This is bullshit…and yet it can be true. Fuck me. I cross my arms, hating how easily she can make me doubt myself. "If it's not Tor-rance or Morrison, who do you think Butterfly Man is?"

"That's what we'll find out when I go on my social media accounts and post this video."

CHAPTER 14

Tristan

"Absolutely fucking not." I cut through her half-formed explanation. "Are you out of your mind?"

"Tristan, I really don't appreciate the way you talk to me."

"And I really don't appreciate the mere suggestion of using you as bait!"

"I'm only giving back to society. Nothing is wrong with that."

Blood simmers in my veins. "You want to go live and out your husband's addiction, saying it's what led to the stalker fiasco with the press."

"When people know he's a drug addict, any word he says will be discredited and inadmissible in court. He won't be able to use Aaron against me or contest the divorce."

"But in the same video you wanna tell *people* Saldana's unfortunate death, also due to drug abuse, urged you to reflect deeply on the issue that you decided to give back to society by going to your *roots* and teaching *at-risk youth* creative writing."

"It'll give them an opportunity to build a career instead of ruining their lives with substance abuse."

"Cut the crap." My hands clench at my sides, fighting the need to grab her and shake some sense into that reckless yet brilliant mind of hers. "You think you're being clever, sending a message only your stalker would truly understand. Your roots mean Miami. At-risk youth means the school. You're practically telling Butterfly Man where to find you. All that's missing for your *date* is the time."

Something flashes in her eyes. Surprise or a hint of respect for figuring it out so easily, I don't know or care. All I know is that I'm not letting her sacrifice herself for this hunt.

"Think about it. Seeking him out will convince him I'm no longer pushing him away. I'm falling for his game," she insists. "Once he hears that message, it'll catch him off guard, but he won't be able to resist. It'd be the perfect trap to draw him out. He'd be as vulnerable as possible, and you could finally catch him.

I know he will follow me to Miami and—"

"And that's exactly why it's not happening. You're not using yourself as bait. Not now, not ever."

Her fingers run over her lips. "We need to do something. We can't just sit here hiding forever."

"It's been less than twenty-four hours since we came here, Birdie, and we've already done something. Did you forget about the other two traps we've set?"

"Those traps will be a waste of time if Butterfly Man turns out to be someone other than Morrison or Jacob."

"You're not posting that video. End of discussion."

"Since when do you get to decide what's the end of any discussion?" Her voice carries that dangerous edge that usually precedes her doing something monumentally risky.

"Since I'm the one keeping you alive and safe. You hired me to protect you. Let me do my job."

"I hired you to find him," she counters, not backing down an inch. "How are we supposed to do that if we're just reacting? Always one step behind while he controls everything?"

"By being smart. By being patient." My voice drops. "Not by painting a target on your back and hoping we catch him before he catches you."

A shadow crosses her face, fear finally breaking through that iron determination. Good. She needs to understand the stakes here. This isn't one of her novels where the heroine can take wild risks and trust it'll all work out because it's a Happily Ever After. It's a dark and twisted reality where the stakes are etched in blood.

"You want the internet, I'll give you thirty minutes on my secure computer. I watch everything you do. No exceptions."

"Whatever you say, *sir.*"

My stupid cock pulses at the word again despite the scorn she pours behind it. "Don't make me regret this, Birdie."

"You already do." She moves past me, close enough that her ass grazes my thighs. If she leans back an inch, she'll feel how hard I am for her. And I could just grab her hips, bend her over, drop her pants and show her what happens to women like her when they taunt men like me. "But that's what makes it fun, isn't it?"

CHAPTER 15

Birdie

"I'll get you set up with a secure connection." Tristan guides me down the hidden bunker. It looks like a secret military operation in action down here. Computer monitors lined up, playing on them squares of every room in the cabin, the woods and the beach. Other equipment I'm not familiar with but looks expensive. A cot and a cupboard filled with water bottles, canned food and guns. Lots of them.

"I thought we kept the guns upstairs in the bedroom safe," I say.

"Here too." He reaches for a satellite phone and works his magic. Then, within seconds, he points at one of the computers, grabs the one chair in the room and sets it for me. "It's ready."

"You're so fast. How have you become so good with high-end technology? They teach you that in sniper school?"

"No, but there's so much you can learn when you can read, and decide to run a security company." He bends to work some buttons on the keyboard, and his cologne, mixed with raw masculinity and heat, invades my senses. My imagination runs wild. A man and a woman in a dark, tight place like this, too intimate, built for making wrong decisions and sweet regrets.

His chest nearly touches my back as he reaches around me to type, his muscled arm brushing against mine. The heat from his body envelops me, and I fight the urge to lean back into him. "Your thirty minutes," his voice drops lower, rougher, his breath hot against my ear, "start now."

I shift in the chair, hyper-aware of every point where we almost touch. "You're going to stand there the whole time?"

"Right here." His palm flattens on the desk beside the keyboard, caging me in. "Where I can see everything."

I cross my legs to ease the ache building between them. "Everything?"

He chuckles. "You're not as subtle as you think, Birdie. I know you've imagined my fingers, my tongue and my pierced cock in your pussy so many times more than you care to count just like I know you don't only picture me between your squirming legs now, you need it." His other hand moves, and for a second I think he's reaching between my thighs. But it only rests on the back of my chair. "Twenty-nine minutes."

Breath catching, skin flushing, I reach for the mouse. "Fuck you."

"You wish." He taps the desk, rushing me. "Your agent first, then your lawyer. We need to know what Blake's been saying, what he might be planning."

I videocall Martha, painfully conscious of how his body towers over mine, how trapped I am between his arms, the desk and this damn chair.

The connection seems to take forever to start—courtesy of the extra layers of security or the silent tension between us. At last, Martha's face fills the screen. "Birdie, thank goodness. Where have you been? I've been trying to reach you for—" Martha chops off her words, and her brows knit. "What is this place? Where are you and why are you calling me on an *app*?" She waves at Tristan. "And why is your handsome bodyguard breathing down your neck with his serial killer face on?"

A laugh finds its way to my heart despite everything. "It's a long story. Listen, I don't have a lot of time. When was the last time you talked to Blake?"

"I don't know. The day Saldana died or the day after, I'm not sure, but I haven't spoken to him since you sent me his termination notice email, if that's what you're worried about."

Blake hasn't tried to reach Martha. It's a good sign. He hasn't intended to expose me to her—not yet—or the media or she would have known about it. I exchange a glance with Tristan. "No, it's just that he's been MIA for a few days. After what happened to Gia, I was worried about him."

"Gia? What happened to her?"

"You don't know?"

"No. What's going on, Birdie?"

Gia's murder hasn't made it into the press yet? My head jumps automatically to Jacob. He has his way of controlling the press. Perhaps he's protecting me behind the scenes, making sure no news about the murder or the stalker gets leaked.

I fill my agent in. Gia's murder. The police interrogations. "And Martha, there's a big chance Blake is involved, and honestly—"

"Birdie," Tristan warns.

I stare at him. "She needs to know to stay safe. I can't let anything happen to her."

"Know what?" Martha's eyes go full dinner

plate size. "What's gonna happen to me?"

"We think," I swallow, "the stalker might be behind all this."

"Oh my God. Oh. My. God. You think he killed Gia? Why?"

"She and Blake were having an affair."

"Holy shit! No way!"

"Ms. Goldman, please know this is privileged information and can't be disclosed under any circumstances, not even to the police," Tristan interrupts.

Martha's image breaks and blurs, cutting off to a terrified face, and then a funnier one somehow, before it stabilizes. "Of course. Birdie made us all sign NDAs. Anything involving that crazy-ass freak is off-limits. Not that I'm stupid enough to get on his wrong side. He killed Gia for crying out loud!"

"We don't know that for sure," I chime in. "But it's better to be safe than sorry."

"Mr. Stalker, if you're listening, I'm sorry for calling you a crazy ass freak, and I love Birdie. I've never done anything to hurt her. I even got her that deal she wanted."

I blink incredulously. "You did?"

"Well, not exactly fifty percent, but twenty-five. I can definitely push for thirty."

Thirty percent of what I've made the house, not bad at all. "What about my rights? Will they revert them back to me?"

"Uh…no, but they're offering a seven-fig-ure deal per book in whatever new series you'll write next. I can get you a whole five mil for a trio!"

I mull it over. "No. I don't want to publish with them again. I'll take the thirty percent and my rights. Nothing more, nothing less. But lis-ten, keep stalling them until my divorce is over. Warn them if Blake knows anything about this deal, it's void, and I'll sue their dirty asses pen-niless. I don't know how far Blake is willing to fight, but I won't let him get a single dime out of this deal."

"I understand. You got it."

"Be safe, Martha, and please let me know asap if you hear from Blake."

Tristan presses a few more buttons before he ends the call. "One down. One to go."

I nod, all innocence and compliance. "Of course. Whatever you think is best."

"Good girl," he taunts back.

For some reason, my vagina likes it. *Traitress.*

My email takes painstakingly long to open. "Is this normal?"

"Yes. Routing and rerouting and encrypt-ing—"

"Oh God, I'd rather just watch the page load in silence."

"Really?" He bends lower, his breath tick-ling my ear. "I thought the technical boredom would be a nice distraction from the aching throbs in your—"

"Email!" The aching throbs in my email. Yup. That would totally make a cute line in a cutesy rom com, but my book is definitely not one of those. The emails staring me in the face are enough proof. "Adriana sent me five emails in the past forty-eight hours."

"Open them."

I read as fast as the letters load. "She's reached out to Blake because…he contested the divorce. Fuck." I was hoping he'd be too wasted and miss the twenty-day window to contest it.

"What did he say when she talked to him?"

"I don't know." I read each email thorough-ly. "She doesn't say. But it doesn't look so good if she's urging me to call her that badly."

"Then what are you waiting for? Make the call."

My breath shakes on my fingers, press-ing over my lips, as I wait for the call to go through.

"Hello? Birdie?" Adriana is in her office, stunned. "Is that you?"

"Hi. Yes. Sorry for the strangeness. This is not how we usually communicate. But it's the safest option at the moment."

"Don't worry about it." A frown contorts her face. "Are you all right? Has your husband made any contact with you? Did he hurt you in any way?"

"He didn't directly contact me, not since the day he tried to attack me, but he did leak the stalker issue to the press when he received the divorce papers. It's been escalating since. I'm worried it may escalate even further. I was hoping you'd already talked to him and mentioned our leverage…"

She pinches the bridge of her nose and sighs. "About that…"

That doesn't sound good at all. My heart sinks.

She glances at Tristan. "Is it safe to talk?"

"Yes. Tristan knows everything. He's my bodyguard. You met him once."

"Yes, I remember," she says warily. The way she looks at him sends an eerie feeling through me. What's going on?

"Ms. Lockwood, we don't have much time." Tristan interrupts my line of thought. "We have too much on our plate with the stalker situation. We don't need another active threat. My client would like to know what the situation is with her husband so that we can take precautions and counter his moves."

Adriana hesitates for a second before she speaks. "When I talked to your husband, he didn't agree to the terms of the divorce. So, as we planned, I mentioned the video you gave me, however…"

I grip the desk edge, bracing myself. "What did he say?"

"He said, and I quote, that video could put me in jail for a few months," she swallows, "but what I have on her will send her in for life."

CHAPTER 16

Birdie

The bunker's ventilation hums in the background, a monotonous sound that matches the static in my brain. I grip the desk harder, focusing on the pain in my knuckles to keep my expression neutral.

Tristan's presence shifts from intimidating to protective as he leans closer to the screen. "Ms. Lockwood, did Abel elaborate on his claim?"

Adriana shakes her head, her professional composure cracking. "No, but he said to tell Birdie that he had a long visit with someone called Shane, and she'd know what he meant."

My entire body goes cold, but not from fear—from recognition. I thought Blake was going to use Aaron against me. This is worse.

Way worse.

"Shane?" Tristan asks. "Isn't that—"

"Yes." My first mistake. The past that, even behind bars, poses a threat to end my future. "But I don't know what Blake meant." I whisper, proud of how my voice trembles just right. Years of pain have taught me the perfect pitch of vulnerability. "What could he possibly have on me?"

Neither of them can give me an answer. I don't wait for one I already know. "Did he say anything else?"

"He didn't elaborate any further," Adriana replies. "I've been trying to reach you because this changes our strategy completely. If he's bluffing, that's one thing. But if there's anything—anything at all—that could be used against you, I need to know now."

My eyes go wide and vacant, like I'm searching my memories. In reality, I'm calculating. Blake has gone to visit Shane in prison. They talked long enough, and now Blake knows what he should have never known, what should have been buried forever.

The video I have of him is nothing compared to what he could reveal. The real question is: would he destroy himself just to bring me down?

"Of course he's bluffing," I lie.

"To be honest, his confidence concerns

me."

"I…" I start, then stop, letting the silence build tension.

"Whatever it is, I'm on your side. But I need complete honesty to protect you." Adriana's voice turns gentle, almost maternal. The kind that makes me want to confess everything. "Birdie?"

Almost. "He has nothing. Nothing real anyway. But… Shane was my first husband. He is in prison because of me. Blake and Shane could have come together and fabricated something, created false evidence that could implicate me. They both seek revenge. Blake is also good at working the police in his favor. Who knows what he might have promised Shane in return for a false testimony? Protection in prison. Early parole…" I make my voice small and frightened. It's easier to suggest he's lying than to admit my own lies.

The weight of Tristan's hand lands on my shoulder. I allow myself to lean into it, a wounded bird seeking shelter.

"It's possible," Adriana admits. "But from the way he was speaking, I know this isn't just an angry bluster. He thinks he has something concrete, and he's desperate enough to use whatever this is, regardless of the consequences to himself."

I think of the concrete evidence hidden

where no one will ever find it. "What do you think I should do, Adriana?"

She leans closer to the camera. "Do you have anything else on him?"

Yes. Blake isn't the only one who's been keeping receipts. "No."

Threatening Blake isn't the way to win this game. He's a desperate man in a classic trope. *If I can't have you, no one else will. You* here isn't me. It's my money.

Adriana sighs. "If you're not a hundred percent certain he's bluffing, the best option is to settle."

"How much?"

Another sigh leaves her chest, and her lips purse. "He's asking for forty percent."

"Forty percent of what?"

"Everything."

"Everything? What do you mean everything?"

"He said, and again, I quote, I made her. Every penny she's ever made should be mine. She's lucky I'll let her have something after what she's done to me. But I'll be generous and only take forty percent of everything she's earned and will earn from her author career in perpetuity."

Blood rushes to my ears, drowning out the bunker's hum. Forty percent. Of everything. Forever. A laugh bubbles up in my throat, high, unnatural. I swallow it down before it runs loose. "That's... That's insane. He can't... Fuck this shit!"

"All blackmail claims aside, if this is a regular situation, and we go to court, the judge might see it differently," Adriana cuts in. "Especially if Blake can prove he contributed significantly to your success. Story ideas, character development, plot suggestions..."

My fingers twitch on the desk. If only she knew where my stories really came from. Who really inspired them. "He's a drug addict. He didn't contribute anything," I say, ice creeping into my voice before I can stop it. "Except fear. Except pain. That piece of—"

"Birdie, I understand your frustration, but I need you to calm down because the message isn't finished."

"What else does he want? The house, a kidney, my right eye!"

"No, but he said if anything happened to him, he had one of those apps *Aaron* used. And everything he knew wouldn't just be sent to his therapist. It'd be sent to the whole world."

I am Jack's cold sweat and raging bile duct.

CHAPTER 17

Tristan

Birdie ignores protocol and dashes out of the cabin.

"Brandon, guard the place and stay alert!" I command as I grab a gun and dart after my *client*.

She's bent in the driveway, her hands frantically rubbing her thighs, her eyes squeezed shut.

"You can't just run off like that," I say softly despite the need to reprimand her. I can sense her rage from here, crashing more violently than the waves against the cove behind. "How many times do I have to explain it to you?"

"I needed some air. I…" Her index finger jabs toward the cabin multiple times. "That fucking bastard can't do this to me."

"He won't."

She straightens and snaps her eyes open. "Were you not in the same room with me? Did you not hear his message? All this time, I've been banking on," she glances at the cabin and drops her voice, "Butterfly Man taking Blake out of the picture so I can break free from my violent, disturbing marriage. Now, I can't." A laugh full of wrath bursts out of her. "Not just that. Ironically, I must protect my abusive husband who has made my life a living hell for eight years and ensure he stays alive or he'll spread to the whole world the lies he's spun to destroy my life."

"No. I won't let him hurt you, Birdie. I'll find him, and I'll deal with it."

"Like you found my stalker? Like you stopped Butterfly Man from assaulting me in my bedroom? I mean, you told me you had eyes on Blake all the time. How the fuck did he get out of your sight? How did he go to Florida to see Shane in prison when you were supposed to monitor his every move?"

A sharp pang of guilt twists in my chest. She's right. I failed her when she needed protection most. That night in her bedroom still haunts me, knowing I was too late to stop him, knowing what could have happened if...

"You're right about my failures, and I'll carry that responsibility." But I push the guilt away. Now is not the time to fall for classic Birdie manipulation, whether conscious or not. I've taken my time learning her tells. I know when she uses a person's weaknesses against them to deflect. I know when she's hiding something. "But right now, you gotta tell me the truth."

"What truth?"

The one she wouldn't tell her lawyer. The one she's terrified of coming out. "Why is your husband talking to your ex in prison a threat that could ruin you? What does Blake Abel really have on you, Birdie?"

She whips around, her eyes blazing. "After everything I've shared with you? You of all people? How dare you?" Her voice cracks, but the anger doesn't waver. She stalks toward me. "I told you when Blake beat me, when Shane… When he… I trusted you and told you everything, and now you're standing here acting like I'm some kind of liar?"

"I'm not calling you a liar." I level my gaze with hers. "But you didn't tell me everything. You told me how Shane and Blake hurt you, but that's not all there is to the story."

She stills, the kind of stillness that sends a chill down to my bones. "Some things should stay buried, Tristan." Then something shifts in her eyes, a flicker of raw darkness, before fury crashes back in. "You of all people know that."

"Oh, I do. But not if they're putting you in danger. Not if your pieces of shit husbands can use them to hurt you." She is hiding something. A secret so destructive even recalling it is a menace. I won't stop until I find out what it is one way or another.

She shakes her head and wraps her arms around herself, her eyes darting back to the cabin walls. "Remember, you asked for this." Then she sighs in defeat. "Walk with me."

I don't leave her side as we go deeper into the woods. The waves from the cove grow distant, replaced by the whisper of wind through bare branches. Dead leaves crunch beneath our feet, marking our path like breadcrumbs. Part of me wants to stop her—we're too exposed out here, too far from backup—but her confession won't come within those cabin walls, not where Brandon or anyone else can hear.

When it comes to her darkness, I'm the only one allowed to listen. A privilege. A curse.

She walks ahead, arms still wrapped around herself, until the cabin disappears behind the treeline. Only then does she stop. "Do you know how long a man who beats his wife serves in prison?"

As a matter of fact, I do. I've looked it up a million times, hoping with each search for a better answer that can put me and my mom out of our misery. An answer that never came.

"One year and a thousand-dollar fine."

"Maximum." She scoffs. "Unless the charges change to aggravated assault. That can put him away for a whole five." She exaggerates the way she says the number, making a humorless face.

Pain squeezes around my soul. "You said Shane smashed your bones. He should be in for aggravated battery, which is up to fifteen."

"He should, but you know as well as I do that never happens."

I've spent my life watching monsters like my father, like her husbands, walk free because the system is rigged against the victims. Even when justice comes, it's never enough to heal what's broken.

"If Shane wasn't charged with aggravated battery, and he's still in prison after eight years…" A gust of wind whips through the trees. My pulse quickens as pieces click together. "What is Shane really in for? And for how long?"

Dead leaves crunch under her feet as she retreats a step. Her eyes dart between the trees as if checking for shadows that shouldn't be there. And I see it, the weight of something much darker than she's ever told me, something that's kept Shane locked away all these years.

"Birdie." My tone softens, but the urgency remains. "What did Abel frame Shane for?"

She goes dead still, and the hair on the back of my neck stands up. When she finally meets my eyes, there's an inferno of blue I've never seen before. I can hear the word before she speaks it. "Murder."

The confession hangs in the frigid air between us. Eight years makes perfect sense now. Shane is in for murder. He's got a life sentence to serve. He deserves the electric chair—a lethal cocktail ending his miserable life would be an act of mercy. But I wasn't lucky either way. They never pushed for the death penalty.

"Whose murder, Birdie?"

"Some woman who would have been another cold case. Blake planted evidence that linked Shane to her murder. I was Shane's alibi, but I testified we weren't together at the time of the murder. Shane couldn't afford a good lawyer, and with his history of violence and biker gang affiliation, it wasn't hard to stick."

"And now Shane is in for life for a crime he didn't commit."

"It was the only way I could live knowing he couldn't hurt me or another woman again."

"You asked Blake to do this for you, and he did it because he loved you that much?"

"Because it earned him a detective shield." She scoffs again. "It didn't hurt that he got to be the hero for the weak and broken battered wife, the one he could marry later and manipulate into being anything that satisfied him, one he could abuse without consequence."

Something Abel said the day he tried to attack Birdie echoes in my head. *Everything I do is to protect you. Who has been protecting those secrets for you all these years? Who has been running to your rescue all this time like a damn dog?*

Even then he was trying to guilt her, to manipulate her into believing he was her savior, when all he did was use her to build his career. He made himself look like a hero while planting false leads, manipulating the system he was supposed to protect, all so he could swoop in and use Birdie even more, only to become the very monster he claimed to be fighting.

Will you tell your new savior? Do you think he's gonna stay and protect you after he finds out what a monstrous little bitch like you is capable of?

"Pelotudo! He was threatening to expose you that day at the house. All this time, why haven't you told me?"

"Tell my bodyguard on his first day on the job that I'd asked my sick husband to falsify evidence to put a man in prison for life for a crime he didn't commit, and I gave false testimony to make it stick?"

Maybe she couldn't trust me enough then. Maybe Blake's questions got to her head. Maybe she didn't know I'd have answered yes. Yes, I'd have stayed and protected her. I'd always stay and protect her.

"Maybe not then, but you had a hundred other chances to tell me the truth, Birdie."

"I told you, Tristan. Some secrets should stay buried. I was never going to tell you or anyone else because I've never thought in a million years that Blake would lose it to the point that he'd risk serious jail time just to bring me down with him."

"He wouldn't. An ex-cop junkie in prison… He wouldn't survive a day without being someone's bitch. He's bluffing."

"Is he?"

The doubt in her voice stirs mine. We need facts, not speculations. "Birdie, you have to be very honest with me. Does Blake have any proof that you asked him to frame Shane or that you gave false testimony?"

Years of paranoia flash across her face. "No. Not that I know of. But eight years ago, I was young and vulnerable and naive. I trusted Blake so much back then. Now that I know the kind of monster he is, how can I be so sure he didn't record our agreement or anything like that?"

I mentally catalog what we know about Blake, about his methods. "I don't think he did. A person so ready to expose you would have shown your lawyer a hint of the receipts he kept, if he had any. But he only mentioned the prison visit to rattle you because that's all he has."

She shakes her head, unconvinced. "Perhaps, but I'm not taking any chances, Tristan."

"You're not. If he says anything, it'll be your word against his. You have proof he's a drug addict. You have proof of his violence. He has nothing. His lies will crumble down on him, not on you."

The look she gives me is pure acid. "What an optimistic scenario with a glorious happy ending! Do you live in the same world I do? Because I don't remember seeing unicorns farting rainbows in mine." Her voice takes a harsh turn. "Have you forgotten about Aaron?"

Aaron. The skeleton in her closet that could bring everything crashing down. "No, but everyone related to him is dead. Blake has no proof for it either."

"It's a sexual assault scandal, Tristan. It doesn't need proof. Guilty or innocent, one word out and I'm done. No coming back from that."

The blood in my veins turns to ice. How did I not think of that? How did I not see things from her perspective?

"Now imagine a man who is spending the rest of his life in prison and another who is penniless, who suspects his days are numbered. Imagine these two coming together with this knowledge, with this power…" She paces between the trees, twigs breaking under her feet. She's terrified. And now I understand why.

"Blake and Shane are two men who, in their sick minds, think you ruined their lives. They're angry, and they want revenge. But above all, they have nothing to lose and everything to gain."

"Exactly. Shane would say anything, do anything, to get out of prison. Blake would do the same to save his life and take my money. What if Blake promised to get Shane out of prison if he lied for him?"

"Lied about what?"

She whirls to face me, eyes blazing with a desperation I've never seen before. "Everything. Aaron, the beating, the testimony. There's a story in everything, Tristan, and it can be told in so many ways, where heroes and villains are one and the same."

My pulse hammers against my throat. How far can those two scumbags twist the truth to destroy Birdie?

She moves again, faster now. "Here's one where I'm the unredeemable villain. Aaron is innocent, and I'm the predator. Shane, my loving husband, finds out. He loses his mind and beats the crap out of me. It's the worst thing he's ever done, and he can't be sorry enough, but put yourself in his position. The woman he loves so much not only does she cheat on him, but with her student whom she rapes.”

Jesus Christ. My stomach turns as she wields their twisted version of events.

“But my monstrosities don't stop there. Afraid Shane will tell on me or kill me, I report him for domestic violence. The one cop that empathizes with my case and tries to help me, I seduce. Then I ask him to abuse his power to put Shane away for life because I'm too afraid.”

I want to stop her, to shelter her in my arms and tell her none of this will happen, tell her that everything is gonna be okay. But I can't. Because she's right. This is exactly the kind of story they'd tell.

“Blake thinks he's doing the right thing helping me get rid of the monster. But then, he realizes it's a mistake. His guilt is unbearable. It leads him to substance abuse. He visits the man he's wronged to apologize. There, Shane tells him about Aaron, the parts Blake doesn't know. Blake is devastated. He wishes he knew the truth about the woman he's lost everything for. Now, it's too late. All he can do is come clean and free an innocent man.”

“Holy fuck.”

Her feet halt, and the bitterness on her face spreads to mine. “Do you still think I'm safe from Blake, Tristan?”

CHAPTER 18

Birdie

The silence that follows is a noose tightening around both our necks.

Since I saw Butterfly Man's first sick note on my pillow, I've wanted to prove something to the deranged man who thought he owned me. I wanted to show him he didn't.

Now, I end up with two of them.

"Tristan, I have to post that video we talked about. It'll temporarily discredit Blake and buy us some time, giving us a chance to tell Butterfly Man he can't touch Blake, until we figure out what to do."

My bodyguard laughs incredulously. "Tell your stalker he can't kill your husband now? What the hell, Birdie? He's not your personal hitman. He's a lunatic murderer who operates on his own psycho whims. I'm pretty sure you can't just send him a memo to reschedule."

I'm too angry to respond to the sarcasm. "Butterfly Man doesn't kill on a whim. He does it for me. If he finds out about Shane, about Blake's blackmail, he won't kill him. If anything, he may come up with something that will help."

"You're not meeting your stalker, Birdie. End of story."

"Do you not realize the kind of danger I'm facing? If anything happens to Blake, and that app sends whatever fucked-up story he plans to expose, I'm done. Everything I've ever worked for, my freedom, my life, is at stake, Tristan. I must update Butterfly Man on the situation or I'll lose it all."

"I can't put you in danger!"

"Do you have another solution?!"

Tristan runs his hand through his hair. "That app… I think I might have a way to find it, and when I do, I'll destroy the message."

"*Might* is not good enough, Tristan."

"I will find it."

"How? You don't even know where Blake is."

"You said he's in Florida, and he'll stay there. A coward like him won't come back here, not after what happened to your assistant. I'll track him down from that prison visit. Junkies are the easiest to find, Birdie."

"You'll go there yourself?"

"Yes."

"Then let me post that video and take me with you. We find both Blake and Butterfly Man and end this once and for all."

Frustration etches across his face. "You're asking me to put you face-to-face with a serial killer. Do you even hear yourself?"

"I hear a woman desperate enough to consider every option, even the unthinkable."

"This is insanity."

"No, insanity is sitting here doing nothing while my life implodes!" I push past him and walk deeper into the woods.

"Where are you going?" Tristan demands, following close behind.

"Away from here. Away from you telling me what I can and can't do."

"Birdie, wait."

My steps widen. "Don't follow me."

"I'm your bodyguard. Following you is literally my job description."

I spin around, fury shaking my voice. "Then guard me from a fucking distance."

I head down the narrow footpath that leads away from the clearing. The afternoon sun filters through the dense canopy of trees surrounding our hideaway, creating dappled patterns on the forest floor. The thickets close in around me as I walk, wild berry bushes catching at my clothes. I push deeper into the woods, away from the cabin that has become both sanctuary and prison.

Tristan's footsteps crunch behind me, maintaining a distance but never straying too far. His persistence only fuels my anger. I take a deep breath of the pine-scented air to calm the storm inside me.

The ocean's distant roar grows louder as I unconsciously head toward the hidden beach cove. Maybe the crashing waves will drown out the noise in my head, the constant fear that has become my unwanted companion.

I pause at a fork in the path, the trees opening slightly to allow more sunlight through. A flutter of movement catches my eye—something out of place among the static green of the forest.

Squinting into the dense part of the woods, I listen. Nothing.

"Tristan?" I call out, confused. He should be behind me, not off to the side.

No answer.

Then—there it is again. A flash of dark fabric between trees.

My heartbeat quickens. I scan the surrounding forest more carefully, piercing through the layers of foliage with my gaze.

A gasp chokes in my throat when I realize I'm not alone. About thirty yards away, partially concealed behind a massive pine tree, a figure in a dark hoodie stands perfectly still. Even at this distance, I can make out the grotesque print on the mask covering his entire face.

A butterfly.

My blood turns to ice. "Tristan!" I scream, stumbling back on my feet.

The hooded figure steps fully into view now, tilting his head as if curious. The butterfly mask catches the light, its intricate patterns somehow more terrifying in daylight.

I turn and run, no longer caring about the path, just putting distance between myself and the nightmare made flesh. Behind me, I hear Tristan shouting my name, the confusion in his voice telling me he hasn't seen what I've seen.

I crash through ferns and low-hanging branches, the sound of my own panicked breathing drowning out everything else. Sharp thorns from berry bushes tear at my arms as I push through, but I barely feel the sting.

A quick glance over my shoulder, and my heart nearly stops. The hooded figure is following, his movements eerily smooth as he navigates the forest.

"He's here!" I shout, hoping Tristan can hear me. "Butterfly Man is here!"

I trip over an exposed root, stumble, but manage to keep my footing. The path slopes sharply downward now, leading toward the hidden cove. If I can reach the beach, the open space will give me nowhere to hide, but at least I'll be able to see him coming.

The trees thin out ahead, revealing glimpses of grey sky and the ocean beyond. Almost there.

The sky thunders, and rain pours out of nowhere. Something catches my ankle. A hand? A branch? I don't know, but I'm falling, tumbling down the last section of the slope, loose dirt and pine needles sliding with me.

The roar of waves is now deafening, yelling over my screams. Dazed, I roll over, spitting wet dirt from my mouth. Then a shadow falls over me.

I look up, heart hammering in my chest. The butterfly mask stares down. My stalker has found me. Butterfly Man has come to claim what is his.

CHAPTER 19

Butterfly Man

"Got you, little butterfly."

The rain washes over us like a baptism. My little butterfly, sprawled before me, drenched, her eyes wide with recognition. With fear.

"Tristan!" she screams, and I drop to my knees and place my palms on either side of her head. My body hovers over hers, caging her beneath me. She scrambles backward, but I move with her, my knees now bracketing her hips, trapping her against the muddy forest floor. The rain cascades down my mask onto her face, our breaths mingling in the narrow space between us.

"Don't be afraid." I caress her cheek with the back of my hand and watch her flinch. So fragile, so beautiful in her terror. "I would never hurt you, Reagan. Never you."

"I have every reason to fear you. You've left trails of blood in your wake," she whispers.

"For you. And you like it." Can she argue with that?

"How did you find me?" Her voice trembles.

I tilt my head, studying her, my hand sliding down to her throat. The rain slicks her hair against her face, dark tendrils framing those eyes that haunt me. Her pulse flutters at her neck like that of a captured animal, her chest heaving with each panicked breath. "I've always known where you are. Every moment. Every breath."

"No. You couldn't."

"Couldn't I?" I lower my face closer to hers. I want to kiss her so badly. God, she's beautiful. But she's never been more beautiful than in this moment of surrender, this perfect culmination of our chase. The fear in her eyes ignites something savage within me, something primal. Predator and prey. Hunter and hunted. "And yet here I am, darling. The question is, why did you run from me? Don't you know I'll always chase after you? It makes me hard as fuck." I push my hips forward, letting her feel the proof.

She whimpers a gasp, and I smile behind the mask. "You like it, too, don't you, darling?

You told me so the last time we met. Being chased by a masked man, your stalker, in the woods… The moment he catches you and you lie helplessly while he fucks you like a hungry beast." I press my cock harder against her and hiss. "On the scale of one to ten, if I slide my fingers now inside your pussy, how wet will you be?"

"Get the fuck off of me."

"That wet, huh? I bet wetter than when I put a gun to that sweet little cunt. I know I'm harder. Nothing compares to the primal thrill of capturing you, my little butterfly. Nothing compares to watching my prey tremble beneath me, caught at last after the pursuit…and vice versa."

"Tristan!"

The distant shout of her bodyguard echoes through the trees. I have minutes, perhaps seconds.

"Why are you calling for him? You're the one who ran into the woods away from him. He doesn't understand what we have, what I've done for you. He can't give you what you really need, so you came here, looking for me."

"You're insane. I didn't know you were lurking in the woods."

"Didn't you, darling? Didn't you, at least, hope I was?"

Lightning flashes across the sky, illuminating us in stark white light. In that moment, I see her completely, vulnerable, terrified, mesmerizing. Her hands are pressed against my chest, neither pushing me away nor pulling me closer. Suspended between rejection and acceptance.

"Tell the truth, Birdie. Isn't there a part of you that hoped I was listening? Who else would solve your little problem? You want more of the gifts I've been giving you."

"Gifts?" Her chest rises and falls rapidly beneath me, rain droplets clinging to her eyelashes like tears. "You mean the people you've murdered."

"The people who hurt you," I correct her with a surge of pride. "The ones who deserved their fate. I've watched them all, Birdie. The ones who used you. The ones who think they own pieces of you. I couldn't let that happen anymore. They had to pay for what they did. They had to know the truth. You are mine. All of you. Mine."

The shouting grows closer. Her bodyguard, crashing through the underbrush. "We don't have much time."

"You can't kill Blake."

"Your husband," I say the word like poison on my tongue. "He thinks he can control you with his threats. But don't worry, little butterfly. I will take care of it."

"I'm serious. You can't kill him now."

"C'mon, darling. Drop the act. We both know that's not really the message you're trying to give me."

"What are you talking about? The things that will come out about me after his death will ruin my life."

"Whatever he has on that app is retrievable and easy to destroy. You already know how good I am with technology…and finding people."

She shakes her head in disbelief. "How did you know about the app? You couldn't have been listening to us in the woods. I'd have noticed. Tristan would have noticed if someone was there eavesdropping."

"Guess he just sucks at his job."

Her eyes narrow at me. "Or you had the same training and know exactly every procedure, every security measure to counter it, because you work in the same company."

This is cute. "Or I've been tailing your lawyer, listening to her calls, reading her emails. I've done it before. I followed her to get Saldana's book. Or, unlike your lousy bodyguard, I didn't lose your husband's trail and know exactly where he is and what he's been up to. These are more believable scenarios than my being Morrison, don't you think?"

"Morrison? How the hell did you know

about Morrison? I only had this conversation with Tristan in the cabin. We'd only just arrived. There is no way you could have already known where I was then or had the time to bug the cabin."

"Then it's Brandon. He's too young to be your stalker, but he could be an accomplice. You trusted the wrong bodyguard, the one who has been working with me all along. He let me in your house that night, and he told me about Morrison."

"That's impossible. We never told Brandon which bodyguard I suspected."

"Then, my darling butterfly, the only explanation left is," I trace the line of her throat down and back up, "I'm not really here, and all of this is happening in your head."

She bares her teeth at me. "Don't you dare. Last time we met you punished me for telling the world you were a lie, a prank. You are real, as real as the blood you spill in my name."

"You're right. Last time we met was amazing, too good to be true, but it was real. A memory branded on my soul. But now… Your bodyguard did his job this time. No cell service. He didn't tell anyone where he took you. No trails. Nothing to track, even the internet proxies route your location to… Where was that again? Hmmm… It looks like I don't remember that…because *you* don't remember it."

A new terror blanches her face. "I'm not crazy. I didn't hallucinate you."

"*But there is also always some reason in madness.* Isn't that what the man with the motorcycle said to you the night he saved you from me?"

She looks like she's about to cry. "How did you know that?"

I chuckle. "Don't worry, darling, you're not crazy. You just tripped and hurt your head. It explains a lot, like how the hell he hasn't shown up yet. You've been screaming for him, and he's been calling out to you for so long. He should have found you by now." I lean closer and rest my head on her shoulder. "But you don't want him to. You want *me* here now, the man who would sacrifice everything for you, who sees you beneath all the masks you wear for the world, and I know why."

"Why?" That shaky whisper isn't a question. It's more of a necessary evil.

"One, you want to send me a message, remember? And it's not about postponing your husband's demise. What you really want me to do is kill Blake *and* Shane." I tilt my head to meet her gaze. "And you're absolutely right. Putting him behind bars for life isn't enough. I heard you, my queen. Loud and clear. He, too, must die."

"You'd do that?"

"Of course. I made you a promise. I always

protect what's mine."

"What's two?"

"Huh?"

"You said, 'one I want to send you a message.' What's two?"

I lift my head and pull up the mask just enough to let her see my smile. "Two is… you're a horny little slut, and you want me to make you come again. This time, here in the woods, and maybe not just with my fingers… Why else would you lie beneath me, like a little bunny about to be devoured by a big bad wolf?"

"What? No. No!" She squirms.

"There's nothing to be ashamed of, little butterfly." I slide my thumb over her lips. "I've been missing you so much, too. I know I still have to earn you, but since that night, I can't stop myself from wanting more."

Her breath trembles and crashes on my skin. "Get off of me now. Tristan!"

I wrap my fingers around her neck and pin her head down to the ground. "He's not here, darling, and there's nothing you can do to stop me from taking what's mine."

"I'm not yours."

Her eyes, her breath, every fiber of her being, betray her lips. Her resistance is a performance, a compulsory pretense when the truth is too dark to bear.

"It's just us now," I murmur, my lips brushing against her ear, my hardness digging into her pelvis. "No one to perform for. No one to pretend for."

"This isn't real," she whispers, but her body arches beneath mine—an involuntary confession.

"Isn't it?" I challenge, my fingers still wrapped around her throat, applying just enough pressure to remind her of who really owns her. "Your mind creates what you truly desire, little butterfly. And here I am."

A tear escapes the corner of her eye, mingling with the raindrops on her cheek. Beautiful consummation. "I hate you," she says, but there's no conviction behind it.

"No," I trace the tear's path with my thumb. "You hate that you want this. You hate that after everything," I tear open her shirt, and our gasps collide. I bite on my lip as I marvel in the beauty of her skin, the shape of her tits, her waist, her belly, "I'm the one who understands the darkness inside you, the one who obsesses and worships it as much as he obsesses and worships your body." I can't help myself. My palm takes its time exploring how it feels to touch her without a barrier. I study every curve, every bone, every sensation that shatters the edges of sanity and paste it all to memory.

Thunder rumbles overhead, vibrating

through the ground beneath us. Her body-guard's voice has faded, lost to the storm or distance. Or perhaps he never was here at all. Perhaps it's always been just us, predator and prey, locked in this eternal dance.

"Tell me what you really want," I command, leaning until our foreheads touch, and my lips are a breath away from kissing hers. "No more lies. Not between us."

"I want—" Her lips part, words forming and dissolving before they can take shape.

"Louder," I demand, tightening my grip on her throat, her pulse racing beneath my fingers.

"I want you to stop."

Desire and rage twist together inside me, a blend that leads to pain and mayhem. How dare she lie to me, even now? How dare she deny what burns so obviously between us?

"Even here, in the darkness of your own desires?" I shake my head slowly. "I thought we were past that, Reagan."

My free hand trails down her exposed skin, savoring the goosebumps that rise in its wake. Her skin is feverish despite the cold rain, burn-ing with the same fire that consumes me. "If you can't be honest with me, then you don't de-serve what you truly want."

Her eyes widen as I rip open the buttons of her jeans. She squirms, kicking and screaming. Her strength is nothing against mine. All her resistance can't stop me from punishing her now. I unzip her pants and pull them down with her panties below her ass. Then I shift my weight, my knee pressing between her thighs, parting them just enough to see the slickness of her pussy.

A needy growl seethes out of me. I've killed for this moment, just to worship at this altar. Her fear, her struggle, her unbidden arousal, all feed that primal hunger I have only for her.

This was always inevitable. She was created to be found by you, to be taken by you.

I hate that voice, but it's right. "Yes. A masterpiece designed solely for me."

"No—" she begins, but I press my thumb against her lips, silencing her.

"Shh. No more lies. Not when I can read the truth in your body. Not when I can taste your desire in the air between us." My lips crash against hers—not gentle, not asking permission, but taking, claiming, branding.

Her surprised gasp melts into something hungrier, and her lips respond to mine with an eagerness that calls her out on her bullshit. When I pull away, her eyes are glazed, her lips parted in shock and need.

"That," I murmur, "is what honesty feels like." I taste her rain-stained skin, her cheek, her jaw, and leave a trail all the way down to her pussy. My whole body trembles, not with hesitation but with the overwhelming power of having her completely at my mercy, pinned and helpless beneath me, with the sight of her wet pussy that is all mine to finally own.

With my fist on her throat, I press my lips to her pussy. My first taste of heaven. No, of hell. Her wetness in my mouth ignites all my vices at once. Possession, hunger, violence, a savage need to claim what I've hunted for so long.

Groaning, I devour her. I lap my tongue inside, outside, over and under many times like a depraved animal until I savored every drop. Only then do I come down from my feverish delight and realize she's not fighting me anymore. She's moaning with me, moving into my mouth, needing more.

"No, butterfly. Last time, I let you come and denied myself pleasure." I pull down my mask. "Today, it's a different story." Then I work my pants and pull my cock out. She wriggles as my hardness pries its way between her thighs. I take my hand off her throat and pin down both of her wrists. "I'm not gonna fuck you either. I've made you so horny you're gonna come all over my cock in no time. You don't get to come today…but I do."

She protests when I slide the tip inside her. Then, when I rub myself, teasing her to the point of whimpering, her protests turn into pleas.

"Yeah, little slut, beg for my cock. Beg for your stalker to fuck you like an animal. Beg to make you my little bitch. Isn't that what you want? A fucked up monster to pursue you, chase you and make you his fucktoy when he catches you, to show you what it is to be loved by a predator?"

Her moans grow louder, pumping fire through my veins. My breath catches as my fist works faster, and I know I'm tormenting her clit.

"Last time I was in your bed, what were you going to say before they cut us off?"

"What?" she moans again.

"When I counted how many times your pussy clenched to orgasm…" My balls grow heavier. I'm so close. "I thought you'd think it was sick or plain psycho, but you were about to say something else. What was it?"

"I'm never going to tell you." She arches her hips, trying to take more of me inside her. But I don't let her. Just when she rubs herself around my shaft, I pull out and choke her again.

I howl at the thunderous sky. Angrily, my cum spurts all over her, on her pussy, on her stomach, on her neck, on her cheek.

I marvel at the sight of my marked prey sprawled beneath me, drowning in a need she denies, begging for a darkness she can't re-sist, and a sated smile creeps under my mask. "That's for hiding from me." I tuck my cock back inside my pants and rise to my feet. Then I push my cum inside her pussy, where it be-longs, and smear some of it over her lips be-fore the rain washes it away. "And that's for not answering me, lying to me and…believing I'm only a dark fantasy you can control."

"I… You… This… is all in my head. It's the only explanation."

"Is it?"

The rain pelts harder, erasing the evidence of our encounter, the mud, the sweat, the tears. But it can't wash away the connection that binds us—predator and prey, stalker and stalked, two damaged souls orbiting the same dark star. Two broken pieces that only together are whole.

"Until next time, my butterfly." The forest swallows me as I become one with the dark-ness and rain. But not before I glimpse the war in her eyes—anger battling desire, fear wres-tling with longing, madness defying sanity. She can deny me with her words all she wants, but her body has already surrendered.

The next time we meet, I won't be wear-ing a mask, and I'll claim every inch of what's rightfully mine.

For now, the hunt continues.

CHAPTER 20

Birdie

I bolt upright, disoriented, my body damp with sweat. It's pitch black. Where am I? Tristan's name rips from my throat, raw and desperate.

A shadow moves in front of me.

Panic constricts my chest. My eyes dart around frantically. My fingers claw at the surface beneath me. It's not mud and pebbles. It's warm and soft. Sheets. I feel the blankets tangled and trapping me. The shadow moves closer, and my pulse hammers against my ribs. "Tristan! Tristan!"

"Hey." His voice cuts through the darkness. Then a lamp flickers on. The light reveals wooden walls, a quilted blanket twisted around my legs, moonlight spilling through curtained windows. The cabin. The safe house. And Tristan. He's rising from a chair beside the bed. "I'm here. You're safe, Birdie."

Suddenly, he moves to the edge of the bed and pulls me into his arms. Tristan, the man who flinches at the slightest accidental brush of fingers, who maintains a calculated space between himself and the world—between himself and me—whose entire body coils with tension at proximity, crosses all his lines and hugs me.

The shock of his touch, of his arms encircling me completely, pulling me against his chest with desperation, eclipses my terror. I feel the thundering of his heart, the shake in his hands as they press against my back. His body is tense, but he doesn't let go. "I was so worried about you," he murmurs, his voice unusually soft, thick with an emotion he's never allowed me to hear before.

A sob rips from my throat, violent and unrestrained. My fingers dig into his shirt, my body wracked with tremors. "He had me," I gasp. "Butterfly Man, he was there. He caught me, he… Tristan, he was on top of me. He did it again."

Tristan pulls back just enough to look at me, his brows furrowed. "What are you talking about?"

The words tumble out in a frantic rush. I tell him everything. The glimpse of the mask through the trees, the desperate flight through the rain-slicked woods, the feel of my legs giving out beneath me, and then... him. The weight of Butterfly Man crushing me into the mud. The whispers. His touch. My helplessness. When I finish, I'm shaking, my fingers clutching Tristan's shirt like it's the only thing keeping me from drowning.

"Birdie," his voice drops, threaded with concern, "that's not possible."

"No. He tried to convince me I hit my head and imagined it all, but he was there. I saw him. I ran, and he chased after me. He pinned me down in the rain. He—" The memories flood back in vivid flashes—the mask, his mouth on my lips, his words in my ear, his hands on my throat, on my body. I bury my face against Tristan's shoulder. "I can't believe he found me and did it again. How does this keep on happening to me? I kept calling for you, but you never came."

"No, Birdie. I was there the whole time. You asked me to keep my distance, but I was watching you."

"Yes, but then I saw him, lurking behind the trees, and you weren't there anymore."

"That's not what happened. I've never left your side. You kept going farther into the woods until you tripped and fell on the rocks by the cove. I ran to catch you, but I wasn't close enough. When I reached you, you'd already passed out, and your head was bleeding. I carried you and hurried back here. I did the best I could to clean the cut and stop the bleeding, but since then, you've been out for hours. I thought…" He doesn't finish, but his arms tighten around me.

My skull and temple throb with pain as if on cue. I touch my head and feel the bandage covering it. "That's… But I… No, Tristan, please, not again. He's trying to make me look crazy, just like before. Why are you falling for it again?"

"I'm not, but what you think happened couldn't have. I think I'd have remembered if you were drenched in cum when I found you."

"The rain must have washed it away."

"No, because all of the things you told me aren't real. It must have been a nightmare. I can prove it. Look at your clothes."

I lift the blanket and glance down at myself. I'm wearing a clean black T-shirt—Tristan's—and sweatpants. "Where are my clothes? Who took them off and put me in these?"

He swallows. "I did." His eyes drop to where my fingers clutch the hem of his T-shirt against my thighs, then quickly back to my face. A flush creeps up his neck.

"You…" My voice trails off. The thought of Tristan's hands on me while I was unconscious, touching parts of me no one has touched in a long time except in violence, sends an unexpected tingling through me.

"Your clothes were soaked through," he explains, his voice lower, rougher. "You were shivering. I was afraid you'd get hypothermia on top of the head injury." His thumb absently traces small circles on my arm. "I had to."

His scent surrounds me, embedded in the fabric of his clothes I'm wearing. Now, I'm hyperaware of how his T-shirt drapes over my body, how the neckline slips off one shoulder, how nothing but thin cotton separates his hand from my skin.

I should pull away. Put distance between us. We're both too raw right now, too vulnerable. But I lean toward him, drawn by some gravity I can't control. "Thank you, for taking care of me."

His eyes spark, and for a moment, I think he might—

He clears his throat and reaches over to the nightstand. "Your clothes are here." He hands me the folded stack, without breaking our embrace. "They're intact. I washed them. They're still a little damp, and there may be some mud stains that didn't go away, but they're not torn."

I force myself to shift focus from the heat of his proximity and the lingering sensation of his fingertips against mine to the clothes, to the presumed evidence of my insanity. "This doesn't make any sense," I whisper, my fingers trembling as they trace the unmarred fabric. "I felt him tear my shirt open, my pants, I heard them rip."

Tristan hesitates, then pulls out a phone, not his usual device— this one is bigger. "There's something else you should see." He swipes through it a few times before handing it to me. "After what happened last time, I... I needed to make sure you were safe. Even when you needed space."

A video feed pops on the screen. The time-stamp shows earlier today, around the time I left the cabin. The camera angle is strange, bobbing with movement. "Are these the woods outside?" The angle is from the perspective of someone walking in them. Then it hits me. "This is me walking, isn't it? You put a camera on me without telling me, Tristan?"

"A micro-GPS with a camera attachment. It was on your shirt collar. I put it there during our sparring in the kitchen." His eyes are pleading for understanding. "I had to be sure I could find you and protect you if he tried to come near you again. I don't know what I would do if anything happened to you. I can't…"

I want to be angry, but the desperation in his voice stops me. Instead, I watch the footage.

There I am, walking through the woods alone. The camera catches glimpses of trees, the ocean in the distance, my shadow stretched ahead of me. No one follows. No one watches. Then the view abruptly tilts, spins—I'm falling. There's a sickening crack as the camera catches the ground, rain pattering against it.

Tristan calling my name follows. Seconds later, he appears, running into view. His face is twisted with terror as he drops to his knees beside me. His mouth forms my name again and again as he checks my pulse, my breathing. Then he lifts me into his arms, my head lolling against his chest.

Tristan calls out for Brandon as he reaches the cabin. They're both running. We're in the bathroom, where Brandon is filling the tub with water, and then Tristan lays me in the tub. He reaches a hand toward me, I assume to take off my shirt because then the footage ends.

"Are you saying the only thing that happened out there in the woods is that I hit my head, then you brought me here and you've been up all night, keeping watch, afraid I wouldn't wake up?"

"Yes. I was scared shitless." He rests his forehead on mine, his eyes squeezing as if in pain. "Don't do this to me again. Please, Birdie. I can't lose you."

I stare at the screen, trying to reconcile

what I've just seen with the vivid horror etched into my memory. "But it felt so real. I can, literally, feel him inside me."

"I was there the whole time. There was no one else there, Birdie," he says softly, holding my gaze. "But you hit your head pretty hard. I should have taken you to the hospital right away." His thumb gently brushes near the bandage on my temple. "Get some rest. I'll arrange for a secure trip to the hospital first thing in the morning. I don't think what you had was just a nightmare. You may have a concussion."

I lean into him, too exhausted to fight anymore—against the memories, against the evidence, against the comfort of his arms that defies everything. "No. We don't have time for this. We must go to Florida. Now."

"Birdie, we talked about this. I get that you want to send your stalker a message so badly you fantasized about it when you passed out, in a disturbingly dark erotic way of all things, but I can't let you go see your stalker. Besides, we've already narrowed him down to two possible suspects. Both we can easily contact and subtly tell about your husband's blackmail. There, message delivered."

I draw back. "Are you sure I'm the one who hit my head and not you? Whether the creep bodyguard is Butterfly Man or not, maybe that would have been the easy way to do it, but if we tell the detective the truth and he turns out to be just that, a detective, what do you think he's going to do with the crimes we voluntarily confess to him? He'll slap our wrists and tell us not to do it again? Are you crazy?"

He just stares at me. He must know I have a point.

"Besides, we can't rule out the possibility that Butterfly Man is neither of them, not yet," I add. "We must go to Florida. You have Blake's trail to follow from the prison in Jacksonville that will lead you to where he's hiding his app to destroy it, and I must stall Butterfly Man in Miami until you do."

His jaw tightens as he pulls away from me. The warmth that had been in his eyes moments ago hardens. "You still want to offer yourself as bait. After everything that's happened." His voice is controlled, but the fury building beneath the surface isn't hard to miss.

"We don't have another choice. You know that."

He stands abruptly, running a hand through his hair. "No. What I know is that you collapsed in the woods today. What I know is that you're having such vivid hallucinations that you can't distinguish between reality and your own fears." His eyes pierce mine. "What I know is that you're in no condition to face anyone, let alone the man who's been tormenting you for months.”

“Tristan—”

“But I also know that every minute you’re away from me is dangerous. I promised I wouldn’t let you out of my sight.” He nods to himself. “You’re coming with me.”

I sigh in relief. “Thank you.”

“But you’re not posting that video or meeting your stalker.”

And just like that, the relief slips away. “But—”

“No buts. I’m not gonna stand by and watch you walk into danger. Not again.” He turns off the light and moves toward the door. “Get some sleep. We leave first thing in the morning.”

With Tristan halfway out of the door, as the last flicker of light fades, panic surges through me at the thought of being alone in the darkness again. “Wait!” I call out, my voice breaking. “Don’t leave. Please.”

He pauses, hand on the doorknob, his back to me.

“I’m scared…of being alone tonight. Of what I might see when I close my eyes,” I whisper, hating the weakness in my voice, but I don’t care. “Would you stay with me tonight? Even if you can just sit in the chair until I fall asleep.”

For what feels like an eternity, he remains

frozen, silhouetted in the doorway. Then, without a word, he closes the door and turns back to the room. He doesn't move toward the chair. Instead, he walks to the bed.

"Scoot over," he commands.

I blink, surprised by his directness. "Really?"

"I've been sitting for hours in that chair. My neck is still sore from watching over you all night. And I meant what I said about not letting you out of my sight."

A smile sneaks up on me as I slide over, making room. "Of course."

He sits on the edge of the bed, his back to me, and removes his shoes methodically. The mattress dips as he stretches out beside me, keeping a careful distance between us. He places his gun on the nightstand, within easy reach.

He lies rigid, staring up at the ceiling. Even in the darkness, the tension radiating from his body is palpable.

"Who else can have access to that footage from the GPS camera?" I ask.

"No one but me. Don't worry. I've already deleted the part when we had our heart-to-heart chat. Do you want to see for yourself?"

"I don't need to. You always have my back."

"Good to know that you can finally trust me, at least when it comes to protecting you."

"I know you're furious with me," I say quietly.

"I'm not furious." His head shifts toward me. "I'm terrified."

The admission catches me off guard. Tristan has never been one to acknowledge fear.

"Does that shock you, that you can make me feel afraid?"

Yes. But I don't say it. I don't know if it's the right thing to say.

He stares back at the ceiling. "You have your way of bringing out the worst in me."

"I didn't mean to fall and cause all that panic." I was running from my stalker, or so I thought. "I'm sorry I scared you."

"Don't." The command is clipped, harsh. "I know it wasn't your fault, but, for the love of God, you can't put yourself in danger again." He rolls on his side, and his breath fans my face. "When I saw you fall… When I couldn't wake you up... I've watched men die, many by my hand. But seeing you lying there, blood on your face, not knowing if you'd open your eyes again—" He cuts himself off.

"Tristan—"

"I can't lose you." The words rush out, violent in their intensity. "You don't understand what it's like," he continues after a long pause. "I've lost everything that mattered to me once before. I won't go through that again."

My heart stutters. This isn't just about the job anymore or his promise to protect me. This is something deeper, something neither of us has dared to name or voice.

His eyes find mine in the darkness. The walls are down, and my breath catches at what I see.

Slowly, deliberately, he breaks the invisible barriers he's set between us and reaches across the void. His fingertips brush the back of my hand where it rests on the blanket.

He swallows audibly. "Touch was a weapon used against me for a long time."

I can relate. We both had monstrous parents who used us as punching bags. They took something from us that wasn't theirs to take. "Tristan, you don't have to. I know how hard it is for you."

"It's different with you." The confession is dragged from somewhere deep inside him. "I don't know why."

I let my fingers slide among his, and he squeezes them gently without hesitation. "Maybe because I've been through the same kind of pain. I understand how it steals a piece of you that you'll never get back, how it leaves a dark void that alters you forever, one only someone like us can fill…or fall into without remorse."

He moves closer and pulls me toward him, until my head rests against his chest, his heartbeat racing beneath my ear. His arm encircles me, protective rather than restraining.

A smile stretches my lips. "I should fall and hit my head every day."

"Don't ever say that, not even as a joke."

"Tristan—"

"You should try to sleep. Tomorrow will be..." He doesn't finish the sentence. We both know what tomorrow holds.

I shouldn't push for more, but I have to give it one last shot. "If I see him tomorrow, he won't try to take me, you know, because he hasn't earned me yet. And we both know he won't kill me either."

"Birdie," he starts, not in reprimand or agitation, but in sinister affirmation, "there are worse things than death. Ways to keep someone alive but make them wish they weren't."

A chill runs through me at the darkness in his tone. I lift my head to look at his face, shadows playing across his features. Before I say anything, he pulls me back to his embrace.

"Sleep, Birdie," he murmurs into my hair, his lips brushing against the back of my neck in a ghost of a kiss. "I've got you. I'm going to keep you safe. Whatever it takes."

The vow speaks of blood and consequence. I should worry. I should remember that this man has killed, has destroyed lives without a blink. I should be afraid of what he might do to keep his word.

Instead, I close my eyes, oddly comforted by his presence even as fear of what's to come gnaws at my insides. Tomorrow, we face our demons. But tonight, we're safe, two broken people finding unexpected strength in each other's jagged edges.

For now, it has to be enough.

CHAPTER 21

Butterfly Man

I have been watching.

Every anxious glance, every feigned moment of control, every desperate little scheme.

"Even when you're hiding, I know you want me to find you. Fly as high and far as you wish, little butterfly. In the end, I'll always catch you." Memory floods back. Not the first time I saw her face, but the moment I truly saw her. The darkness behind her eyes. The pain that matches my own. The line in destiny that wrote her mine.

There were men before me who tried to own her, to shape her into something lesser than what she was. Men who try to take her from me now. The detective. The man with the motorcycle. They don't understand her like I do. They don't see the darkness inside her the way I do. The hunger. The need. They will fail like the others before them.

And they will pay like I've made the others pay.

Every threat I eliminate brings me closer to her. Every potential rival removed makes her more dependent on my presence. Soon, she'll realize the monster I've become to keep her safe, the one I'm ready to become to make her mine, is the only constant in her world of chaos.

Unlike her *bodyguard*—it makes me laugh every time—I haven't lost track of her husband. Lingering in the shadows, my breath a whisper against the night, I've followed Blake. He moves with the desperation of a man who knows his time is running out. A coward, seeking refuge in lies. I know exactly where he is. I can see him now like I see my reflection in the mirror.

I didn't even need to hack his phone to track him. I simply cloned it. One text from the cheater's phone to his, and I'm in with a little backdoor that allows me to clone his entire phone.

Every contact, email, photo, phone call. Apps, passwords, timings, patterns. Everything I can control. I have the son of a bitch by the balls.

Except…

The dead man's switch app. The same kind of app the pervert had. The one I wished I'd known about seven years ago.

I hate those. They get more advanced by the day, and Blake uses one of the most complicated ones when it comes to security. It needs more than a password or passkey to open. It is device-bound with a biometric sequence of authentication to get in. It means only Blake can open the app, and if I create a spoof system to mimic his check in pattern or attempt to open it on my device, it will trigger a security alert that will tell Blake he's being breached.

Whatever message he sends from that app if he doesn't check in can't be good. After his phone call with the lawyer, I don't need to see what he has inside the app to know it's a threat to Reagan meant to destroy her.

Nobody threatens my little butterfly and walks away with it. Nobody threatens my Reagan. Period.

My hand slides into my pocket and closes around the blade handle, the familiar grip molding perfectly to my palm. The thought of sinking it into Blake's flesh burns through me. Not the clean kill of a mission, but something primal, a taste of the divine, final and euphoric.

I imagine the moment, the sharp gasp as he

realizes, too late, that he is not the predator but the prey. The way his blood will spill across my hands, a final offering to my queen, the—

My phone buzzes with an alert. It nudges me before the rush of the fantasy consumes me too soon.

The notification is for a post on Birdie's Instagram. I open it. I watch it. I watch it again, and again, and again, like I'm some sort of an obsessed maniac—a very angry one.

The video is a direct message to me. *Meet me at the school in Miami.* A trap so obvious it's laughable. But there's another message encrypted in her face, in her hidden eyes behind the shades, in her carefully crafted words, in the lies, like the location of the video. It says Miami when she's in Jacksonville.

Yes, I know where she is, too. I can see her like I see my reflection in the mirror. She's here with her bodyguards, where Blake is, where Shane is.

Shane. The name sits heavily in my mind. A man rightfully imprisoned for a heinous crime or a pawn in a larger game? Pawns can be useful. Especially when they're desperate.

Blake's prison visit with Shane isn't just a random encounter. In Blake's book, it's a calculated move. In mine, it's a mistake. A misstep that has unraveled everything. That video proves it.

Blake and Shane are working together, trying to expose her, to hurt her. Trying to destroy what we have. She is afraid now, tangled in a web of threats. Blake holds something over her, something dark enough to make her come out of hiding and try to stall me with that message. But she underestimates me.

My fingers trace the edge of the phone, feeling the electricity of anticipation. My queen is summoning me into an ambush. And despite everything—every warning, every rational thought—I will go to her. She knows me. She knows I can't resist. Our connection transcends logic. Our hunt is written in blood and desire long before it's begun.

I play the video again and smile. "I'll answer your calling, my sweet butterfly with a message only you will understand."

If life has taught me anything, it's patience. The wait for the perfect moment. Her video is confirmation of what I've already planned. "Don't worry, my love. Tonight has never been about Blake. His time hasn't come yet. I have a different prey to catch for you."

Tomorrow, she'll wake up to a gift wrapped in crimson and steel, a reminder that I am always watching, always listening, always taking care of what is mine.

CHAPTER 22

Birdie

Jacksonville. My city of firsts.

First crush. First kiss. First secret. First broken bone. First heartache. First nightmare. First sin. First blood.

Jacksonville, my city of pain.

The hotel room walls press in around me like a confession booth, all beige monotony and recycled air. Outside, the St. Johns River cuts through downtown like a scar, reflecting the neon signs of dive bars and late-night diners. I swore I'd never return to this place, but here I am, trapped forty stories above it all, watching my past spread out below like evidence at a crime scene.

The keycard beeps in the hallway. Tristan's footsteps. I know that deliberate, measured gait anywhere. Four weeks—feels like four years, even more—of having him shadow my every move has taught me to read his moods in the rhythm of his walk. Tonight, each step carries the weight of barely controlled fury.

I don't turn from the window when he enters. In the glass, the extra foot and a half he has on me towers over my reflection. His expensive suit can't quite hide the gun holstered on his left side or his massive muscles. He looks exquisite even when his jaw is set in that particular way that means I'm about to get the lecture of my life.

The door clicks shut behind him, followed by the sound of the deadbolt sliding home. "What the fuck, Birdie?"

I trace a finger along the condensation on the window, drawing a small heart before wiping it away. "Go on. Get it all out. I deserve it. I promise I'll just stand there and take it like a good girl."

"You have the audacity for snark after what you've done? I don't think you understand the gravity of—"

"Believe me, I understand."

"Really? Because from where I stand, you're playing Russian roulette with your own life, and I'm the one who has to watch."

How can I make him understand when every threatening letter, every photograph slipped, every shadow that has been following me is a dark love song written in a language only I can understand? How can I show him Butterfly Man isn't a threat to my life, not yet? I turn to face him with a shrug. "I had to."

"No, you didn't. That's the whole point of having me here. So you don't have to do anything. So you can be safe."

I'll never be safe if Blake or Shane use my secrets against me. In my *nightmare*, what I really needed to be safe was clear. Both Blake and Shane must die before they get a chance to utter a single word about me. And Butterfly Man is the only one who can do it.

"Did you get the list of the people who worked at the school, locate Blake or find his app?"

His jaw clenches, and then he scoffs, shaking his head. "I can't believe you right now. I'm working on it. My whole team is working on it. You could have just given me a few hours before you—"

"I have no doubt you'll come through." I stare back at the window. "Until then, Butterfly Man will be in Miami, waiting for me, away from this city, away from Blake."

"So this was your plan all along? Just to get your stalker out of the city until we find Blake?"

Part of it. "Just like you ask me to put my faith in you and trust you, Tristan," my gaze wanders to Jacksonville's skyline as it glitters like broken glass, beautiful and sharp enough to cut, just like everything else in this city that has shaped me, "you're going to have to do the same with me."

CHAPTER 23

Tristan

I regret giving Birdie her phone back. Of course, she would post that video. She's so desperate she'd do anything to reach her stalker, and I'm starting to believe it's not just to solve the Abel situation. She *wants* to meet him, the masked man she fucks in her head, in her dreams.

A chime comes from her pocket. The look on her face when she sees the name on the screen tells me who is calling. She swallows, and her finger, trembling, hovers to make a bigger mess than the one she's already made.

I snatch the phone out of her hand. "Don't even think about it."

"Give me that back. It's Blake," she rasps.

"I know. How your face pales, your eye

twitches and then your nostrils flare every time you see his name gives you away." Switching her phone off and pocketing it, I stare her down. "But you're not answering until we figure out a way to deal with him. You told the whole world he's a drug addict. He must be pissed. What if he blows the whistle and goes through with his threats?"

"He won't, if you just let me talk to him and—"

"And what? Talk some sense into him? Your sober, clear-headed husband, who has zero anger issues that make him destroy everything without thinking? He's a junkie. You're one drag away from his ruining your life forever just because. What were you thinking? Way to mitigate the threat, Birdie."

"I've been married to that asshole for seven years. I know what matters to him the most. I'll just tell him I'm ready to settle. I'll set up a meeting to negotiate, which not only will get us to know where he is but also buy us some time, hopefully enough for you to get that app."

"Smart. It's all part of the plan, isn't it? You know what else is smart? The word us you keep using now, as if we've been in this together all along, as if you didn't go behind my back and did all that on your own without asking me."

"If you'd been listening to me, I wouldn't have—"

"Don't you dare turn this on me. Everything I do is to protect you." I step closer and closer until I back her against the window. "And don't you dare lie to me anymore. We both know your little plan isn't about Abel. This whole thing has never been about your husband."

Her breath stutters on my face. "Of course it is. What else?"

"Yeah?" My beautiful liar. "Then I'll answer him myself and set up a meeting, here in Jacksonville, where the three of us are. Yeah, I managed to track him down and found out where he was staying in the city, by the way."

"You did?"

"Yes, and his dealer, too. I told you junkies are easy to find."

"Okay. Great. But…I need my lawyer present, and she's in Boston."

"We'll easily get her via a video conference." I bend my head and look her straight in the eye. "Then, once I get the app, we'll go back to Vineyard's Haven, right away."

Her lip quivers, and her eyes widen. "But…"

"But what, Birdie?" I challenge. "Tell me."

She lowers her gaze. "I'm tired, Tristan. My head still hurts. Those pills the doctor in Edgartown gave me before we got here make me sleepy."

"I'm not leaving until you say it. Until you tell me what you're really here for, until you tell me how much you want to see him, how much you crave him, your Butterfly Man—"

"—You're crazy—"

"—until you confess that when I thought you were describing a nightmare, all this time, for you, it was a dream you wished would have come true."

She tries to push me aside. "You are crazy and completely out of line. Get out of my way."

I snort. Does she really think she can use strength against me? Swiftly, I collect both of her hands and bind her wrists together in my grip above her head.

"Tristan!"

"You wanna see crazy, Birdie?" My eyes drop to her lips, and then down to her T-shirt. The letters on it have been taunting me since I entered the room. STFUAEYPLAGB. Why the fuck would she wear something like that? Here? Now? "Take it off."

"Take what off?!"

"Your T-shirt. Off. Now."

"You really lost it, didn't you? Let me go, Tristan, or I'll scream."

"Will you say Gatsby this time? I bet you will. With me you use your safeword, but with him…"

"Tristan, you're scaring me. What's wrong with you?"

You. You are what's wrong with me. "Scare you? I scoff. My nose nuzzles along the side of her neck, and, fuck, her scent pulls me into a delirium. A spell that disperses anger and spins it into something wild and hungry. It blurs the world at its edges until there's nothing left, no reason, no sanity, no man. Only her and the soul I'd sell just to make her mine.

"Easy, Mrs. Abel. I'm not telling you to take it off so I can touch you," I whisper in her ear, "so I can fuck you." With a hiss, I drag myself away and drop her shaking hands. "If I want to get you out of your shirt, I won't have to pin you in place and scare or force you to do it, because you'll be desperate to take it off yourself, and then you'll beg me to STFUAEYPLAGB."

Cheeks blazing, mouth gaping, eyes sparkling wide, she fixes her clothes and crosses her arms over her chest. "You know what it means? Of course, you do."

"And it's not hard to guess for the rest of my men either. They knew exactly what you were doing with the rose under the sheets when you thought you were being discreet. And Brandon just picked one of your books at the airport. It won't take him long to know exactly what those letters stand for, if he hasn't already. Is that what you want? The attention of every man in the vicinity?"

"I didn't wear it on purpose. I didn't get to choose which clothes to pack, remember? When you took me to the cabin, you told Brandon to bring some of my things, so I just packed whatever he got, not that I need to explain my wardrobe to you, Mr. Morra. Now, get the fuck out of my room."

"Or what? You'll scream? Fire me?"

"Don't try me."

"No, you don't try me because I've had enough." I storm to the door, but before I leave, I glance at her over my shoulder. "In which prison is Shane serving his sentence?"

"Florida State Prison in Raiford. Why?"

"Just like you ask me to put my faith in you and trust you, Birdie, you're going to have to do the same with me."

CHAPTER 24

Birdie

The light filtering through the curtains isn't warm. It's sterile, fluorescent—hotel light. *Am I sleeping? Have I slept at all?* I'm awake before I open my eyes. My skull throbs. I don't need a bandage anymore, but the headache is still there, a dull, pulsing reminder that I fell. Or imagined I did. Or…

I swing my legs over the edge of the bed and reach for my phone. Not there. Right. Tristan took it. My head throbs more painfully. I pop a pill and get up.

When I crack open the door, Brandon's massive frame blocks it like a wall of muscle. He doesn't flinch. "Good morning."

No. "Where's he?" I don't care about my hoarse voice or messy hair. I need that asshole to give me my phone back.

"Raiford."

"What?" That wakes me up faster than caffeine. "No. No. What's he doing there? Does he think he can just go there and visit Shane, without me, without even telling me?"

"He didn't say, but I don't think he's there to visit an inmate. You need to apply first and get approved before you can, which takes several days, if not weeks. It'd be such a waste of time."

The kid is right. "How do you know so much about visitation rules?"

His eyes flick to the hallway behind him for a split second. Then he shrugs, too fast, uncharacteristically casual. "I was a private detail for a guy whose brother got locked up. Same routine. Applications, background checks, fingerprinting."

That's the first time I catch Brandon in a lie.

I step forward, testing his boundary. He doesn't move, doesn't even shift his weight. But it's too late. I know a made-up story when I hear one. There's no hiding it from me now. I'm not interested in the reason or the truth behind it though, not at the moment. What I'm looking for is leverage and distractions. "Can you go into Tristan's room and bring me my phone please?"

"No."

"No?"

"Mr. Morra said you'd ask for your phone and left strict instructions not to give it to you."

Looks like Mr. Morra's words are more intimidating than my leverage. "Fine. Can I use *your* phone?"

"To call Mr. Morra?"

Smartass. "Sure. I need to remind him of his promise never to let me out of his sight, which he broke, again."

"Technically, he didn't let you out of his sight. He has active surveillance and tracking apps on his phone. Also, I report security stats every fifteen minutes, and I'm keeping my eye on you at all times."

"Your phone, Brandon."

"Sorry. He said no calls or internet until he returns."

No internet as well. That means my laptop is a dead piece of metal, too. No wonder Tristan never bothered to take it. "Did he also tell you to keep me locked in here like a prisoner?"

"He said to keep you safe."

I smile, slow and sharp. "From whom exactly?"

No answer. Just silence and the faint tick of the hallway ventilation. I study his face. He's good at keeping expressionless but not perfect. There's a flicker of doubt in his eyes, a shadow of something deeper. Guilt?

"Take me for a walk, then," I say. "Around the block. Down the hall. To the goddamn ice machine. I don't care."

"Can't. I must stay here and guard not just you but our rooms. If your stalker is close or watching, the second I take you out or leave the floor unattended, he could make a move. This is a hotel. There's staff and—"

I slam the door shut and haul myself back inside. Brandon is wired. Tristan's little bitch. There's no hope with him, but if I don't get out of here soon, I'll scream. I need to call Blake, and I need to know what the fuck Tristan is doing at the prison.

Glancing at the windows, I curse. Tristan has chosen these rooms on the fortieth floor on purpose. No escape whatsoever. What am I supposed to do? Wait for Tristan and beg for permission like I'm some wind-up doll?

I spy the landline by the minibar. It's black with a golden trim, almost quaint—designed for pillow service and overpriced champagne, not desperation. Still, I snatch it up and dial.

Silence, no ringing. Then a soft click echoes. "Front desk," a woman answers, chipper and professional.

"Hi," I say, as calmly as I can. "Could you please connect me to an outside line?"

A pause. "I'm sorry, Mrs. Abel," she says

with the warmth of scripted politeness. "Outgoing calls are currently restricted from your suite."

I stare at the receiver. "What?"

"I've been instructed that all outgoing calls from your suite must be approved by your security liaison. Is there someone on staff I can connect you with instead?"

My voice sharpens. "This is an emergency."

"Then I can transfer you to security," she offers quickly. "What's—"

I slam the receiver back into the cradle before she finishes the sentence. The minibar hums beside me, its small screen reflecting the tick in my jaw. He'd thought of everything. Every goddamn thing.

There's a knock on the door. I know it's Brandon. I thought he'd barge in the second I held that phone. Now, I realize why he didn't bother.

"Ma'am, please open the door," he says.

"I'm not getting lectured by a twenty-one-year-old. Go ahead, report me to Tristan and return to guard the hall like the good do—boy you are. Do whatever he told you to do. I'm going to take a bath."

In the bathroom, every muscle in my neck is tight. My scalp feels like it's shrinking, and the pounding in temples intensifies.

I want to cry, but I don't. Innocent, real

tears always come with a price.

When I was little, I learned crying made everything worse. My mother couldn't stand the sound of it. Not the hiccupping breath or the trembling lip or the stifled sniff. She said it grated on her nerves, that it scratched her ears like nails on glass.

Every time I cried, she'd slap me, and when the pain made me cry harder, she'd hit me some more. And more. And more. She wouldn't rest until I passed out and couldn't make any more "noise."

"Shut up," she'd say, like I was some broken radio she couldn't unplug. "You're too loud, you little bitch. Always whining. Why do you have to ruin every goddamn moment?"

That was how she saw me. I wasn't the innocent baby she carried in her womb. I wasn't the life she was supposed to nurture and protect. I was the bitch who ruined every goddamn moment of her life. As if it was my fault that my father cheated on her when she was pregnant with me. As if I was the one who got her too depressed to drink herself to sleep every night until she became a violent alcoholic.

As if I deserved to have my jaw shattered because I coughed too loud in the kitchen. As if I deserved to be locked outside on Christmas Eve because the snow globe my father gave me made a soft jingling noise that pissed her off.

As if I deserved to be held in the basement, bleeding and starving for days, because…

I keep my jaw clenched, my eyes dry, my voice calm. You learn not to cry when it costs you something every time. You train your body to obey. You shut your tear ducts like vault doors and freeze your face mid-panic.

Because tears are dangerous. Because silence is safer. Because, even today, when I know she's rotting in a grave and can't lay a hand on me anymore, somewhere deep down, I still believe someone might hit me if I make a sound.

I twist the gold handles and wait as hot water gushes out and fills the oversized marble tub. Steam fogs up the mirror. I strip and slide into the water before the tub even finishes filling. I need to disappear.

The thing about silence is that it builds. It expands in your chest until it becomes something else. Something that curls around your ribs like a wire, twisting tighter and tighter.

The heat wraps around me, too hot at first, then just right. It doesn't soothe me, though. It stirs—like slipping into a bad memory.

Shane's voice echoes through the steam like a heartbeat underwater. Not words. Just laughter. Sharp, cold, the kind he used when something ugly was about to happen and I didn't yet know it.

My mother's hands in a sink full of red water.

Her voice as she told me I was just like my father. A whore.

The crack of my bones.

The dripping of my own blood.

I dunk my head under to silence it, to shut it all up, to make it stop. It's quieter beneath the water, like I'm going into a different world or rather seeing the world differently. A change of narrative. A story told from a different side. But the water follows me. Fills my ears, my nose. My arms feel too heavy.

The steam rises, but I'm slipping lower, face tilted toward the ceiling, breath held too long.

My body finally goes still. I see and hear nothing now. No water. No light. No voices. Just—

CHAPTER 25

Birdie

"You can't fall apart, little bird. Not yet."

I know that voice. I know who it belongs to, but I just can't get the name in my brain. I struggle to open my eyes, to make out his face, but they are too heavy to open, stinging. From the bathwater or have I shed those tears at last?

It doesn't matter. He's here. I can hear his voice. Low. Familiar. Dangerous in its softness. I should scream for help. But I'm limp and soaked and too tired to shout. "I hate that name…little bird. Why are you calling me little bird?"

"I think you know why."

"Get away from me," I whisper, or maybe I don't. Maybe I just think it.

He crouches in front of me. My vision blurs to take in the shape of him: black clothes. Leather gloves. A face obscured by a hood and mask.

Butterfly Man.

"You're real," I murmur. "You're not—"

"A hallucination? Maybe. You hurt your head the other day, and now, you're sleeping in the tub, head underwater, perhaps for too long…"

"What?" Disoriented, I try to take in my surroundings, but I can't move. This is another nightmare, where I've been paralyzed.

His gloved fingers push damp strands of hair from my face. I flinch, but I don't move away. If anything, I press my cheek to the leather and purr like a horny cat. This is definitely a nightmare.

"Why are you here?" Not that you can be here. There's no way you'll get past Brandon. Unless you killed him. Dare I ask?

No. You wouldn't. You don't lose control—you ration it. Every touch, every word, every gesture, every silence, precisely calibrated. You don't act on impulse. You drip-feed your madness like venom, just enough to paralyze without killing.

You enjoy the unraveling, don't you? Watching me flinch while you stay so precise, so calm—like a god dissecting his favorite creation. You administer chaos like it's medicine—your twisted cure for a sickness you believe I have but can't see.

"Why are you here now?" I repeat.

"To remind you that you're not safe."

"Because of you."

"No, darling. Not from me. From yourself." His head tilts slightly. "You think you're trapped in this hotel. But you've always been trapped, Reagan. Since long before Blake. Since long before me."

I swallow, water in my throat, in my lungs. "You don't know me," I cough, a small muffled noise, like my voice doesn't belong to me anymore.

"I do," he says gently. "I know the sound you make when you're about to cry but don't. I know the way your breath catches when you lie. And I know what they did to you."

"Don't."

"No matter how hard you try not to remember it, it still lives in you. It will always live in you."

"I said don't."

"You think I'm the monster? I'm not the one who locked you in closets and basements or slammed your head against the edge of a porcelain sink. I didn't punish you for crying. I didn't strip you of your own voice. I didn't rip—"

"You're punishing me now," I snap, though it comes out too soft, a breath laced with ache. "Stalking me. Playing your little game. Controlling me, just like…"

"Like who? Your mother? Your husbands? Your bodyguards?" He leans in. "It's time you woke up, Reagan."

"I don't want to be awake." The confession comes out raw. Ugly. Too honest.

He smiles under the mask. I know it, even if I can't see it.

"I know," he says. "That's why you married him."

"Blake?"

"He's the reason you're in this hotel. Blake and Tristan, they're playing each other to own you. You're the prize, little bird. Not the player."

There are noises disrupting the water. A knock on the door? A door breaking?

It's finally catching up to me. The water I'm under, filling my lungs. I can't breathe.

No. Mom. Please! Another voice joins.

Is it a memory or the here and now? The voice is so distant underwater. Is it mine? Have I made that plea before?

"But I'm different," Butterfly Man says, as if we're alone, as if I'm the only one hearing that, now screaming, voice, and his gloved hand brushes my neck. Just once. Just enough to make every nerve in my body seize. "I'm not playing," he whispers. "I'm saving you."

You think you're saving me. That dragging me into the dark is some kind of mercy. And maybe the worst part is…sometimes, I almost believe you. Because you don't just haunt me—you know me. The parts of me I bury in fiction and pretend aren't mine. You see them. And instead of running, you…stay.

That's what makes you dangerous. Not the way you stalk me. But the way you make me wonder if I want to be found.

"You're not my savior," I slur.

"And yet here I am, dragging you out of the water when the people guarding you didn't even notice you went under."

My heart slams so hard against my ribs, and yet the beat is so faint. "You're lying."

"Maybe. Maybe I'm just the part of your mind that doesn't want to die. The part that refuses to be caged."

"Or maybe you're just what I deserve."

He leans in until his masked lips are inches from my ear. "No, little bird. I'm what you created."

CHAPTER 26

Tristan

Brandon's panicked voice crackles in my earpiece. "Something's wrong—she's in the water, sir, she's not—she's not moving—"

I don't remember crossing the hallway. I don't remember shoving guests aside. I only remember the bathroom door, splintering off its hinges. And the tub. The water is high, Birdie's head tipped back like a fallen doll, hair floating around her face, eyes half open, glazed and vacant.

And Brandon's shaking hands pressed against her bare, lifeless shoulders. "She's not—she's not responding—"

I slam into him, dragging him out of the way. I don't see the marble. Don't feel the water. I just see her.

I'm in the tub without thinking. My suit, my shoes, my gloves drenched. None of it matters. Only she matters.

"*Dios mío, no!* No, no, no, Birdie, *no me hagás esto, por favor!*" I pull her out, one arm braced under her back, the other gripping her legs like I'm holding her together. I check for her breathing and pulse. They're so faint. She's barely there. "*Respirá, mi amor! Respirá, por favor! No te me vayas. Te necesito! Te necesito, carajo! Te juro que no puedo sin vos…*" Her head lolls. Her skin is pale and slippery. Her lips— "*Puta madre, no te mueras!*" I shake her and slap her cheeks lightly. "Breathe, baby, come on."

Brandon hands me a towel from behind. "I'm calling an ambulance."

"You haven't yet?! What the fuck are you still doing here? Get out! Get the fucking hotel doctor. It's faster." I tilt her forward, one sharp movement, forcing the water from her lungs.

She coughs.

A soft, horrible sound. Then another. Her body convulses once, twice, and suddenly she's gasping, wheezing, alive. ALIVE.

Every fiber in me quakes. I crush her to me. My fingers curl too tight into her skin. She shudders in my arms, lashes fluttering.

"Birdie, Birdie, look at me," I whisper, cradling her against my soaked chest. "Don't move. Just breathe. That's it. In and out. Good girl."

Another wheeze escapes, and I can't help the tears rushing out. "My God, what did you do, Reagan? What did you do?"

"I didn't—" she rasps, taking in the surroundings, and realization tightens the corners of her eyes. "I didn't mean to—"

"Don't talk." I wrap the towel around her body and cup the back of her head. "Just breathe, baby. Please."

"No, Tristan. I wasn't trying to hurt myself," she murmurs. "I just… I needed to shut the thoughts down. Anything to keep me from running into *the bad thoughts*. The memories… They would take over and send me into a spiral. I didn't want to feel anything for a little while. That's all. I was just shutting them down." She looks me dead in the eye. "You believe me, don't you?"

God help me. My whole body is screaming, but all I manage is a nod.

"It must be the meds, the ones they gave me for my head. They make me drowsy," she says as I pull her out of the tub. "I'd never hurt myself, Tristan."

I walk out, carrying her, and lay her on the bed. Then I grab more towels and dry her hair, her body. "I'm gonna take care of you, okay? I'm gonna take good care of you. *Estás bien, vas a estar bien. Estoy acá. Estoy acá.*"

"Say you believe me."

I nod. Again. And again. An automatic reflex. Because if I speak, I'll shatter. I tell myself that I do believe her. I need to because the alternative might tear something in me I won't be able to stitch back together.

I almost lost her. I almost walked back into this room and found a corpse in the bath, her skin cold, lips blue and mouth open in drowned silence.

My Birdie. My Reagan. Gone.

The images won't stop. Her body—limp, boneless in the water. Her eyes—dead. My arms—too late. I wasn't there. I left her. I fucking left her.

Maybe she didn't intend to leave this world without me, but accidents happen. What if I didn't get here on time? What if he got in?

What if while I was playing spy at Raiford, pretending to control this game, he was here, watching her, touching her?

He doesn't get to do that. He doesn't get her. She's mine. Not Blake's. Not Shane's. Not Jacob's. Not Death's. And sure as fuck not his.

Mine.

Mine to save. But even when I try, the world finds a way to pull her under. I'm losing her. To her past. To Blake. To Torrance. To him. To her memories. To her own fucking mind.

"Tristan? Why would you not say it? Why would you not say you believed me?"

That's all it takes. Fuck me, the towel drops from my trembling fingers, and I break into tears. My head falls into her lap, and I cry until I can't breathe.

"Hey." Her fingers brush over my hair ever so gently. I don't flinch, not anymore. I lean into her touch. It encourages her other hand to comfort me, too. I become the one she's cradling, the one she's taking care of. "I'm okay. You will be, too. We're okay, Tristan."

I lift my head to her, and she smiles, wiping away my tears. "I've never seen you cry. Not like this. It's not like the first time you thought I was going to die." She chuckles.

"Don't ever joke about this."

"Too soon? I'm sorry. I meant I bashed my head on a rock a few days ago. It was more dangerous than falling asleep in the tub for two minutes. Why—?"

"I wasn't there. This time, I wasn't there for you."

She puts her hands on either side of my face, and I let them stay there. I welcome *her* touch, seek it, fucking need it. Warm. Anchoring. Bringing me back to life. "But you came for me, and I'm alive. You saved me…again. Don't you see? We are survivors, Tristan. It's what we do. We survive. That's why you have to believe I'd never hurt myself."

"I believe you." I push the words out.

"I'm okay now," she whispers. "You found me. You always do."

"If anything happened to you, I'd burn down the world. I'd carve a hole in the sky just to follow you."

"Oh, Tristan, that's so sweet." She stares at me, and it feels like she can see all the way into the back of my skull. "But you keep forgetting one thing."

"What is it?"

"You, too, are a survivor." Her stare is not invasive or uncomfortable but a brutal type of kindness, a shared understanding of the wounds that shaped us. "That's why you're here. That's why you understand."

Not without you. I won't survive it. The world wouldn't either.

CHAPTER 27

Tristan

The monitors flicker in my hotel room. Twelve feeds. I focus only on her angles, only on her. I should look away. Give her privacy. But I can't. Not after what happened. Not after I pulled her half-dead body from the bath. She said she didn't mean it, and I believe her. I do. But belief doesn't make the images go away.

Birdie is asleep now. Her hand twitches against the blanket, restless even in her dreams. She's fighting something in her sleep, like she always is. I watch the curve of her jaw, the way her lips part and then close again. The way she curls into herself. The way her toes twitch. The way she pulls the sheets over her face like they can protect her.

I tell myself it's for security. That I need to monitor her for signs of distress. But if I'm honest, it's worse than that now. I'm studying her. Memorizing her. Obsessing over her. I'm slowly turning into the thing I'm supposed to protect her from.

I've become worse than her stalker.

An email pops up on the screen. It's from the techs at Monarca. The final and complete list of the people who worked and studied at the school in Miami when Birdie was a teacher. Janitors. Staff. Teachers. Students. Volunteers. Substitutes. The list is long, and the notes are longer. Background checks, employment history and red flags. They've color-coded it for her to review. Green for cleared. Yellow for low threat. Red for urgent.

The hum of electronics is the only sound in the room. I lean back in the chair. I should go over the list myself before I give it to her, but I can't keep my eyes off of her. That's not going to help.

I shove my phone in my pocket, grab my laptop and, slowly, open the connecting door to her suite. Watching her through a screen isn't enough. If I'm going to get any work done, I need to be in the same room with her.

The carpet muffles my steps. Her room smells like lavender, her favorite color, her favorite scent. I sit in the armchair by the window, far enough not to disturb her, close enough to hear her breathe.

The laptop balanced on my thighs hums softly. List still open, I go over parts of it, names blurring together. I switch my gaze toward her instead.

She shifts under the sheets again and turns her face toward me, half-covered by a strand of hair. Her brow furrows like she knows I'm here. A chill climbs my spine. Does she sense me?

She lets out a sound—a soft, broken moan—and I'm up before I realize it. Standing over her. One hand gripping the laptop. The other curled into a fist I can't unclench. Her eyelids flutter. She's waking.

What would I say when she sees me here? Who am I going to be today? Her protector or the man who keeps crossing lines, convincing himself it's in her best interest? The man who would kill to have her in his arms, to taste her lips, to fuck every hole she has and carve every sound and face she makes to memory until the day he dies?

Her eyes blink open, hazy with sleep and shadows. For a moment, she looks confused, caught in the quiet limbo between dream and reality. Then her gaze locks onto me.

She doesn't speak. Just stares. Her lips press into a line hardened by suspicion. She draws the sheets tighter around her body, as if only just remembering I shouldn't be there.

I wait for the regular question, *what are you doing here*, my mind ready to deliver a lie.

"You're watching me sleep," she says. Not a question. An indictment.

Shutting the laptop screen, I put it on the chair. I can blurt out so many rehearsed lines. *Security check. Distress monitoring. Protocol.* Instead, I opt for the truth. "Yes."

"Because it's protocol after saving a principal from drowning in a tub?"

"Because the monitors aren't enough. They don't let me hear the sound of your breath. It's the only thing that keeps me sane. Without it, everything inside me starts to unravel." I lift my shoulder in resignation. "It's crossing a line, so many lines, but I don't care anymore."

She sits upright. "Lucky for you somno is my favorite kink."

Heat creeps up my neck and cheeks. Birdie has no filters. "Concha de la lora. What the…"

She chuckles. "You're no stranger to my inappropriate word vomit. You cross the line, and I tease back. It's our thing."

"Our thing…" We have a thing. I like the sound of that.

"The way you blush, though, gets me every time."

"Gets you how?"

A mischievous smirk plays on her mouth, plays with the strings of my heart. "In all the right spots."

I imagine just that. All her right spots, raw and buzzing and wet. "Yeah?"

"You blush to my smutty words like a virgin, and that… Nothing beats a virgin man trope who has been saving himself for the woman he can't have, not even a masked stalker who kills to have her."

All my blood pumps into my cock. There are words, and there are Birdie's words. They're spells written precisely to enchant my soul… and cock. At this moment, the spell is a voice that says, "Take her. Take her now." It's a dark mantra that doesn't stop until all I can think about is taking her right here in that bed right now, fucking all her right spots over and over again until she passes out.

I take a deep, loud breath, gathering every ounce of willpower I have to turn my brain back on. "You think I'm a virgin?"

"You blush like one but no. I don't think a guy like you can stay abstinent for twenty-seven years, not even if he wants to."

"A guy like me?"

"Tall, dark and handsome, tattooed, *pierced*, scarred with a tragic backstory, protective and successful, who rides a bike and smells like trouble. You're a classic— Tristan, are you okay?"

My breath gets louder. I'm moving toward the bed. *Yes, take her. She's not yours, but take her anyway.*

"Why are you looking at me like that?"

Like what? An animal closing in on prey? A man with the hardest boner he's ever had ready to fuck you senseless regardless of the consequences? I'm towering over her now.

Her smile vanishes, and fear jumps into her eyes. She leans back. "Tristan?"

Take her now. No one can stop you. Make her yours. Only yours. I don't fight the voice. I don't tune it out. I'm only moving closer, bending my head and—

My earpiece blares. I blink fast as if snapping out of a trance, swearing. Brandon is talking. "What?" I huff.

"Sir, we have a breach."

I grab my laptop fast and open it. "Where?"

"Vineyard decoy cabin."

"The one where you told the detective Birdie would be." I cock a brow at her, and she blanches.

"Yes," Brandon confirms. "Someone tried to break in. They used a jammer, disabled the perimeter cameras, but we got a shot before they did."

CHAPTER 28

Birdie

My heart leaps. I'm standing next to Tristan now. He works buttons and shifts angles until he captures it. A blurry figure in all black. Head down, hood up, mid-stride outside the decoy cabin on Martha's Vineyard.

My eyes must be the size of dinner plates. I study the frozen image, the man who is supposed to be my stalker, Butterfly Man, who has been terrorizing me awake and asleep. The man who, according to the traps we've set and this image, must be Jacob Torrance.

Everything inside me screams *no*. "That could be anyone. Can you zoom in?"

Tristan glares at me sideways as he enlarges the footage as much as possible. "You won't see the truth if it looks you straight in the eye. We told no one that cabin was where we'd be except the police. Look." He points at the shot we have. "It's from the side, but it's clear that he's wearing a hoodie and a mask. What more proof do you need?"

When I baited the stalker, part of me didn't think I'd actually catch him. And I didn't think it would be Jacob. Not the gentleman who cares. Not the person who looks at me like I'm more than just the wreckage of something that could be cut to pieces for sale.

"It just doesn't make sense." But it does. That's the worst part; it fits too well.

"What exactly doesn't make sense?" he asks incredulously.

I turn back to the screen, the blurry shape frozen mid-step. The curve of the jaw. The angle of the shoulders. My stomach twists. It *could* be Jacob.

But it can't be right. "Jacob isn't Butterfly Man. I can't be that stupid."

Tristan doesn't look away from me. "You're not stupid, Birdie. You set those traps, and now we got him because of you. This was all your plan, and it paid off. We found out who your stalker is. You just didn't want it to be him, but deep down you knew. It's the detective." He points at the image again. "Jacob Torrance is your stalker."

I shake my head hard. "No. No, this is too easy. Why would he let himself get caught on camera? The man who was in my bedroom that night was so smart. He would never…"

"He had no access to you. It made him crazy, and he made a mistake. That's what *you* were counting on, remember? Think about it, Birdie. He transfers from God knows where around the same time you started getting those notes. He shows up to your fucking date with flowers your favorite colors, the real ones, not what you feed the fans, picks your favorite restaurant, owns dog-eared copies of your books with annotations and NSFW drawings of every spicy scene, memorizes their fucking page numbers, allegedly, in the span of a few days, who does that?"

An obsessive maniac.

"And if that's not enough, think back to the time of Saldana's murder investigation," he continues, eagerly, too eagerly. "You suspected someone in the police was involved, someone who could manipulate evidence, right?"

I nod once.

"And then the radio incident, the only logical way the stalker could have tracked our movements without a trace to know exactly when to strike."

"But…but…"

"No buts. We got him, Birdie."

I stare at the screen again, this time longer, like if I just keep looking, it will change. Like the pixels will rearrange themselves and reveal evidence that points to a different person, not the one who has made me laugh with dumb puns, and for the briefest moments, has made me look forward to the future.

"If Jacob was Butterfly Man, he would be on his way to Miami." I jab the screen with my index finger. "What is he still doing there?"

"How is this not obvious to you?" Tristan's jaw is clenched so hard it tics. His fists twitch at his sides. His whole body vibrates like a machine powered by rage. "He's making sure you're not bluffing, Birdie. He wants to know if you really left the island to wait for him for your *date* in Miami."

I stop in my tracks. "Miami, the school… Did you get that list?"

"Yes."

My heartbeat thunders in my ears. "Is Jacob's name on it?"

"I haven't had a chance to go through all the names yet, but—"

"Give it to me."

"Sure, but what difference does it make now? We already got him."

"No. Not until his relationship to the school is established and validated."

"Are you serious? After all this glaring evidence, you need to see his name on a list to believe?”

"You and I figured out Butterfly Man was someone who knew me from the school. How else would he have found out about Aaron and the people involved in the cover-up and murdered all of them? If Jacob's name isn't on that list,” my eyes flicker at the masked man in the black hoodie, “then he is not that person. He is not Butterfly Man.”

CHAPTER 29

Birdie

"What were you doing in Raiford?" My question halts Tristan's storming out.

He pauses, his back to me. "Did you know Florida had rolled out a statewide electronic communication system across prisons?"

"I'm sorry what?"

"Inmates are allowed tablets." He spins to face me. "They can read books, listen to music, watch videos, finish their education and… send and receive messages."

I swallow involuntarily. I don't know where exactly this is going, but my heart jumps at every possibility. Shane's direct and unrestricted connection to the outer world, to journalists, to podcasts, to groupies, to Blake…

Question after question bullets through

my head. I don't let them out. I only stare at Tristan. He's examining me, testing me with his eyes. I hold still and try to dig my way past the scrutiny, to decipher whatever is hiding behind.

"I stumbled on some interesting information at the prison," he says.

Now, it's my heart that bullets. *What did you find out, Tristan?* "Care to share?"

"For starters, Shane doesn't have a tablet."

My eyebrows shoot up. "H-he doesn't?"

"No. You need money to buy one and use the apps. From what I've gathered, he doesn't have much because his parents are unavailable and his MC shunned him after the conviction."

That's a lot of info gathered in one visit. Those prison guards have big mouths.

"You know what else I found?"

And it's not over. I hold my breath.

"Shane Fletcher's file is sealed."

That is no news to me. The case was automatically sealed because of the victims involved, and I paid a lot of money to keep it that way over the years. "It doesn't matter. I already told you everything that's in there. Was that why you went to the prison, to investigate my ex-husband's case? Such a waste of time."

Tristan steps closer. His voice drops, low and lethal. "You think I went there to play detective? I went there to assess the threat…in case I'd have to neutralize it."

In other words, kill Shane. Just like he said he'd kill Blake. Just like I want Butterfly Man to do for me. I gulp. "Tristan…you can't. I'd never—"

"I'm your bodyguard. It's *my* job." He's not blinking. Not breathing. His eyes are locked on mine. "If Shane so much as breathes in your direction, I need to know how to cut off the air."

I flinch. Every syllable is soaked in intent. Not rage. Not jealousy. Something worse, twisted and terrifying and yet loyal, dedicated.

Obsessed.

"Your job is to protect me, but not—"

He marches out of my room and into his. I run after him. "You can't ignore me. This is crucial."

Abruptly, he returns, blocking my way the second I cross the threshold. "Take this."

I glance at his hands. He's holding a tablet. "What is this?"

"When I knew Shane didn't have a tablet, I made a generous donation to him and inmates like him that allowed them all to get tablets."

"What?! You let Shane have the means to contact anyone outside?!"

He glares at me like I'm a fool wasting his energy. "I let him have a gadget I can track. The one I'm holding is a clone."

"What the hell are you talking about?"

"Every message he sends, every app he opens, every name he searches—it's mirrored here."

My fingers tighten around the device. "You bugged him."

A smug smirk curls up the corner of his lips. "If Shane decides to open his mouth, he won't just be talking to the outside. He'll be talking to us."

"Any message we don't want getting out…"

"I'll intercept and make sure it never reaches the intended audience."

I sigh in relief and smile at him. "You're a genius, Mr. Morra."

"Not a waste of time after all, is it, Mrs. Abel?"

CHAPTER 30

Butterfly Man

Manipulation. Intimidation. Deceit. Bribery. Blackmail. Shank. My list goes on and on. Top ways to take care of scumbags like Shane Fletcher and Blake Abel.

Like Tristan Morra.

As of yesterday, Shane Fletcher, DC number: F39284, didn't have a registered tablet on JPay. Today, he does. The same day Tristan Morra visits Florida State Prison. Coincidence? My ass.

I'm guessing the man with the motorcycle didn't get Reagan's ex-husband a tablet out of the goodness of his heart.

What is his plan? Manipulation. Morra makes Shane believe he's a philanthropist to gain his trust. Intimidation. Morra pretends to be someone he's not, someone with leverage that intimidates Shane to leave Reagan alone. Deceit. Morra pretends to be a liaison of Blake, his lawyer maybe, to get Shane to spill whatever the fuck he's planning with Blake. Bribery. Morra offers Shane a better deal than Blake's. Blackmail. Morra bugs the tablet, tracks Shane, and gathers any information he can use to blackmail Shane into silence.

All of these ideas came to me first. *They say great minds think alike, but you're not great. Obviously, you're a copycat. You're trying to be me to get her attention since you've failed to get it any other way.*

Whether you like it or not, Reagan likes me more than she'll ever like you. She wants me more than she'll ever want you.

She will love me, never you.

"Because unlike you, I don't waste time with fruitless plans. I'd have given you credit if, let's say," I retrieve Blake's mirrored device on my computer, "you'd figured out a way to open that fucking dead man's switch app without triggering it."

It was easy to get my hands on his phone. The tricky part was to clone it without Blake noticing. The text from the cheater was only a door, but I needed to enter through without making any noise. Lucky for me, Blake and I had someone in common, someone we could charm into doing anything for us, like dropping her pants and betraying her best friend's trust, like slipping Blake drugs to borrow, for a few minutes, his other phone where he saved the authenticator app that opened the dead man's switch app…

Oh, Gia. I understand why she helped me. After Reagan explained what kind of monster Blake was, Gia wanted revenge. She didn't need any convincing to steal his phone for me. What I couldn't understand was how she'd thought for a second I'd have spared her life.

I mean, yeah, she was trying to redeem herself, but doing one thing in my pretty little butterfly's favor isn't enough. *You should have thought about that when you spread your legs for that motherfucker, Gia. You should have known that your soul was the only price I'd take for redemption.* I lean back in my chair behind my desk, sighing, "What a shame."

You know what else is a shame? Blake Abel being a smart piece of shit. Not smart enough to stay loyal to the most beautiful, intelligent, creative and kind woman in the world or treasure and protect her instead of hurting her, or say no to drugs. But smart to turn this fucking app into a fort even I can't infiltrate.

With every step I take to get closer to retrieving the message he's hidden in there, I find another obstacle. The authenticator was enough to open the first layer of security, but to get to the message or the interception settings, he's made sure no one, but him in person, can.

I've thought about sending the cloned phone to Reagan to show her I'm on track, but that will give the man with the motorcycle access to it. I doubt he can do any better with it, if not worse. He cloned Shane's tablet for fuck's sake.

"Can't you see? Manipulation. Intimidation. Deceit. Bribery. Blackmail. They don't work here. While Blake clings to a trump card that lets him slither through another day, Shane doesn't. Because for vermin like Shane, I opt for shank."

CHAPTER 31

Tristan

Birdie is completely absorbed in the screen. Her dark hair falls like a curtain around her face as she hunches over her laptop. I've secured it first and made sure she can't use the internet. I can't afford another one of her impulsive solo *plans*.

The blue light illuminates her features, casting shadows that pronounce her cheekbones more. Her lips are slightly parted in concentration. She's beautiful when she's thinking. Hell, she's always beautiful, but there's something about the way her mind works—the intensity, the determination—that mesmerizes me.

I sit across from her with my own laptop. She's scrolling through the list my team curated. Eighty-seven names. Faculty, staff, third parties and janitors who have worked at or for the school during her time. Even their male family members are included. Anyone with a dick is on that list.

Her fingers work methodically, making notes in the margins of a notebook beside her. Her pen taps against her bottom lip every few seconds, rubbing there, instead of her usual index fingers.

She has no idea she's wasting her time.

The stalker isn't some creepy professor or administrator from the school. The man who has been watching her, following her, leaving those twisted little gifts and notes, killing for her, brings her coffee and takes her out to dinner. The man in her mind she's secretly building a future with and hopes she can trust to keep her safe.

Detective Jacob Torrance.

How could she see that footage of the man in the hoodie and deny the truth? She even made me verify Morrison's whereabouts at the time of the breach, and I complied. She spoke to Marcus directly, and he sent her the security footage of every single detail on Martha's Vineyard. None of them left the house. Marcus confirmed, beyond doubt, that he was doing rounds at the time of the breach and personally accounted for each detail.

Still, she sifts through names like she's chasing ghosts. Her brows hook deeper with each scroll, each note she scribbles. She's trying to solve a puzzle that's already been solved, refusing to look at the piece that fits too perfectly.

I'd laugh if I didn't want to put my fist through a wall.

I get up and lean against the kitchenette counter, arms crossed, pretending to make coffee. What I'm really doing is maintaining a casual distance while I study every micro-expression that crosses her face. The way her eyebrows furrow when she seems to recognize a name. The slight shake of her head when she dismisses someone as unlikely. The unconscious way she worries her lower lip with her teeth when she's deep in thought.

She's so focused, so trusting in the process. If only she knew how close the truth really is.

I've suspected Torrance for weeks. The timing of his arrival in her life, his transfer to Oak Bluff right when the stalking escalated. The way he always seems to show up just after an incident, playing the concerned protector. The convenient way evidence keeps appearing and disappearing. The access he has to police databases and equipment.

But suspecting and proving are two different things. I thought capturing him on screen would be enough, but Birdie won't let herself believe Torrance, the man she's allowed herself to trust, to dream with again, is her stalker because then the world she's built around him collapses, and she's not ready for that kind of ruin, not after every other man in her life has let her down.

She glances up suddenly, catching me staring. "Find something interesting on the wall behind me?"

Heat creeps up my neck. "Just thinking."

"About what?"

I need Torrance gone. Whether he is the stalker or not. Not just because he's a threat to her safety, though that would be reason enough. I need him gone because every day she stays with him, every day she looks at him with those trusting eyes and accepts his protection, is another day she's not seeing me.

She sets down her pen and stretches, her sweater riding up slightly to reveal a strip of pale skin above her jeans.

I force myself to look away. "Any names stand out?"

"A few." She turns the laptop screen toward me. "Mr. Henley, head of my department, was eerily supportive during Aaron's fiasco. Sam Crane, a fellow teacher, seemed a little too interested in my personal life during office hours. And there was this IT guy, Sumesh Kapur, who always made weird comments when I needed help with computer issues."

I scan the names she's highlighted, knowing none of them are right. However, I nod instead of walking over to her, shaking her and telling her it's fucking Torrance. She'd defend him. Make excuses. Maybe even stop trusting me entirely. I need to be smarter than that. I need to let her discover the truth herself, or at least think she has. "I'll cross-reference their whereabouts this year—airports, ferries, credit card activity—and see if any of them has set foot in Massachusetts."

She scoffs.

"What?" I ask.

"You've done that already, haven't you?"

Insulting her intelligence with a pathetic lie won't do me any good. "We…have. Yes. My team vetted all of them. That's why it took a little longer to get the full list." I point at the screen. "See, the names are color-coded based on the information we found. The green ones are clear, yellow ones are inconclusive and the red ones are the names that couldn't be traced."

She turns the laptop back to her side. "Two greens and one yellow."

"Which one is yellow? I'll double che—"

"No, you won't. You think this list is a waste of time."

"Nonetheless, I'll look into any name you suspect myself, Birdie. You have my word."

Our eyes meet across the space between us, and for a moment, something electric passes between us. Understanding, maybe. Or just the weight of secrets—hers she doesn't know she's keeping, mine I can't afford to tell.

She leans forward. "Where are the students?"

"Hmm?"

"The list of students that were enrolled in the school when I taught there. They're not included in the list you gave me."

Clearing my throat, I retreat to the coffee maker. "That was a harder list to make."

"The hard lists are usually the important ones."

Nothing gets past Birdie Abel. "You're absolutely right."

"Please tell me you have that list. I'd flip if I had to wait again—"

"I have it, Birdie. I just didn't want to overwhelm you with all the names. It's a much bigger list than the one you have. How about you finish going through the names you have and then I'll send the rest?"

She looks back at the screen. "Just send it over, Tristan."

I pull my phone out of my pocket with a sigh and send her the file. "As you wish. The names are segregated by class. The ones you taught and the ones you didn't. Their family members are included, too. Same color code applies. Knock yourself out."

She's writing down notes again, back to her methodical search. I pour two cups of coffee and set one beside her laptop. She doesn't look up, but when she reaches for it, our fingers brush.

It's barely a touch—skin against skin for less than a second—but it detonates something in me, like my body has been waiting for this exact contact. The effect is immediate and devastating. My pulse kicks up. Heat spreads from the point of contact like wildfire through my veins. That single brush of her fingers is enough to unravel me, and yet I crave it. I ache for it.

I want to grab her hand, hold it, feel the warmth of her palm against mine. I want to thread my fingers through hers and never let go.

Instead, I step back like I've been burned.

Soon, I promise myself. Soon, I'll have more than a fleeting touch and scorched tension. Soon, she'll know the truth about everything, who she can and can't trust.

Soon, she will be mine. Once Torrance is out of the picture, once she realizes what he really is, she will be mine.

Going back to my own computer, my mind races through the possibilities. I need evidence against Torrance, something solid enough to convince her. Something that can't be explained away by coincidence or circumstance or by a skilled liar with a badge.

I need something irrefutable. Something that will shatter her faith in him completely.

His phone records, maybe. Financial information. Travel logs that match up with the stalking incidents. Where the fuck has he transferred from? Why can't I find those records anywhere?

I read somewhere that cops sometimes work under different aliases for security reasons, like if they work on sensitive cases that put targets on their backs. What if Torrance transferred after one of those cases and Jacob Torrance isn't his real name? That must be why the precinct won't reveal his information, and his name doesn't pop up in any database.

Puta madre, why haven't I thought of that?

A text from Marcus buzzes with an update on the Torrance situation. I've had him digging deeper into Detective Douchebag's background, looking for anything that might serve as proof.

The text says one thing. Torrance isn't at the precinct. He's been on emergency leave since yesterday.

Could you be any more sus, pelotudo?

In front of me, Birdie makes another note.

She'll exhaust every lead there first before seeing what's right in front of her. She's trying so hard to solve this puzzle, to find safety in logic and lists and methodical investigation. She doesn't understand that some monsters can't be caught with spreadsheets and color-coded databases.

Some monsters wear badges and bring you coffee and wish you goodnight.

While she's chasing shadows in academic databases, I'll be gathering the real evidence she needs. The kind that will bring her back to me, where she belongs.

CHAPTER 32

Birdie

"Jesus." I scroll through the student names. "There are so many."

"Three hundred and forty-seven," Tristan tells me without looking up from his screen. "That's just the males. We included female family members of students, too, in case the stalker is using a female relative as a cover."

"This is going to take forever," I sigh. "What's that?"

Did he not hear me or is he mocking me? He thinks I'm chasing ghosts, drowning in shadows and wasting our time. He's certain Butterfly Man is Jacob. My chest tightens because Tristan may not be wrong. Some part of me knows Jacob doesn't add up. Too many coincidences, too much convenient timing.

The footage of the masked man I can't explain.

At the same time, Tristan is too eager to get Jacob out of the picture. He wants Jacob gone, and it has nothing to do with the stalker and everything to do with the fact that he can't stand that I like the detective. Would my bodyguard risk my safety because of jealousy?

I open my work in progress and write that down.

"What did you just type?" Tristan asks, and I catch the quick flick of his eyes toward me.

"Notes."

"You write your notes on suspects in the notepad next to you, but you just typed something."

I raise a brow at him. "Are you really watching me that closely?"

His mouth tips into that infuriating smirk, but I don't let him answer before I add, "Careful, Tristan. Pay that much attention to my every move and I might mistake you for my stalker."

With a scoff, he leans back, cool and composed, like my jab didn't land at all.

I'm back on the list, scrolling further. Lines of names blur together until I hit a familiar class. Tristan used to be one of them. A student. My student.

My pen hovers over my lips. "What was your last name back then? When you were in my class?"

That gets his full attention. For a heartbeat, something flickers across his face—hesitation, bewilderment and almost blame—but then his expression slides back into neutral, even playful. "You wanna find me in there to cross me out or add me to your list of suspects?"

"Who knows?"

He lets out a short laugh, but there's tension in it. "That's reassuring."

"I'm just curious," I admit.

"You really don't remember me at all, do you?"

"Three hundred and forty-seven names, Tristan, and that was eight years ago," I say, as if that is enough for a good defense.

He puts his laptop aside and leaves his seat. "Well, I was hoping you'd find out on your own. Honestly, it was my intention to tease you about it."

"But you remembered you were a gentleman and decided to put me out of my misery by simply telling me?" I bat my eyes as cutely and charmingly as possible.

Crossing his arms over his chest, he slouches against my desk and bends forward, close enough for me to fill my nose with his cologne and appreciate the gold flecks in the green of his eyes. "Is that what you want? For me to be a gentleman?"

Oh, he's going there. Tristan Morra is starting the game he never seems to win. The muscle in his cheek ticks as he leans closer, clearly determined to play it cool.

I rub the pen playfully against my lips and then lick the edge of my bottom lip, deliberately slow, just to see the way his gaze drops there before darting back up like he didn't mean it. He did. He always does. It's almost unfair, but then again, he's the one who keeps stepping into the ring. "God, no," I whisper, "gentlemen are boring."

"Yeah?" The corner of his mouth twitches. His cologne curls around me, warm and spicy, and I can feel him recalculating, looking for a move that won't leave him defeated again.

Brandon's voice cuts into the room. "Sir, your bike just got here."

Tristan's shoulders tense as he straightens, the moment dissolving like it's never happened. He clears his throat and looks toward Brandon. "Thanks. Tell them I'm coming down."

"Your bike?" I ask.

"It's a beast. Pretty sure it costs more than my yearly salary," Brandon says.

I get off my chair. "Have you just bought a new bike, Tristan?"

He shrugs. "Mine broke down in Boston and I had the garage ship it back to the island, but then we came here so…"

What the fuck? "But we're just stopping by. Are you planning on moving to Florida soon?"

"No, of course not. I'll have the new bike delivered back to the island as soon as we're done."

"From Jacksonville to Vineyard Haven?" *Or wherever we'll be after we get out of this state.* "Is that even possible?"

He shrugs again, like having a motorcycle shipped across states is no big deal. "Anything is possible for the right amount of money, not that it's expensive to ship bikes. It's like a grand or so, with insurance."

I stare at him. "You throw a grand or so to ship a bike you don't even need? Are you in the mafia or something?"

"What? No." He laughs.

"Just how rich are you?"

"Rich enough."

"That's not an answer."

He dismisses Brandon and turns back to me, his smirk returning. "What do you want to know? Net worth? Assets? Stock portfolio?"

"I want to know what kind of rich you are." Blake comes to mind, and the way money has poisoned everything between us.

"My money is legit, Birdie. The military pays well and so does security work. When you risk your life every minute on the job, it'd better make you loaded."

"Good to know, but that's not really what I meant."

"Okay. Well, then I'm the kind of rich that can take care of someone as wealthy as you without ever needing to touch a dime of hers. The kind that, if you were mine, you wouldn't have to sell your soul to publishers who control you, kill yourself for meeting deadlines or attend another event you were forced into ever again. The kind that, *if you were mine*, you'd be free to be whoever you wanted, do whatever you wanted without a single worry."

His eyes beg me not only to understand what he's offering but to take it. The picture of life he's painting for us, one I've never dared to dream of.

He approaches me, his face softening, yet dead serious. "The kind that, *if you were mine*, it would be because I loved and wanted you, not because of what you could give me."

My breath catches in my throat. The way he says it—if you were mine—like it's not a possibility but an inevitability. If you were mine. Three times in a row, each carries more weight than the one before, a promise he's made himself and would do anything to keep, no matter the danger or cost.

"You don't know what you're saying," I whisper, even though part of me—a lonely, desperate part—wants to believe every word.

"I know exactly what I'm saying." His voice is low, rough. "I've known for a long time."

"Tristan…" I start, but my voice comes out breathless.

He glances toward the laptop with its endless list of names, then back at me. "You've been cooped up in here for so long, staring at screens…" He gestures toward the door. "You wanna go for a ride? Get some air? Try the new bike with me?"

"I…" *I can't believe you let me off the hook so easily.* I look at the monitor, at all those names I still need to go through. God, I'm so tired of being trapped in safe houses and hotels, tired of staring at screens and feeling like I'm drowning in suspects and suspicions. Then I look at Tristan, at the way he's watching me like my answer matters more than it should.

"What do you say? Trust me for an hour before you come back and find out, of all three hundred and forty-seven names, mine is your stalker?"

I laugh under my breath. "How can I trust this is not your kidnapping me?"

"I'd be the dumbest kidnapper ever if I chose this city to take you. This is your hometown. You know it better than I do. You'll know where to escape."

"Fair point."

"So? Show me around?"

"Eh, why not?" I say, as if I'm doing him a favor. As if I'm not desperate for that one hour of being free. Freedom, a big part of Tristan's promise, of the life he's picturing for us. Am I too naive to allow myself to want that? With someone like him?

A smile slithers its way to my face even though I know the answer is yes. I guess I'm too tired of fighting whatever this thing is between Tristan and me.

CHAPTER 33

Tristan

Birdie's face lights up when she spots the new Ducati in the parking lot. "Is that a Superleggera V4?"

"Yes, ma'am."

She sprints toward it like a child who has seen a Christmas present. I don't bother reprimanding her for breaking protocol for the umpteenth time. Let her be happy for once.

Her fingers run along the sleek purple metal, and her grin couldn't be any wider. Pure joy. When was the last time I saw that on Birdie? She has no idea how long I've been waiting for this——to give her something that isn't just protection, something other than blood and surveillance and suspect lists. To give her freedom, even if only for an hour.

"She's beautiful," she breathes.

"Just beautiful?" I tease. "C'mon, use your words. If that was a scene in one of your books, how would you write it?"

She lowers her sunglasses and cocks a brow at me. "Oh. You sure you can handle it this time?"

I rest my back against the bike and smile at her. "Maybe if you go easy on me."

"Can't make any promises." She circles around the beast and grabs the spare helmet. "It crouched like a predator in repose—sleek, angular, and unapologetically rare. The body was cloaked in a matte violet-black, a color that shifted with the light: regal in shadow, electric under streetlamps. Every curve of carbon fiber whispered of speed and precision, sculpted not just for aerodynamics but for desire."

"Wow."

She lifts a finger in an 'I'm not done. Don't you dare interrupt me' warning. She's still circling the bike, taking in every detail she's just described, memorizing it, like I'm memorizing her. The way the afternoon light catches in her hair, the effortless grace in her movements, the passion in her voice when she talks about something that moves her.

Then her eyes pin me in place. "Gold glinted from the suspension forks and brake calipers, not garish but deliberate—like armor on a warrior. Even idle, it radiated majesty, as if the road itself were beneath its notice." She inches closer, and my breath catches when her scent fills my nostrils. "Bold but refined, like a woman who commands attention without raising her voice. It wasn't just a motorcycle. It was a statement—of wealth, of taste, of danger wrapped in elegance."

Only Birdie Abel can make poetry out of steel and chrome that somehow gives a man a hard-on. "In other words, it's you."

"Should I take that as a compliment?"

My fingers move of their own accord and caress her cheek. Her skin is impossibly soft beneath my calloused fingertips. "Always," I whisper, a confession weighted with everything else I can't say.

Flustered, she pushes her shades up her nose and looks around. We're in public, and Abel is in the city. Even though I've secured the hotel parking lot before I let Birdie out of the room, there's always a chance he's following from a distance, taking pictures, twisting things around. I should have been more careful.

Pushing off the bike, I clear my throat. "Do you like her?"

She studies the Ducati one more time. "Well, it's in my favorite colors, and it's definitely different from your other bike."

"Different how?"

A small smile plays at her lips, the kind that

tells me she's about to say something that will completely demolish my ego. "Let's say this one is more sophisticated than your BMW."

"Do *you* like it, Birdie?"

"*I* love it, Tristan. But if I'm being brutally honest, it doesn't exactly scream Tristan Morra."

Perfect. That's exactly what I was hoping she'd say. "Then it's yours."

"What?" she laughs dismissively.

"I'm not a bike fanatic or an adrenaline junkie. I can survive a few weeks without riding. I got her for you."

Her laughter continues, but she chops it off when she seems to realize I'm serious. She blinks rapidly, her hands open in the air, demanding an explanation.

"Ever since you told me about your car, how Abel chose it for you when you'd have preferred a bike, I wanted to take you on a ride with me, just for fun. But everything was happening so fast. I was hoping to do so when the garage sent my bike back, but we had to leave and come here. Then…"

I trail off to that moment in the dealership. The way the Ducati calls to me, not because I want it, but because I could so clearly picture her on it. Free. Happy. Fearless. Mighty. Herself.

"Then what?" she prompts, her voice softer.

"On my way back from Raiford I saw it and thought of you. I thought maybe when this was all over, I could take you to the dealership and if you liked it…"

"What? You'd buy it for me as a surprise gift?"

"Pretty much, yeah. You've been cooped inside houses and hotel rooms for weeks. Brandon told me you asked him to get you out of the room for a while. I know how you must feel."

"Then take me in your car to get some coffee or just for a spin around the block." Stunned, she gazes at the Ducati. "But this… A six-figure *gift*… It's too much."

Too much. As if I wouldn't mortgage my soul to see that look of pure joy cross her face again. "Nothing is too much for you."

"Tristan, it's extravagant, insane."

"There's nothing too extravagant or insane when it comes to you." The words come out more intense than I intended. I'm scaring her. I can see it. The tension in her arms. The parting of her lips. The way she takes an imperceptible step back. But it's true. I'd give her anything, everything, if she'd let me.

"Stop. What are you doing? This is not how you make you love you."

The accusation lands like a rusty bullet

in the bone. As if I'm no different from every other man who's tried to manipulate her. "You think I don't know that? I'm not buying your love, Birdie. I just saw her, the colors, the design, and thought she was made for you. I found something beautiful and wanted to give it to someone who deserves beauty in her life. *You* deserve to have someone give you something nice with no strings attached for once."

"There's no such thing, Tristan."

My chest clenches at the resignation in her voice. She rejects the idea despite the evidence. This is what years of abuse and control do to you. You reject kindness. You suspect good. You only accept malice and evil because they're the only things that make sense. "That's what the likes of Abel and Shane made you believe, but that's not true. Not with me. All I ask, all you gotta do, is let me be that someone."

"Tristan," she murmurs. Her chin wobbles, and her cheeks and nose redden. Is she crying? She looks away, before I can find the answer, and presses the back of her finger to the tip of her nose. "The idea of someone caring for me without an agenda is so foreign it scares her."

"I know." No one knows that better than me.

A nervous chuckle escapes her. "You said you were going to wait until this was over before taking me to buy it. Why didn't you?"

The real reasons flash in my head, but the truth is more vulnerable than I want to admit. "Because…life is too short."

"In other words, because you pulled me out of a tub half-dead." Her voice is flat, matter-of-fact, with a touch of humor for fuck's sake. "So this is what, a *congratulations you survived a maybe suicide please don't do it again* gift?"

"Don't do that. It's not funny. It'll never be funny."

"I know. But you know me. I say weird, unfiltered shit when I…feel. I hadn't been allowed to express emotions without heavy repercussions for a long time. It's a defense mechanism."

The raw explanation stabs deeper than the dark joke. She was robbed of her simplest of rights, the right to feel. Years of walking on eggshells, of having every emotion policed and punished, have taught her to hide behind sarcasm when things get too real. I wish I could tell her she never had to hide her feelings from me, that she was entitled to show every emotion without fear of consequences. I wish my words could be enough for her to believe it. But we both know words here mean nothing, only patience, actions of unconditional love and time would.

"If it's anything, it's an *I'm sorry* gift," I mutter, my voice hushed and thick, "not that anything could make up for what you had to go through."

"Sorry for what?"

"For wasting so much time." It tears out of me. Every regret, every what-if, every night I've lain awake thinking about how different things might have been. "For not being strong enough or old enough back when I first met you. If I'd been, none of those terrible things would have happened to you."

"Oh, Tristan." She stares at me with tenderness I don't deserve. "You were a nineteen-year-old student of mine living in a hell of your own. There's nothing you could have done."

"There's plenty I could have done." I could have been braver. I could have fought harder. I could have not ignored the signs or pretended everything was going to be okay. I could have…

"No. Do you not remember what you taught me on your first day as my bodyguard? You can't possibly blame yourself for other people's choices. I chose to marry Blake. Blake chose to treat his wife as a slave, cheat on her, beat her almost to death and blackmail her to spend her money on his drug addiction. But you," she reaches out to touch my arm so carefully, so gently, and it steals my breath away, "you chose to come back for me. You chose to be here now, doing everything you could to protect and save me. That's all that matters."

The sincerity in her touch, the way she's trying to offer me the same comfort I've been trying to give her, swirls inside me with an unexpected force. She sees my being here, after leaving her to rot for eight years, as enough.

But it doesn't feel like enough. It will never feel like enough to make up for the years she spent suffering while I was working my way out of my father's grip, building myself, telling myself I was getting strong enough to deserve her.

"Can we take this boss lady for a spin now?" She puts on the helmet, and it brings the first time she rode with me to memory, when I had to put it on her and buckle it myself. "Or will I have to wait for road security protocol measures first?"

"Now that you mention it, we need a vehicle tailing us with at least two details."

She blanches. "What? What about Brandon? He can be enough, right?"

"Brandon has to stay on floor duty to secure the rooms. Maybe if you can go over the lists and clear a couple of details from the team, make sure they have no ties to anyone from the school, then I'll fly them over here and we can go for a ride."

"Oh my God. Then why did you say that we could go for a ride now if I—"

I chuckle. "Relax. I'm just messing with you.

When it comes to bikes, I'm all you need."

She stares at me for a beat. Then her eyes narrow dangerously. "Oh, you…concha de… la…lora."

A wholehearted laugh bursts out of me as she stumbles through Argentinian cussing. "You're adorable when you're trying to be mad at me."

"I'm not trying," she hops on the bike and settles on the back, making room for me at the front, "I am mad at you."

"Remember our first ride, when you fought me every step of the way, and I had to practically carry you and put you onto the bike myself because you'd rather have faced your stalker than trusted me enough to get on?"

"Doesn't ring a bell."

I snort. "Well, I remember it like it was yesterday." How rigid her body was, how she felt when I lifted her anyway, how furious she was right up until the moment we hit speed and the world cracked open around us. That sound she made—half shriek, half laugh—is burned into me like my own first breath. "*That* was mad at me, but now…"

Now, when I climb on, her arms wrap around my waist voluntarily, and fuck if that doesn't mean everything.

"Remember how to hold on?" I ask.

Her chest presses into my back. Even

through my jacket, her warmth seeps through me. The heat of her thighs cages me in. "What do you think?"

I bite down a groan. "Perfect."

The engine thunders, and I roll us out onto the street. Jacksonville rushes past us in blurs of palm trees and strip malls. The air smells of salt and asphalt. Humid air lashes our faces, the Florida heat shimmering everything like a mirage. The city hums like it knows we're escaping.

I weave through streets like I've lived here all my life, but she's the one who guides me without speaking. The way her grip shifts when I turn one street over another—it's her telling me where to go. She leans into the turns with me, fluid, trusting, her laughter muffled but real against my shoulder. That sound—her laughter—undoes me more than anything. She hasn't laughed like that since this nightmare began.

I could ride like this forever. Just her and the open road and the choice to go wherever the hell she wants. Her arms holding me like she will never let go, her body molded to mine, my heart not my own anymore.

For a few miles, I believe in miracles.

But gas doesn't. The needle on the gauge glares red at me. I curse under my breath. To think when you pay one hundred thousand dollars plus tax, they'd fill up the tank. I pull over at the next light and cut the engine.

"What's wrong?" she asks.

"Need gas. Sorry, should have checked before we rode on." I twist around to face her, pulling out my phone to open the GPS. "Any gas stations nearby?"

Her eyes dart around. Her shoulders hunch up under her jacket. Prey that has wandered too close to danger. "Not here."

My instincts flare. I scan the area. A small church on the left. A grocery store on the corner. A few kids, squealing, awestruck by the bike. It's just an old neighborhood. Nothing stands out as alarming. "Okay." Even though the GPS shows a gas station four blocks from here. "How far?"

"Anywhere but here." Her voice cracks.

"Hey, are you okay? Is something wrong with this place?"

"Please just go. There's another station about ten minutes out," she says quickly. "We can make it."

I glance at the gauge again. "I don't think we have ten minutes, Birdie."

"Please, Tristan. We're too close."

Close to what? Her childhood home? Is that why she's so nervous? She is afraid of being recognized? I want to ask, but how she's pressing her sunglasses against her face, how she's coiling behind me, making herself small, unseen.

"All right," I say, even though every protective fiber in me screams something is off. This is Jacksonville, not Miami. No one here knows about Aaron. If someone realizes she's Reagan, so what? That panic is beyond the fear of recognition. "I'll try to make it to that other gas station, but if we don't, we'll have to walk there and get the gas ourselves because waiting for a tow service will take much longer. Is that okay with you?"

"Yes." Her voice is barely a whisper now. "Just get us out of here."

I shove my phone in my pocket and fire up the engine. "Tell me where to go. I'll follow your directions."

Her directions come in clipped yells over the engine. Left here, straight ahead, avoid that street. But the Ducati has other plans.

The engine sputters. Her grip tightens desperately around my waist. "Tristan."

"I know. I'm trying." We make it maybe two more blocks before it starts grinding so loud I know we're done. I coast to a stop on a side street, my jaw clenched. "Birdie, I'm sorry, but—"

A pack of motorcycles roar past in formation.

"No." Birdie is off the bike before I can finish, backing away like it's betrayed her. "No, no, no."

I'm beside her in a flash, pushing her behind me, hiding her rather than protecting her. The bikers slow down in tight single file and glance in my direction. I'm on high alert, assessing the threats, hands ready for guns.

One of them flashes his teeth at me. One is gold, two are missing and the rest are brown. "Nice ride."

It's normal for bikers to admire a good machine when they see one, but Birdie's reaction can't be ignored. Until I decide if the compliment is genuine or if they're here for trouble, I nod, hand on hip, closer to my Glock. "She's a rare breed."

"She giving you trouble?" His Southern accent shows.

"Not this beauty, no."

"All right," he drawls, heavier on the accent. "Get home safe."

"You too."

He revs the engine and motions for the rest of them to move. Their stares linger on us for a while until they all follow him and tear down the road.

"What the fuck was that? Do you know these guys?" Behind me, Birdie is shaking like a leaf.

"Hey, it's okay. They're gone. I'm right here with you. I won't let anything happen to you."

"We have to leave."

"Sure. Scratch the gas station. Let me call an Uber back to the hotel. I'll tell Brandon to come get the bike."

"No. You can't leave it here for long. It'll get stolen."

I point a thumb back at where those bikers went. "By them?"

She nods once.

"I don't give a shit about the bike. You're spiraling. Your safety is my top priority, Birdie. Who are they anyway? What did they do to you?"

"Did you not see their cuts? It's an MC." She swallows. "Shane's MC."

"Holy shit."

"They usually run on the other side of town. I didn't expect…" Her breathing accelerates. "I don't know if they recognize me… This was a mistake. I shouldn't have left the hotel."

"Hey, hey, breathe. They can't hurt you. You're safe. Do you hear me, Birdie? You're safe here with me."

She nods, trying to even her breath. "Thank you, Tristan, but we really need to get out of here. Can you push the bike until we get to the gas station?"

"Forget about it. I'll figure something out."

She starts pushing the Ducati herself. "If

they recognize me, not only will they take the bike but they'll find out it's you who bought it and track me down through you."

The bike doesn't budge. I take it from there before she pulls a muscle. "Then we'll go to another hotel. I know how to cover our tracks, Birdie. Don't worry. They can't know who you are. Why the hell are you so scared of them?"

"Because if you think they shunned Shane for the atrocity of his crimes, you're wrong." She walks next to me as I haul the beast in the other direction of the street. "They shunned him because he left the MC, for me. They blame me for everything. I took Shane from them, and if it weren't for me, he wouldn't be where he was now."

Every muscle in me tightens. It makes a lot more sense, her panic. It runs deeper than just being recognized. This neighborhood—this whole city—holds something darker than just bad memories of a terrible childhood.

I peer down the road right and left as I angle the Ducati toward the curb and keep us moving, my body between her and the street.

We round the corner and I guide the bike into the lee of a shuttered barber shop, half-hidden behind a busted soda machine tagged with old stickers. The gas station looms from a distance.

"We're almost there," Birdie announces.

I'm scanning the area, looking for threats, when I see boots coming out of a flower shop. They're heavy on the concrete. Confident. The kind that announce themselves.

"Well, I'll be damned."

Birdie turns to stone at the voice. The boots belong to a woman walking toward us—leather vest, worn jeans, graying hair pulled back in a ponytail.

The woman stops a few feet away, hands on her hips, studying Birdie like she's a ghost made flesh. "Reagan, is that really you?"

Birdie goes white. Completely, utterly white.

I step forward, ready to intervene, to get Birdie out of here before this gets any worse. "No, she's not. Sorry, ma'am. You've mistaken my wife for someone else."

The old woman steps closer, squinting. "No, no, I'd know that face anywhere. You're little Reagan Fletcher." Her face crumples with sympathy. "Oh, sweetie, I was so sorry to hear about what happened. Such a tragedy. Your mother, Shane…and Mason. And then you just disappeared. We heard you were dead."

"You're mistaken." Birdie utters. "My name is not Reagan."

But the woman isn't buying it. She's coming closer. I step into her line of sight. "Ma'am, she said you're mistaken." My tone is polite. My body isn't. I widen my shoulders, give Birdie my left side so she can tuck in under my arm, and angle my stance to block the woman's view from the street. "Now if you'll excuse us. We're in a hurry."

The woman's gaze lifts to mine. There's no fear in it, just a weary recognition of men who take up space on purpose. "You're her husband, you say?"

"Yes."

Her head shakes slowly, and then she gazes back at Birdie. I incline my head to tell Birdie to get behind me so I can handle that woman, but, for a moment, I hear Birdie whisper, "Please," and then she mouths something to the woman.

Suddenly, the woman drops her head, backing away. "When they told me they saw some girl who looked like little Reagan, I had to come down and see it for myself. Too bad they were wrong. Some things are too good to be true. I'll make sure those old farts know that poor girl is still dead." She throws another glance at me. "You take care of your ol' lady. She deserves a good man."

CHAPTER 34

Birdie

"We need to leave immediately." I drop my half-unpacked suitcase on the bed and almost rip the zipper off.

Tristan closes the door to my hotel room. "It's been taken care of. Brandon arranged for everything. We're going to another hotel as soon as you're done packing."

"No. We need to leave the city. And can I please get my phone back?"

He starts getting my clothes out of the wardrobe. "We can't leave the city yet. What about your husbands, ex and soon to be?"

"You have Shane's tablet clone, and I told you I could stall Blake until you found a way to disable his goddamn app. All I need is my fucking phone."

"You're not calling him."

"Then you do it," I throw my things inside my suitcase, "like you said you would."

"Fine. I'll call him and set a meeting tomorrow. What's the farthest place in town from that MC?"

"Not in Jacksonville, Tristan, because we're not staying here a second longer." My face twists with all the pain this city has caused me and continues to cause me. "I should never have come back here. What the hell was I thinking, going for a ride on the most conspicuous bike?"

"Hey, don't blame yourself for trying to be happy for once."

"Happy?" A mocking laugh chokes and dies on my lips. "Happy feels like stealing, like taking something that was never meant for hands like mine, calloused from holding onto people who take and cut and ruin.

"Happiness is a borrowed dress, always belonging to someone else. My parents taught me that joy was selfish, a luxury I hadn't earned through enough suffering. So when it comes— that fleeting, golden thing—I hold it like a soap bubble, knowing that even my breath might be too rough, too desperate, too much. Happiness for me is like trying to hold water in cupped hands while walking across broken glass. Every step forward costs me something, and by the time I reach safe ground, my palms are empty, stained only with the memory of what might have but never has been."

"Birdie, I'm so sorry. I thought I was doing something nice. I didn't know it'd ruin everything."

"You were trying, just like I was. Maybe trying is what happiness is. Maybe the moments when we forget to brace for impact, when we let our guard down just enough to feel the sun on our faces without fear, those seconds of forgetting we're not supposed to have this, are the only brand we're allowed."

"No." He shakes his hand sharply. "We deserve more than that. You deserve more than that."

Do I? I walk to the bathroom to get the rest of my stuff. Tristan is right about one thing, though. I shouldn't blame myself for trying to be happy for once. I should blame myself for believing I didn't deserve to try every single day.

When I return to the room, Tristan is holding my phone. "Where should I tell Blake to meet?"

A deep breath fills my chest. "Home."

His head shoots up. "You're not setting foot in your house until I capture the stalker, and Abel isn't stupid. He's got ties to the police and must know by now he's the prime suspect in your assistant's murder. He will never return to the island willingly. He'll see this is a trap, which will escalate the situation, not defuse it."

"Then you choose. It's a five-hour drive from here to Miami. Any town in between will suffice."

"Miami?!"

I busy myself with finishing packing. I'm not ready to have the same argument again.

Tristan grabs my wrist away from the suitcase and slams it shut. "You're sure as hell not offering yourself as bait. We're not going to Miami."

"Get your hands off—"

"No." His grip tightens, not painful but unyielding. "You want to run straight into the arms of the psychopath that stars in your wet dreams? The piece of shit who has been pretending to be a good cop to get close to you, to get you to trust and fall for him so when you find out the truth you'll be too far gone to be saved?" His face is inches from mine now, eyes blazing. "Not happening."

"Jacob is not Butterfly Man, Tristan. You're blinded by jealousy and it's going to cost me everything." I yank my hand out of his. "And for the record, who I decide to trust or fall for or FUCK is none of your business. You don't get to make that choice for me or any other choices. You can't stop me from going to Miami."

He steps forward, backing me against the bathroom door until I'm trapped between his body and the wood. His hands brace against the wall on either side of me. His chest rises and falls heavily, so close I can feel the heat radiating from him. The air between us crackles when his eyes burn into mine and he growls, "Watch me."

When his voice drops into that low, dangerous grumble, when his gaze pins me like he's staking a claim he hasn't earned yet, my breath stutters. My chest brushes his with every sharp I inhale. "You want to control me, Tristan? You want to tell me where I can go, who I can see, who I can fuck?"

His jaw ticks. His breath scorches my cheek.

"You'd like that, wouldn't you? Locking me down, never letting anyone else so much as breathe my name."

He smirks. "Nice try, but your mind games won't work today, Birdie. No amount of guilt, shame, doubt or uncharacteristic weakness will make me cave. I'm not jeopardizing your safety, no matter what you say."

Damn.

His eyes dip to my mouth, and for a second, I swear he'll kiss me. My pulse slams in my ears. My hands curl into fists at my sides—not to shove him away, but to stop myself from pulling him closer. Tristan Morra is the only man who can make my fury feel indistinguishable from desire.

Instead, he says, "Why didn't you tell me about your beef with the MC before?"

"I thought it was inferred. I told you about Shane, about us leaving. You heard he was shunned. I mean, you ride a bike, you read my books. I thought you knew how it was in motorcycle clubs. Their code, their rules."

"Who's Mason?"

My heart lurches, tripping over itself. I school my features into confusion, tilting my head as if I've never heard the name in my life. "Mason?" I echo, soft, feigned bewilderment.

With unnerving precision, he studies me, peeling back my skin to find the lie underneath. "The biker woman, she said she was sorry to hear about what happened. She mentioned your mother, Shane and Mason."

"I don't know any Masons. Maybe he's a guy in their club, and something bad happened to him, too. It's a one-percenter MC. A lot of bad things happen in those."

He grunts. "And the woman?"

"She's an old lady. I don't remember whose exactly, maybe the road captain's or the VP's."

"What did you mouth to her at the end?" He presses. "What did you say to make her back off?"

A shaky laugh escapes me. "You're imagining things. I didn't mouth anything. I was begging her to leave me alone, that's all."

His stare sharpens. He doesn't believe me. I know it. I haven't had enough time to weave the perfect story that kills his suspicions. Have I lost his trust? Have I ruined everything with my lies?

My phone vibrates in his hand. The sound jolts through my chest like a gunshot. "Is it Blake?"

Tristan glances at the screen, and venom twists his face. "Worse."

"Who?"

He flashes the phone in my face. His lip curls like the words taste rotten. "Your stalker."

Jacob.

I reach for the phone, but Tristan jerks his hand out of reach before my fingers even graze the screen.

"Give it to me," I snap.

"No."

"I have to take that call. What if it's about Gia's case? What if he has something we need to know?"

He doesn't hand it over. Instead, with a muttered curse, he thumbs the call open, puts it on speaker and holds the phone between us. Then he tilts his chin at me, challenging me.

"Birdie?" Jacob's voice spills into the room.

"H-hey," I answer, my glare on Tristan.

"Where have you been? I've been trying to reach you for days? Are you okay?"

"Yeah. Yes, I'm okay."

"Thank God. I was worried sick."

Rolling his eyes, Tristan exhales another curse.

"How are you holding up?" Jacob asks, not in his detective tone. It's warm and caring. How could he be the same man violating me in my sleep, the one caught on camera in a hoodie and a mask trying to break into my decoy safehouse?

"I've been better," I say.

There's a pause. "Birdie, listen. I came across something."

"About Gia's murder?" I ask warily.

"About Blake Abel, your husband."

My eyes widen at Tristan. His expression sharpens. He prompts me to keep the conversation going. I clear my throat. "What about Blake?"

"It's hard to explain on the phone. I need to see you in person. I tried your new location and your house, but you weren't at either. Where are you?"

Tristan's head jerks up, eyes narrowing. He mouths it across the charged space between us, "Don't you dare."

Is this call another ploy to pinpoint my location? Jacob once called me at the weirdest time of the day and asked me where I was. I've suspected him then, and now, I feel exactly the same way I've felt. The weight of my secrets and trust issues presses down on me all at once.

Back then, my doubts about Jacob cleared up. Am I mistaken to suspect him now? Have I been mistaken to clear him then?

"Birdie, this is very important," Jacob emphasizes. "You need to see this for yourself. I shouldn't even be doing this, but I must show you the evidence. Just tell me where you are, and I'll come to you."

The cadence of his words crawls under my skin. It's too smooth. Too polished. A net cast, waiting for me to swim willingly into its center. Still, if Jacob is genuine, if this is about Blake, I can't afford not to know.

Tristan's face is a hard no. He is watching me like a hawk, his body coiled and ready to snatch the phone away if needed, 'I told you so' written across his expression.

I can't stop thinking what if Jacob isn't who he claims to be, no matter how much I want to believe he's not Butterfly Man. "Wait, did you say you stopped by the *retreat* and my house?"

"Yes," he answers, and I gesture for Tristan to contact Marcus to confirm.

Tristan pulls out his phone and walks toward the chair he's left his laptop on. I follow him and ask Jacob, "When?"

If Jacob's story checks out, that means he's not my stalker, and I can trust him.

"Yesterday, and then I tried your house again today because that cabin didn't have any-one in it."

Tristan, reluctantly, shows me Marcus's text in response. *Affirmative. He showed up at the cabin before the breach, and then at the house. I told him she wasn't in. Same thing today.*

"Before the breach?" I mouth to Tristan. That doesn't make any sense. Why would Jacob go there and then, later on the same day, put on his stalker getup, go back to the cabin, where he must have seen the security system, and let himself get caught on camera?

I shake my head, angry but relieved. Jacob can't be Butterfly Man. Period.

"Uh, what does that have to do with any-thing?" Jacob asks. "Birdie, are you listening to me? This is no longer about the investigation of your assistant's and rival's murders. I have evidence that could change everything you know about your husband. I'm seriously wor-ried about you and your safety. You could be in real danger. Please let me know where you are."

Tristan warns me with his glare. His fingers are working fast on his keyboard.

No. I'm done listening to the doubts he's

sowing in my head. Jacob has done nothing but help protect me. He can't be my stalker. He's warning me about Blake. He must have something concrete to make him call me with this urgency. I need to listen to him. I must see that evidence myself.

"Jacob, I'm not on—"

Tristan's phone chimes with an alert. He bolts, eyes wide, and then he blinks at me three times, shoving his phone in my face.

"—Martha's Vineyard."

"Okay. Where are you?" Jacob insists. "I can still come over wherever you are. Just tell me."

On Tristan's phone there's an image. A photo of a police academy graduate. It's Jacob's, a younger version of him, but the name under it is different. Reid Ashford.

Then I read the last line under his name, and my hand flies to my mouth. *Florida Law Enforcement Academy, Miami Dade College.*

"Birdie, you still here?" Jacob—Reid—asks, and I'm going to be sick.

Detective Torrance is a liar. He lied about his name. He graduated from Miami Dade. He must have worked in Miami PD, too.

This can't be a coincidence. Tristan has been right to suspect the detective. All evidence is pointing at Detective Reid Ashford.

He is Butterfly Man.

"Birdie?" he repeats.

My eyes squeeze shut. *I think you know exactly where to find me.*

CHAPTER 35

Tristan

Knuckles white against the steering wheel black leather, I navigate through Jacksonville night traffic. In my rearview mirror, Birdie curls up in the backseat, eyes blocked by sunglasses, breathing too controlled to be natural sleep. She's avoiding any conversation. She hasn't even asked where we're going.

I keep my eyes on the road. "I know you're not asleep."

She doesn't respond, doesn't even twitch.

"As a diversion, Brandon is taking the bike to Daytona. He's making sure he'd be seen. If those MC punks decide to follow, he'll know how to lose them. Then he'll leave the bike there with a trusted friend of his, a girl,"

I laugh under my breath, "and meet us at the new hotel. It's in Ponce Inlet, by the way."

No response.

"You're into lighthouses, right? Ponce de Leon is the tallest one in Florida. I figured you'd wanna see—"

"We're not on a vacation, Tristan," she hisses.

But I got her to talk to me. I glance at the rear mirror. "It's also where I texted Abel to meet us tomorrow at ten a.m."

Her head shifts a little. I can't see her eyes behind her dark shades, but I know she's looking at me.

"Thank you, Tristan." That's all she volunteers.

Thank me? I count the numbers Birdie has ever thanked me for something she's been pushing for against my will, and I come short. She must be really sad, defeated. I don't like it. I hate it.

That ass doesn't deserve a second of her distress. He doesn't deserve a second of anything hers. Where is her sass? She should be angry, plotting her revenge, not moping over that useless prick.

Silence stretches for a mile or two. I turn on the radio. A mindless pop song plays. Maybe, I should give her some space, time to process and lick her wounds, but I can't. I can't keep quiet. "I'm sorry, Birdie. I should have dug deeper. When he evaded every question about where he transferred from, my first thought was Miami. I looked up his name, pulled some strings at Miami PD, but there were no police records of a Detective Torrance anywhere in Florida. It threw me for a loop. I should have done better."

"You have contacts in Miami PD?" she asks without moving.

"I do, several other precincts, too. In my line of work, it helps to have connections in the police."

"Did you ask them about Detective Reid Ashford?"

"Yes. I pulled his complete file. Apparently, he's been working there the entire time you lived in Miami." He's had years of access to Birdie's—Reagan's—life, her routines, her vulnerabilities. Years of laying groundwork. "Specialized unit for domestic violence and stalking cases. Can you believe it? Perfect cover."

A shaky breath hums out of her mouth. "Did your contact tell you why the detective transferred under an alias?"

Is she still hoping for a different explanation than the obvious? "There is no legitimate reason for Detective Douchebag to change his name and hide in plain sight at Oak Bluffs PD except to feed his obsession and claim you,

Birdie."

"Did they tell you why he transferred under an alias?" she raises her voice.

"Jesus Christ. No, because there are no secret missions where he has to go undercover in Oak Bluffs or a legal reason to change his name. Nothing. He just woke up one day and asked to leave."

"Not that they'd tell you if he was undercover…"

Fuck this shit. I merge onto I-95 South. "He's been planning this for a long time, Birdie. Years."

"I don't want to hear it."

"He knew your routines, your fears, your vulnerabilities before he ever introduced himself. He studied you like a case file."

"I said stop."

"No. You need to hear this. That predator is—"

"Enough!" She sits up straight, ripping off her sunglasses. Her eyes are red-rimmed, furious. "You think I don't know what he is? You think I don't realize what I've done? I let him into my house. I went on a fucking date with him."

The speedometer climbs past eighty. I force myself to ease off the gas.

"I trusted him. I handed him everything he needed to go on with his plan. Me." Her voice breaks. "I should have seen that plot twist coming miles away. I should have followed the breadcrumbs, the tiny hints that get past the average reader, but not me. I put those goddamn clues and hide them in plain sight for a living for fuck's sake."

In a way I'm glad she's stepped into the angry phase, but it still breaks my heart. Birdie has been through enough. She should spend every second of the rest of her life in peace and happiness, and I'll make it my life mission to see it happen.

"I may be terrible at choosing the men in my life, but if there's anything I'm good at, it's my job."

I can sniff where this is going from inside her brain.

"The detective is the ideal suspect," she muses. "His trustworthy camouflage, his ability to manipulate evidence and access to equipment designed to track comms. Add that to his history, and you've built yourself the ideal suspect. Do you know what we call those in books?"

Red fucking herrings.

"Red herrings." She doesn't wait for my answer. "They are—"

"False misleading clues designed to distract readers from the truth," I say through my teeth.

"Exactly." Her reflection in the mirror is

haunted. "In my book, Reid Ashford remains a red herring until I reveal his face from under the butterfly mask."

I mutter a curse. How could she still think like that? *"The truth knocks on the door and you say, 'Go away, I'm looking for the truth,' and so it goes away. Puzzling."*

She pauses for a few seconds. "Robert M. Pirsig."

"You know him?"

"I read *Zen and the Art of Motorcycle Maintenance* when I was thirteen. Not a fan."

Another swear flies from my mouth. The exit for Ponce Inlet appears ahead. I take it, needing something to focus on besides the rage building in my chest. "Fine, Birdie. I give up. We'll do it your way. Abel first, then Miami. We meet your stalker and finish it once and for all."

CHAPTER 36

Tristan

The inn blue and yellow colors come into view, a modest place near the inlet. Brandon's rental car is in the parking lot. I pull up beside it and kill the engine.

Brandon jogs over from the lobby before we get out. I climb out of the driver's seat. "How did it go?"

He scratches his head. "Well, I guess."

"You guess?"

"I took the scenic route, stopped for gas twice, made myself as visible as possible, but…"

"What? Spit it out. I don't have time for this shit."

"Nothing. Nobody followed me. It's like those MC guys just…didn't care."

I frown. That doesn't make sense. If they

don't care, why did they try to scare Birdie? Why was she so terrified that she wouldn't stay in the city a second longer? One-percenter clubs don't just let go of a grudge.

Birdie gets out of the car. "Is everything all right?"

"Yes, ma'am. The bike is secure and so are the rooms," Brandon continues, and then he whispers to me, "top floor, suite covered by the security cameras from all angles. I've already swept for devices."

"Good work." I grab our bags from the trunk. "Get some rest. Tomorrow is gonna be a long day."

Brandon nods, helps with the luggage and heads back inside. Birdie and I follow in silence. There's no elevator, so we take the stairs. It's only two floors, but the stair flights seem to stretch endlessly. Birdie's perfume clings to the air—sharp yet threaded with something sweet. I can't breathe without tasting her.

I keep my eyes forward, jaw locked, but every nerve in me strains toward her. My mind loops with one poisonous thought: she's let the detective too close. She's let him get to her head, touch pieces of her that should have been mine all along.

I should shove her against the wall and take her right here, lay her on these stairs and brand her with my cock so deep she'll never again think of herself with anyone else.

Instead, I dig my nails into the suitcase handle, veins standing out on my hand. I storm into the hallway, checking the security protocol on the go. Brandon points to our units. A two-bedroom suite and an adjacent room.

"Cozy," Birdie mocks.

"Sorry, it's not the Four Seasons." I shove the room key too hard to open the door. "They don't have connected rooms here, but it's the best place to keep a low profile. Daytona Beach would have been too obvious."

Once I'm in, I let go of the bags. They hit the carpet with a dull thud. I check every entry and exit point in the suite. "All clear. You can come in."

She takes in the interior of the living area. Sand-toned walls with white trim, echoing the beach just outside. A plush loveseat in muted linen with nautical throw pillows. Driftwood weathered coffee table, with a bowl of shells and local guidebooks. Sliding glass doors open to a small patio, letting in salt air and moonlight.

"The bedrooms are this way," I tell her. Then I nod at Brandon to leave. "Choose yours, I'll take the other. Brandon will be in the next room."

I walk behind him. I can't stand to look at her, not another second. I'll lose my fucking mind if I do.

Abruptly, just as Brandon steps out, Birdie slides in front of me, presses her back on the door and locks it.

I force my gaze back on her. "What are you doing?"

Her chin tips up, and she slowly takes off her shades. Her eyes…her eyes are molten, reckless, a wildfire set loose just for me.

The pulse in my throat hammers so hard it might crack a bone. "What the hell are you doing, Birdie?" My voice is more growl than words, ruined. That's all it takes. One look in her eyes, and I'm ruined.

Her lips part, letting out a painstakingly slow exhale. "Is it not obvious?"

The way she says it—soft, sultry, threaded with defiance—goes straight to my cock. My hands curl into fists at my sides, fighting the urge to rip her words out of her throat. "Don't you dare. I'm not your rebound or a one-night stand distraction."

"I agree. Those require a…far less complicated man."

My body steps into the heat crackling between us. Her breasts thrust up as she takes in another breath, grazing me. My palms slam flat against the wood beside her head. "Fuck you, Birdie."

"That's precisely the point."

I groan. "*Me estás rompiendo la voluntad. No puedo más, te juro que me voy a perder en vos.*"

She bites her lip. "I love it when you speak in Spanish."

My hips press into hers until she gasps and there's no room left for guessing how hard I am for her. I hover a breath away, yet enough to taste the cherry sweetness of her lipstick. "If this is about our deal, tell me now, because I don't want it. I don't want you out of obligation to square some promise—"

"I know. You want me to beg. I won't, but I'd do this." Willingly, she lifts her wrists, crossing them above her head. A sinful offering of her body. A complete surrender.

The moment I've been waiting for since I laid eyes on her.

"Here," she rasps, "does this look like obligation to you?"

"Fuck it." I seize her mouth, hungry and savage, passion and punishment—except she meets me with equal fury, pulling me deeper, grinding against me like she's been starving for this, too.

I can't process that this is actually happening. That she's here, touching me, wanting this, me.

The world stops.

I've read that line countless times and

laughed at the poetic way people write about first kisses in those saccharine novels, but it's true. When her lips touch mine, it's like someone has pressed pause on reality itself.

My hands shake as I frame her face, and I hate that she can feel it. I've killed men with these hands. I've broken bones and ended lives without a tremor, but right now, with her mouth moving against mine, I'm coming apart.

Eight years, no, twenty-seven years. Twenty-seven years of waiting, of watching, of wanting her with a hunger that has eaten me alive from the inside out. Twenty-seven years of suffering with every other touch, every other offer, because they weren't hers. Because no one else mattered.

She tastes like the nights I carved her name into my mind just to feel something real, like the ache of yearning years, and yet better than every fantasy I've tortured myself with, better than the dreams that have haunted me.

But it's what lies underneath that undoes me: the unmistakable taste of her skin, her pulse, her essence. It's memory, obsession and relief colliding in my mouth.

My tongue slides against hers, clumsy and desperate. Christ, I've read her every book, memorized every scene like a bible, but nothing prepared me for this. Nothing prepared me for the way she melts against me, the small sound she makes in the back of her throat that throbs in my cock.

Reflexively, my hands glide down to her throat. The darkness in me roars to life, demanding more, always more. I feel it in my spine, in my fists, in the part of me I keep locked away. I want to consume her. To make her forget every man who has ever touched her. To ruin her. To mark her so thoroughly that no one will ever question who she belongs to. Forever altered. Mine.

No. Don't rush it. This is the moment you've been living for.

For once, I listen. She's precious. She's perfect. She's mine, finally mine.

When she pulls back for breath, I follow her, needing to capture her mouth again because the absence of her touch feels like death. Her eyes are wide, pupils dilated, and there's something in her expression that bubbles my chest with possessive satisfaction.

She's looking at me like she's seeing me for the first time. Maybe she is. Maybe she finally understands what she means to me, what she's always meant. The lengths I've gone to for her. The things I'd do in her name.

My thumb traces across her bottom lip, swollen from our kiss. She's real. I tell myself again and again. She's here. She's mine.

And this is only the beginning. "This should

have been our first kiss."

"Seriously," her eyes droop, her voice husky, "you choose now to bring up my transgression."

"What?" My heart sinks to my ass. "No, no! That's not what I meant."

"Then what did you m—"

I swallow her words with another kiss. Her protest drowns in my mouth. Then she arches against me, moaning, her body writhing, begging for more. I break from her lips only to trail down her jaw, my teeth scraping the delicate skin of her throat.

"Jesus, where did you learn to kiss like that?" She gasps, tilting her head against the door, offering herself like she knows I'll bite, like she wants me to bite.

"I've never…" I stop myself from talking but not from marking her neck. She doesn't need to know about how I've structured my entire existence around this single possibility. She doesn't need to know that I've imagined this kiss a thousand different ways, that it's played on repeat in my head during countless dark nights.

My fingers tangle in her hair as I glance up at her wrists. Pictures flash in my head. A hundred different ways Birdie is tied to my bed. Birdie's cuffed wrists while she's on her knees and my cock fills her throat. Birdie on a velvet-lined table, wrists bound with silk cords, movement is no longer hers to command, where I keep her exactly where I want her and finally take what I've starved myself of for years, above her a ceiling mirror where she can watch everything that I do to her body. Bound and trembling under me, every inch of her branded.

Birdie's body pinned, arms and legs spread wide…wings stilled… preserved… forever.

Her wrists brush together as she follows the line of my gaze. A crooked smile curves her lips. "What's the plan, Mr. Morra? Tie me up to your bed while you choke and spank me and pull my hair as you fuck me senseless every way you want?" She throws back at me what I once told her in the cabin. "Or are you going to reenact a scene from my books and show me how much of a good student you've been? Who is it going to be? Dom…" she hisses and curls her lip under her teeth, "Tino?"

"The daddiest daddy of all book stalkers. That's your favorite, isn't it?" I can't hide the edge to my voice.

She shrugs playfully and thrusts her hips forward, pressing into me, reseeking proof of how far gone I am for her. "But not yours. I know what you have in mind. *The Nightingale's Whispers.*" A tremble runs through her. "Holy fuck."

You don't know the first thing about what I have in mind for you, Birdie.

I claim both of her wrists in my grip, hard and tight, and savor her gasp and the anticipation in her eyes. But then I separate her wrists one in each of my hands and guide them to my chest.

Her glance drops to where she's touching me. "Tristan, what are you doing?"

I don't answer with words. My frantic heartbeat does the talking. Swallowing, I take my hands off hers. My fingers pause in the air before they drop to my sides. It's not her who surrenders, it's me.

Dazed, she holds my gaze. "You'll let me touch you without your control?"

"Remember that day in the shower?"

"How can I forget?"

"What was the last thing you told me there?"

She roams my body with hooded eyes and licks her lip. "Mine."

"I am yours, Birdie. Always have been."

Something shifts and ignites through her. A different kind of hunger sharpens in the way she looks at me. "Then I'll take what's mine."

Her fingers spread against my chest, hesitant at first but then bolder, skating over my muscles, curling in the fabric of my shirt. My pulse riots. I should hate this. Instead, I burn.

She works the buttons of my shirt and pulls the fabric out of my pants. Then she pushes my suit jacket off my shoulders. I take off my holster and lay it, with my gun and the radio, on the dresser, and she takes care of my shirt. When I stand half-naked before her, she trails every scar, every tattoo with deep concentration, as if she's editing every inch of the man who has been before this moment, rewriting him into the man she now owns.

Her fingers travel up the back of my neck and thread into my hair. Then she pushes me down.

"Fuck." I know what she wants me to do, and I don't fight. "Only for you." I'm down on my knees, my cock aching against the zipper.

"Good boy. Now, keep your eyes on me… all the time."

Growling, I yank her heels out, one by one, and then hike her skirt up her thighs until her panties are on display.

They're red. Fucking red with a huge wet spot staining them. "*Mirá lo que sos… No sabés lo linda que quedás así.*"

She spreads her thighs wider, giving me a better view, and then her foot lifts and lands on my cock. She rubs me over my pants with her foot travelling up and down my hardness, and I almost nut in my pants.

"Oh, God, you're so naughty." I slide my

fingers down either side of her panties and roll them down to her ankles. "I'm gonna take these, too."

"That's not creepy at all." She chuckles. "What do you do with them?"

"What do you think?" When I free them, I take a sharp inhale filled with her soaked scent.

A moan slips from her lips as her eyes and pussy glisten. "You sniff them, lick them like a dog and then hump them until you come all over them."

I push the red silk in my pocket and capture her legs with my hands. "Yes, ma'am." I feel every plump curve up and down until I lock my grip around her hips. Then I align my head with her pussy, winking at her. "Woof."

A laugh starts but dies instantly in her throat as I thrust my nose and tongue inside her wetness. I am an animal, sniffing her pussy, lapping my tongue all over, licking every drop of arousal and salivating for more.

She shudders, pushing down on me, taking my tongue deeper, gasping my name, tangling her fingers in my hair, pulling me in until I'm buried in her taste, drunk on her.

I never take my eyes off her as she's demanded. I dig one hand in the ample flesh of her ass, and use the other hand to drive her to the edge. Fingers plunge into her slick heat. Thumb adds circled pressure on her clit. She wraps her ankles behind my neck and arches her back, legs spreading wider. I'm about to lose it just from the sight.

"Tristan!" She screams and bangs the door. Then she clutches at me, her nails tearing down my neck.

My tongue forces its way as deep as possible, claiming her pussy. Every spot I touch earns me another sound from her, another breathless gasp, another broken moan, until she clenches. She throbs around my tongue, breaking in my arms, flooding my mouth with her orgasm.

It tears through me. My body detonates. Heat surges in my gut too fast. My balls ache, and I can't control anything in me. I curse against her cum, a guttural, violent sound as I break with her. "Fuck, fuckfuckfuck."

"Tristan," she pants, "are you okay?"

My jaw clenches so hard.

She unwraps her ankles and lets them touch the floor. Then she tilts my chin up to look at me. "What's wrong?"

I just shake my head.

She studies me, and then her eyes drop to my crotch. It's a second or two before realization hits her. "Oh… Have you just…"

"Come undone in my pants just by watching you orgasm all over my tongue? Yup."

She freezes for a split second. "God,

Tristan, that's…"

I bury myself against her skin. I could die in shame.

"…so fucking hot."

My head snaps up. "Yeah?"

"Fuck yeah." The look she's giving me along with her face, hot and messy, her disheveled hair, and her cum trickling down her inner thigh, ignite me all over again.

I don't wait. I don't hold back. I lift her at the waist, and she wraps her legs and arms around me. Walking us to a bedroom, she takes my mouth like we'll never get another chance. God, this woman can fucking kiss.

By the time I lay her on the bed, my cock is straining again. I undo my belt and step out of my pants and boxers.

She glances between my cum-stained cock and my backup gun tucked around my ankle. "Too many guns."

I laugh under my breath and take my ankle holster off. "How about now?"

Her eyes zero in on my piercings, and her tongue darts and swipes across her lips. "Perfection."

She crawls out of the bed and wraps her hand around my shaft. I suck in a long hiss. Birdie Abel, my favorite author, my idol, no fuck that, Reagan Fletcher, my forbidden teacher, my unholy fantasy, has her fingers wrapped around my cock while the taste of her cum is carved inside my mouth.

Her palm opens, and she glances up at me before she spits on it.

"Oh, fuck me." My cock hardens even more.

She rubs her wet saliva on the crown and then she bends her head and licks my own cum off.

I fight every urge to fist her hair and stuff her mouth with my cock. I don't want her mouth, not now. I'm desperate to be inside her.

"I need to fuck you, Birdie." My eyes squeeze as I run my fingers through my hair. "But I won't until you say it."

"Say what?"

"Say you want my cock inside you."

"You still want me to beg, Tristan." She straightens and strips down naked. "How is that for begging?" She presses her body lush against mine. "How's that for saying I want you? I want you inside me, Tristan. Fuck, I need you."

That's it. That's all I can take.

I lay her back on the bed and take a mental photo of her gorgeous body, her abundant curves I will worship until the day I die…her scars. Like me, she has plenty of them. A constant reminder of how we belong together. Every mark of pain is a dagger to my heart and fuel to my rage. And yet they make her even more stunning. I fill my hands with her tits, her ass, her thighs, her waist, taste every part until she's writhing again.

But when I straddle her, she shakes her head.

"What? Don't tell me you changed your mind. Are you worried about Abel?" She's cheating on her motherfucking blackmailing husband with me. "No one will ever find out. I swear on my mother's grave."

"I don't give a fuck about Blake anymore. He's a dead man walking one way or another. If anything, I want him to know. I want him to see how a real man fucks a woman like me."

"That's…so hot." The idea of sending Abel a video of how I fuck his wife… "Why do you want me to stop then?"

"Do you have a condom?"

I grind out a curse. "I'm clean. I swear."

"I'm clean, too. Since the hospital, I haven't let him touch me. Thank God. Who knows who he's been sinking his disgusting dick in other than Gia? But…you know this isn't just about being clean."

"I…" *I wanna say the right thing because there's no way in hell I'm inside you with a barrier. Nothing comes between you and me. And I'd love nothing more than to fill you up with my cum, over and over, until I claim your womb, too.* But if I say that, she'll freak out. She's almost thirty-five and has been married for seven years. There must be a reason she doesn't want children or she would have had them by now. "I… Are you… I can pull out." *I won't.*

She giggles. "Relax. I'm messing with you. I… I can't get pregnant."

"You're so mean." I pinch her nipple and bite the other until she yelps. "That's what you get for being so naughty."

She laughs again, but it doesn't touch her eyes.

"Wait, when you say can't…"

Something sinister crosses her face for a split second. It vanishes as she rises to her knees and pushes me on the bed. "I'm on the pill, Tristan. You're safe." She straddles me, her thighs locking me in. "Now, enough talking."

She holds my cock, gives it a rub before she guides it into her entrance.

My eyes roll back as the scalding wetness coats me, as she pushes her hips slowly all the way down on me, taking every inch of my cock, and her lips part with a strained moan.

"Reagan." Her name tears through me, a prayer I've never believed in until now. I force my eyes open to look at her, fragments of every fantasy I've had of her shattering, collapsing, and reforming into something so very real. "I can't believe I get to see you like this."

"Like what?"

"Like a queen." I feel her tit. "Like a slut." I cup the other tit, bring both her nipples to my mouth and suckle. "Like a fucking goddess."

She lifts herself a little and then comes down on me even deeper. "Then start worshipping."

I hold her hips and thrust my pelvis up and down, my cock fucking her, worshipping her, as if I've done it a million times before. Her tits bounce with every drive, her head thrown back, mouth open, moans flying. My head jerks back, my throat stretched, my breath short in my lungs; I'm being possessed.

"You feel so fucking good, Reagan. So fucking good." I break. Her body was carved out just to lock me inside her. I'm not inside her; she's inside me, gutting me from the core out. This isn't just sex. It's trespassing into a sacred place, and the terrifying part is knowing I'll never be free again.

"You feel so good, too. Those piercings… Oh my God. Oh, fuck me. Please. Fuck me harder."

"You feel that?" I growl, pounding into her harder, faster. "No one else will ever give you that. No one else will ever touch you again. Mine. Do you hear me? Mine. Say it."

"Yours," she moans, eyes rolling back, body shaking on top of me. "I'm yours, Tristan.

Fuck, I'm yours."

Her pussy clenches around me, tight and convulsing. Then my name stutters on her lips as her orgasm rips through her. The sight of her coming on my cock—screaming my name, clawing my chest raw—is the best thing I'll ever see in my life.

I bury myself deep, groaning her name, and spill inside her, pulse after pulse, until there's nothing left but sweat, heat and the unbearable truth that I'll never get enough of her.

Another unbearable truth drills through my skull: if I lose this, if I ever lose her, I'll never breathe again.

CHAPTER 37

Birdie

The alarm snaps my eyes open. I turn it off with a wince. Morning is here. In a couple of hours, I meet Blake.

I should shower, but there's something cathartic about meeting my cheating husband reeking of another man's scent and having his cum in my pussy.

A smile creeps on my lips as I roll and stretch my ar— "Jesus Christ!" I pull the sheets over my—very much still naked—body. "Tristan, you scared me."

He, too, is missing his shirt, sheets pulled up to his hips, hair ruffled, his head propped on his hand, wearing the biggest smile I've ever seen on him. "Good morning."

The sun spills into his eyes, turning them golden. The rays glisten on his toned skin, his muscles gorgeous and equally his inked scars. Tristan Morra is a beautiful man and even more exquisite up close. "Morning to you. Have you slept here all night?"

He nods, unable to wipe that grin off his face.

I notice the dark circles forming under his eyes. "Tristan, did you get any sleep last night?"

His head shakes with a no.

"What were you doing then? Have you been watching me sleep?"

"I'm always watching you. It's my job."

It could have been worse. I'd rather have that pretty face watching me in my sleep than the one hiding behind a creepy mask.

"I can't stop looking at you. You're so beautiful." He cups my cheeks and crushes his mouth against mine. His tongue parts my lips and swirls with mine, the taste of his toothpaste filling my mouth.

"Not fair. You've already brushed your teeth and I haven't."

"I don't care." His fingers dig into my hair as he nibbles on my bottom lip. "You're gorgeous in every state, and I can't get enough."

"Tristan," I pull away, "Tristan, let's just slow down a bit. Last night was…"

His face darkens in a heartbeat. "Don't you dare."

I blink hard. "What?"

"Don't you dare say it's a mistake." His voice takes a harsh turn, bordering on panic. "Everything else in the world is a mistake, but not last night, not this, not us."

"I was going to say last night was," I reach a hand for his face and caress his cheek with my thumb, "unforgettable."

Hope springs back to his expression. "Yeah?"

I shrug, hiding the delectable chill tantalizing my body at the memory. "It was for me."

"Me too. God, you have no idea."

"You've proven to be a remarkable student. A+ performance."

"You really thought it was good?"

"Do you have a praise kink or something? Yes, you're such a good boy and know exactly what to do with that pierced anaconda of yours...over and over and over." He's made me come four times, but who's counting? "You must have had a lot of *practice*."

"I wasn't lying when I said everything I knew, I learned from your books."

"Still, in a way, I envy the other girls who got to have you before me."

"You shouldn't be. No one, and I mean no one, will ever compare to you."

He doesn't just know how to give a woman butterflies. He unleashes a whole swarm.

"She thought it was good," he murmurs to

himself, too happy.

"I'm sure I'm not the only one who told you that."

"I… It hits different hearing it from the woman you…" He chops off his words with a sigh. "From you."

He leaves the bedroom before I can say anything. Before I can tell him I see him, and I understand. He's intense and dark and has his own demons to battle. But who can look demons in the eye and hold their ground better than me?

I go to the bathroom to freshen up. Then I put on a bathrobe and go to find some clothes. When he returns, he's wearing pants and carrying a tray, his grin back on. He leans by my side, kisses me again, makes me sit on the bed and places the tray in my lap.

I uncover the plates. "Oh breakfast in bed."

"Hope you like it. I made it all for you."

"How thoughtful." A kitchenette comes to mind in passing. I didn't get a chance to fully explore the suite. "Sure you made it, though? The eggs aren't burned."

He chuckles. "Positive. I wasn't being distracted by the many ways I could take you on that counter."

"Mr. Morra," I feign shock. "You admit to having fantasies of fucking your client on her own kitchen counter?"

"Guilty."

I bite on toast. "I wonder how many other clients you've fantasized about."

"None," he says firmly.

"None? Okay, how about this? How many girls have had the pleasure of tasting your cooking the morning after?"

"None, Birdie," he answers with the same assertiveness.

"So what, you tied them to your bed, made them take your cock all night and then kicked them out before breakfast? You're cruel."

Red bursts in his cheeks. He runs a hand through his hair and swallows.

"He blushes again. What, early-morning dirty words are too much? I haven't called you daddy or asked if you had your way with me in my sleep." I laugh. I love to tease him. Taking a mouthful of eggs, the rest of that conversation flashes in my head, the recollection of my inappropriate verbal vomit. *Nothing beats a virgin man trope who has been saving himself for the woman he can't have.*

Also, I remember the look he's given me after. It's pretty much like the one he's giving my plate now, like the yolk bleeding across porcelain is the most fascinating thing he's ever seen.

I freeze mid-chew. "I mean, there have been others…right?"

He swallows again. "What others?"

My fork drops with a loud clink on the tray. "Are you telling me that all this," I drag my gaze deliberately over him, every broad line of his chest, the delectable abs, the tattoos, the mouth that ruined me against the hotel door last night, the cock that had me screaming like a slut all night, "has never been… ?"

His jaw flexes. Once. Twice. He doesn't deny it.

I jolt forward, part shock, part thrill, pushing the tray aside. "Tristan Morra," I purr, "yesterday, was I your first?"

Finally, his eyes snap to mine. Hard. Unflinching. "Yes."

My tongue darts over my lip like I've just discovered a diamond mine, and my pussy… Holy shit. I'm practically creaming. "Oh my God, why haven't you told me?"

"Because of how you're acting right now."

"How am I acting, Tristan?" I slide out of my robe and throw myself in his lap. "Like a dirty whore who can't wait to jump your bones?" My fingers get him out his pants rapidly. "You don't want that?"

"Of course I do. I want nothing more."

I hold his cock—God, he's heavy and hard as fuck and mine, all mine—and adjust myself to let him in. "Good."

He plunges inside of me, not gentle but raw and savage. His head tips back, a guttural sound ripping out of him. My cry strangles in my throat—it's stretch and fire and home all at once. I push lower, slick and aching, and sink down on him as deep as I can take. "Tell me." I pant between thrusts.

He holds me down on him, hand fisting my hair and the other marking around my hip and ass, and pushes into me hard and fast. He's so strong, doing all the work, bouncing me like I weigh nothing. "Tell you what?"

"Tell me how you did it." I scream into his shoulder, those rings he has hitting all the right spots. "Girls drool over uniforms."

"I couldn't. Believe me I tried, but they were…" He stops for a second. I open my mouth to protest, to beg, but his hand in my hair slides to the back of my neck and pulls me toward him until our sweaty foreheads touch. His eyes bore into mine. "They were not you. They were never gonna be you, Reagan."

Something in me splits wide open. It's not the words alone, it's the way he says them, like it's been engraved into his bones for years.

And when he moves again, I feel them everywhere, in my chest, in the tremor of my thighs, in the ache of my pussy clenching around him. God, he's not just inside me. He's inside every locked place I've spent my whole life barricading.

It terrifies me, not because there's pure

darkness oozing out of every confession he makes, not because it crosses every boundary and blurs the lines of taboo and impropriety, but because I like it. I like the weight of him, the possession, the brutal honesty of his body taking mine like it's always meant to.

My nails dig into his shoulders, probably drawing blood. He must feel it, the sweet pressure building inside me, because he snarls and slams up into me like a rabid beast. My body ricochets with each thrust, pain and pleasure blurring until I can't breathe. His hand wraps around my throat and tightens, holding me there, keeping me with him.

"Tristan," I gasp, "don't stop—please don't stop."

Possessed, he drives into me. Nothing matters beyond this moment, this joining, this claiming. The sound of his breath, the sweat dripping down his temple, the sheer force of him.

My orgasm claws up and rips through me so hard I sob. I clutch him tighter, nails raking his back as I convulse around him, screaming his name—

The door crashes open.

"Ma'am, are you o—" Brandon's voice freezes mid-syllable, horror-struck.

"FUCK!" I bury my face, as much of me as

I could, into Tristan's chest, but orgasms don't care. I'm still clenching around Tristan's cock, my cum dripping, while Brandon stands there.

Unstopping, Tristan roars, "Get the fuck out!"

"Jesus." The boy rushes away. "I'm sorry. *I'm sorry!*"

My jaw hangs low. I don't know if I should cry or laugh.

Tristan, on the other hand, somehow has gotten angrier. He carries me without pulling out of me, lays me on my back and finishes what he's started. "Mine," he groans, his seed spurting inside me, "only mine."

Then, when he finally pulls out of me, he takes some of his spilling cum with two fingers and draws a line from my throat to my pussy, and another across my breasts, staining me, marking me, baptizing me in the name of the Unholy Spirit.

The ride to the lighthouse is silent. Even though the three of us hide our gazes behind sunglasses, we barely look at each other. I hate that Brandon saw me with Tristan. It was supposed to be our little secret, but now we have a witness.

However, I trust Brandon. I've always had. If I'm being honest, I'm more perturbed that I've exposed him to such indecency. He might be an adult, a soldier, but for me, he's a kid who brings out my protective maternal instincts.

At the parking lot, Brandon goes to secure the perimeter. Tristan moves from the backseat next to me to the driver's seat. The second we're alone, I ask, "Did you talk to him?"

"Yes. He was coming to tell us it was almost time to leave, but then he didn't find me and then heard you…"

"How is he?"

"He's never going to talk, Birdie. It's not worth losing his job."

"I mean, how is *he*? It must have been really awkward…for both of you. You're his boss. He pretty much idolizes you. To see you… compromised…"

"Compromised?"

"You're fucking your principal. Is that not against all rules?"

Tristan snorts. "You'll be surprised how many times it happens, though." His jaw clenches. "I'm sure he's laughing about it in his head."

"Okay, what about you? How do you feel about it?"

"I feel like shit!" He slams his hands against the steering wheel. "Another man saw you naked, saw you being fucked. How the fuck do you think I feel about that?"

I flinch at the abrupt fury, at the reminder

of Tristan's unpredictable temper.

"I'm sorry." He twists and holds my hand. "I'm so sorry. I get jealous. I can't help it. I'm the walking talking definition of an OTT JP man."

Over the top jealous possessive characters are my favorites. Perhaps because they're so hot in the way they would burn the world down for their girls. Perhaps because they're the kind I've never had.

He squeezes my hand gently. "Please don't be scared of me. I'd die before I'd ever hurt you."

I nod and pat his hand. "We should go. Blake would be here any minute."

"By the way, Shane used the tab to send a message this morning. I intercepted it."

Blood thumps in my temples. "To whom? To Blake?"

"Yes."

"What was the message?"

"*I'll talk.*"

CHAPTER 38

Birdie

lake isn't here.

I've been waiting at the gallery of Ponce de Leon Lighthouse for thirty minutes, and Blake hasn't shown up.

Tristan has given me my phone earlier after asking him for the millionth time if he texted Blake the right location. I've checked the text myself and Blake's answer. *I'll be there, little bird.*

I try Blake's phone for the third time. He never picks up. "Where the fuck are you?" I mutter. "He ditched me. Why would he come to negotiate anything with me when Shane is playing ball. He must have gone to Shane to finalize their fucking plan that will end me."

"I intercepted the message, Birdie. It didn't reach Abel." Tristan clasps his hands together and rests them on the railing. His gaze scans the place right and left, up and down on repeat. "He's just playing you, making you sweat."

"Well, it's working." I pace frantically. "He's on to us. He knows that I'm stalling with this meeting, that I'm only after the app."

Tristan doesn't speak, but I can feel an 'I told you so' forming on his face.

Clearly, I've underestimated my husband. "Unless…" My heart plummets to my feet. "What if Butterfly Man got to him first?"

"You mean Detective Douchebag?"

I roll my eyes.

"Your stalker didn't get to your husband. Last time I checked, the detective was on the Vineyard when Abel was in Jacksonville."

"You don't know that. Jacob… I mean, Reid could have been anywhere when he called yesterday."

"But I do. I had one of my men tailing him after the cameras caught him red handed. Wish I'd done it sooner. It'd have proven to you beyond doubt he was your stalker." He shakes his head with a grumble. "Anyway, as of this morning, the detective hasn't left the island. Relax. He hasn't killed your husband yet."

For a second, I wish it was true. I wish Jacob was Butterfly Man, and for now, Blake was alive and I was safe from his revenge.

"And if the detective isn't my stalker," I gulp, "and Blake is dead… It'll be hours before my whole life tumbles down on my head and I lose everything."

"Hey, you're not alone. I'm here, and I'm not going anywhere. No matter what happens, we'll figure something out. I promise." He glances at his watch. "For all it's worth, I don't think he's dead yet. The stalker would have made a great deal out of it. At the very least, he'd have let you know. His final offering before he comes to collect what he thinks he's earned."

A flicker of reassurance breezes into me. Tristan is right. Butterfly man said he'd save Blake for last. If he killed him, he wouldn't be silent about it.

"Excuse me?" A man's voice comes from behind.

I turn, and Tristan is a wall separating me from whoever has spoken.

"I'm sorry to interrupt," the man says, "is this lady with you Birdie Abel?"

"Who's asking?" Tristan uses his authoritative voice with an extra dash of menace.

"I'm the lighthouse keeper. Someone gave me a message for her."

My heart skitters. I jump from behind Tristan. "What message?"

The keeper, a man in his late forties, wearing a uniform and a cap, stretches his hand with an envelope.

I drop my gaze to the yellow envelope. There are no butterflies on it. Perhaps it's not from Butterfly Man but from Blake. I reach to take it, but Tristan blocks me.

He pushes his suit jacket just enough to show the keeper his gun. "Who gave it to you?"

The keeper frowns at the weapon, raising a hand between him and Tristan. "No one. I received a message on my phone from an unknown number yesterday. It said there was an envelope in the keeper's room. If I gave it to a lady called Birdie Abel today, I'd find five thousand dollars in a crypto wallet in my name. It gave me instructions on how to access that wallet and a photo of the lady, too."

"Show me," Tristan barks, attracting some eyes from the visitors toward us.

"Unfortunately, the message disappeared right after I managed to access the wallet."

Tristan curses in Spanish. "Did you check your CCTV to see who put that envelope in your room?"

With a shrug, the keeper puckers his lips. "I did, but it was wiped out." He pushes the envelope our way. "Just take it. I thought I'd make a quick buck here on something harmless, but it doesn't look that way. I don't want anything to do with it."

"Put it on the ground and leave," Tristan

orders.

The keeper does as he's told and scurries away.

Tristan mumbles something to Brandon into his mic about grilling the keeper and bends to take the envelope.

My breath trembles out. If this is from Butterfly Man, if he killed Blake, it's game over. "Open it."

CHAPTER 39

Birdie

Some meetings are written in the stars long before we recognize their gravity.
That day I first met you, I looked at my watch and locked in the time. 3:17 PM.
Tomorrow, same time, same place, we write our own destiny.
P.S. In solitude, we discover who we truly are.

XOXO, little butterfly

"**Y**our precious stalker is telling you the time for your date," Tristan seethes. "3:17 p.m. tomorrow."

"And he wants me to come alone." *In solitude, we discover who we truly are.*

"I agreed, against all logic and protocols, to take you to Miami to see him, but you're not walking into his trap by yourself, Birdie. I'll lock you up if I have to."

I take the piece of paper from Tristan's hand and read it all over again. "Putting the note in the keeper's room yesterday means he knew exactly where I'd be today. How is this possible? Who knows about this meeting other than me, you, Brandon and Blake?" My eyes dart around in panic. Will I find another rogue queen butterfly waiting for me, too? "He's watching us, Tristan. He's been following every step of the way, always one step ahead."

"He's been watching, yes. It shouldn't come as a surprise by now. But he's not one step ahead."

Pacing, I throw my hands in the air in frustration. "Of course he is. Every plan I've mapped to capture him comes to bite me in the ass with his mocking grin on top."

"Not this time, Birdie. Because I've figured out who the stalker is."

My fingers rub my lips angrily. "It's not the detective. You said he was still on the island. How could he be in two places at the same time?"

"Because he's not working alone."

I stop in my tracks. "What?"

"Look at the note. It's typed, not handwritten. You told me all the notes you had before the one you found in your bedroom were typed, not handwritten. Now, look at the butterfly drawing."

"It's…blue, just like the old ones."

"Exactly. Why the sudden change, why now? Unless it's someone else, with a handwriting that won't match the new notes, sending this one because the stalker couldn't."

A chill runs through my spine. "I thought he changed the drawings into queen butterflies to send me a message, to tell me he knows who I am, but all this time he…"

"He's been letting someone else do the work for him where he can't be."

"He stays on Martha's Vineyard to deflect any suspicions while he gets someone else to send me the note…from here."

"Think about it. The detective has lived and worked in Miami his whole life. He must have connections with other police departments around Florida. Who is better to trail someone without raising suspicion than police officers?"

"They have the right to be anywhere. He might have even told them I was a suspect in one of his cases, and he needed their help to gather enough evidence to convict me. A connection at the airport could have told him I flew to Jacksonville. Another follows me there, which leads them to Ponce Inlet." My head spins. "But how did he know I'd be at the lighthouse today?"

"I don't think he did. He just took a chance, knowing you loved lighthouses, and it would be highly unlikely you wouldn't stop by."

"And it's paid off." My head spins. "But who? I get that a police officer he knows could be following us and updating him about our location, but they wouldn't deliver creepy notes over the years? Who could possibly agree to be a stalker's accomplice?"

"Must be someone he trusts, a family member?"

"Or someone he knows they won't talk."

Tristan nods pensively. "Because he has something on them."

"A dirty secret." Just like Blake is blackmailing me, the detective could be blackmailing a person, a dirty cop even, into being his courier. "Fuck."

"You still think Detective Douchebag is a red herring?"

"How could I have been so blind?" Regret slices my chest. "I should have never doubted you."

"It's okay." Tristan's gaze burns into mine, even behind our sunglasses. "Love isn't always gentle words and soft touches. Sometimes it's standing guard in the darkness, taking the hatred meant for someone else, being the villain in your story so you can remain safe."

Goosebumps cover me. "Love?"

He doesn't say anything for a while. Then he drags away his stare. "It's what you wrote. I'm just quoting it."

"Right… A quote," I tell him and then murmur to myself, "not the closest thing to a love confession I'll ever get from Tristan Morra."

"No." He hears me and moves closer. "It's not the closest you'll ever get. It's just the beginning." His fingers brush against the railing spot I'm gripping, the closest he would allow himself to come to touching me in an open space. At this moment, I want nothing more than to collapse into his arms, but I can't.

Blake is still alive. The note and the detective being on the Vineyard are proof. Butterfly Man hasn't gotten to my husband yet. That means Blake could be setting a trap for me by not showing up. Perhaps he's hired a private detective of sorts, one of those who hunts for evidence of infidelity among divorcing couples, and they're fishing for compromised photos of me with any of my bodyguards. It's a stretch, but I can't rule out anything.

Dirty cops, like Blake, like Reid, will do anything to get what they want.

CHAPTER 40

Tristan

"Ashford left the island and went to Boston," I read the text I've received from the detail on the detective.

"Boston," Birdie emerges from the suite bathroom, holding a bag of toiletries, "what's in there?"

"Saldana's case I guess. He must be pretending to be on police business, but he's just losing the tail, covering his tracks with an alibi before he flies to Miami."

She packs the bag in the open suitcase on the bed. "Let him think he lost the tail. Let him come to Miami thinking he's the smartest person in the room."

"Copy. I've also sent Dixon and Riley to Miami before us to cover as much ground as possible. They'll be your security backup."

Concern wrinkles her forehead. "What do I need backup for? Tristan, if the plan we've devised puts you in danger, let's make another. I don't want anything to happen to you."

I smile. "Nothing is gonna happen to me. You'll go in the school building alone as planned, and I'll be on the rooftop of the building across, ready with my rifle to take him down."

"And you're sure you're okay with this? Taking him down yourself instead of letting the police handle it?"

"He is the police, Birdie. He'd have gotten away with it. It's the only way to keep you safe. I've told you so many times before, and I'll tell you now. There's nothing I wouldn't do to keep you safe."

She swallows. "I'm still worried about you. If anything goes wrong, I won't be able to forgive myself."

"There's nothing to worry about. It's a clean operation."

"Then why the backup? More details could spook him away," she stresses.

"The stalker isn't working alone. What if he brings his accomplice or accomplices to the meet? We need the backup. Don't worry. They'll be discreet."

"But—"

I place my palms on her cheeks. "Do you trust me?"

A sigh leaves her lips, erasing all doubt from her gaze. "You're the only one I trust, Tristan. That's why I can't lose you."

"You're never gonna lose me." My lips brush hers. "I'll go get my things ready."

In the car, she rests her head on the window and drifts away. I keep my eyes on her. She's mesmerizing in her sleep.

Her jacket slides off her shoulder, exposing her upper arm. I notice one of her scars that looks rather recent. A tiny incision, about two inches on the inner side. I brush my thumb on it and feel something like a thin, small object underneath. My mind instantly thinks of bullet fragments and shrapnel. I've had my share of those, removing them or living with them on a daily basis. But Birdie has never been in combat.

She flinches into awareness. Her gaze dips to where I'm touching her, and she quickly fixes her jacket to cover her arm. "What are you doing?"

"Sorry. I didn't mean to wake you up. That scar… There's something under it. What is it?"

"Nothing." She glances at Brandon in the driver's seat, and her voice drops. "It's just Nexplanon."

"Nex what?"

She laughs under her breath and whispers, "Birth control implant."

My eyes narrow at her. "I thought you said you were on the pill."

"Yeah… It's easier to say that to a man instead of having to explain what Nexplanon is, like I've just done now. It kind of ruins the mood."

Point taken.

She stares out of the window, a line between her eyebrows forming. Then she fills her chest with a long breath and exhales it in a longer sigh.

"Penny for your thoughts," I say.

A fake smile forms and dies on her lips. "You never told me your old last name."

"Umm, if I tell you, will you tell me what's *really* on your mind?"

Her head rests back and bobs with a nod.

"Cáceres, and Tristán is my middle name."

"Cáceres." She tries the name in a terrible accent. "I prefer Morra."

"Me too. Now, I have one for you. Why didn't you change your last name back to your maiden name after you know who went to prison?"

She shrugs. "I didn't have enough time. It was a very hard time for me. Everything went into a downward spiral. Then I met Blake. It was all happening so fast. You know the rest of that story." Her eyes peer at me. "My turn. What is your original first name?"

"That's for you to remember. I gave you enough hints."

"That's not fair. You know I suck at recalling names. I'll never remember."

"Stop evading my question and tell me what's troubling you. Listen, if you don't wanna go to Miami anymore, it's not too late to change your mind."

"No, of course not. I was just wondering."

"About?"

"3:17 p.m., the first time Reid Ashford saw me. We know it was at the school. What was he doing there at that time?"

"3:17 is around pickup time. He could have been picking up a student. A son, a daughter."

"He said he'd never gotten married and didn't mention any children, but he did say he had a sister."

"Do you know how old?"

"Early twenties. That makes her what, fourteen, fifteen back then?"

I pull out my phone and retrieve the student list of suspects. I search for Ashford. A match is immediately found. I show it to Birdie. "Look, Melinda Ashford. Twenty-three. Father deceased. Only known male relative is Reid Ashford, her brother."

Birdie removes her shades and stares at

the screen for a few seconds. She blinks between my face and the name before she scoffs. "That's it. That's how he's connected to the school. All this time, Reid Ashford has been Butterfly Man. And *Melinda*…may be the one helping him."

"You think he's using his own sister to send his creepy notes for him?"

"I guess we're about to find out."

CHAPTER 41

Birdie

The school looms before me, a monument to decay. Graffiti covers the walls, and broken windows stare down at me. The place that shamed and banished me for something I'd never done. How long has it been abandoned, left to rot?

"You're doing great. I'll be here every step of the way," Tristan's voice comes through the wide-range, wireless earpiece I'm covering with my hair.

"Are you in position?"

"Affirmative. You can go in. Remember, let me have visual on you at all times."

I touch the back of my pants, where I conceal one of Tristan's guns under my jacket, making sure it's not showing. I have a knife tucked inside my boots, too. It doesn't hurt to come prepared. "All right. Let's do this. Let's get that asshole."

At 3:15 p.m., the Florida sun casts long shadows through the empty hallways. Heart in my throat, I make my way to the main corridor where it all began.

"Where are you, Detective?" Will he wait in my classroom? At the parking lot where he used to pick up his sister?

I move through the corridors methodically. My classroom first. The science lab where I used to eat lunch alone. The library where I'd hide from Aaron. The pantry where I secretly cried about the men in my life. I check every room and circle back to the parking lot. Nothing. No one.

"Tristan, do you see anyone? Any movement?"

"Negative."

"Well," I check the time on my phone. It's 3:29, "he's not here."

A text dings from my phone. Unknown number.

Right time. Wrong place. This is not where we first met, darling.

My heart skips a beat. More messages follow immediately.

Nice rifle. Not so discreet. I can spot it from miles away.

Naughty, little butterfly. You brought a third wheel to our date.

"Shit," I breathe.

"Birdie, what's going on? Do you see any-thing?"

My phone dings again. *Lose the bodyguard or your precious protector and his two friends join in the afterlife. I'm watching all of them.*

Terror shoots through me. He knows about Dixon and Riley too.

I flinch with another text notification sound. *Café Luna. You know the place. I'll be wait-ing. Ditch the earpiece and the phone. Come alone or they all die.*

Café Luna. I used to get coffee there all the time. The barista—was it Fernandez? Gon-zalez—always remembered my order. That's where Butterfly Man first saw me? That's where the detective and I first met?

"Birdie, what's happening? Talk to me."

"Tristan." I glance around the empty park-ing lot and go back inside. "He knows you're here. He's just texted me. He knows where you are. Dixon and Riley, too."

"Fuck. Get out of here, Birdie. Now."

That would be the smartest thing to do, but he knows I can't do that. I have to see Butterfly Man. I have to see the face behind the mask myself.

The layout of this place I once knew by

heart maps out in my head. There's a maintenance exit near the old gymnasium that leads
to a narrow service lane. If I move quickly, I
can slip out without Tristan seeing me from his
rooftop position.

"I'm sorry, Tristan," I whisper into the earpiece, "but I have to do this."

"Birdie! BIRDIE!"

I pull the tiny gadget out of my ear and
drop it on the floor with my phone. Then I
run.

The maintenance door groans as I push
it open, rust flaking off the hinges. I sprint
through the service lane, my heart hammering
against my ribs. Café Luna. Two blocks east. I
can do this.

My footsteps halt on the street corner
where the coffeehouse sits. The place looks like
it's been closed for years, its cheerful yellow
awning faded and torn. Of course—everything
from my old life has rotted away. Karma is a
bitch.

I approach cautiously, peering through the
dusty windows. Empty tables, chairs stacked on
top of each other. No sign of anyone.

"Hello?" I call out, stepping inside. "I'm
here. I came alone like you asked."

Nothing.

Evening out my breath, I walk among the
tables. My eyes spot a piece of paper on one

of the tables on the left. Quickly, I take it. He's written something on it. *There's a phone behind the counter.*

I rush to find it. It's a burner, sitting right there, but there are no messages left on it or numbers saved to call. I wait for a few minutes. The phone remains silent. "C'mon. Where the hell are you, motherfucker?"

Then it pops. The text I've been waiting for. *Back alley.*

As careful as possible, I make a beeline to the kitchen and into the back alley, where delivery trucks used to unload supplies. The smell of garbage sends a wave of nausea through me.

I fight the urge to gag, my eyes darting between the alley and the phone. "I know you're here somewhere," I say to the shadows. "Show yourself."

A figure emerges from behind a distant dumpster all the way down. Tall, wearing a black hoodie pulled up over their head. And the mask that freezes my blood.

Butterfly Man. I'm face to face with him. Out in the open. The final countdown.

"I know who you are," I gasp.

He doesn't speak. Just stands there, tilting his head like he's studying me.

My heartbeat and breath race after each other. "It's only you and me. No one is watching." My hand hovers behind my back, ready to take my gun out. "Take off the mask," I demand. "Let me see your face, Detective Ashford."

His head tilts to the other side like a fucking creep from a horror movie. Then, abruptly, he twists and dashes away.

"Hey! Stop!" I pull my gun out and chase after him.

My feet pound against the cracked asphalt. He's fast, but I'm not backing down. All these years of rage and fear and pain must end now.

He leads me through a maze of back alleys, past abandoned storefronts and boarded-up windows. My lungs burn, but I can't slow down. I can't let him get away. Not when I'm this close to ending it.

I shoot. For the love of God, I fire at him. He stumbles and ducks, dodging the bullet. Then he straightens and stares back at me, daring me to shoot him again.

"Please stop." I hold the gun steady, pointing it at him. "I don't want to do something we'll both regret."

He stands still for what seems like an eternity, and then he scoffs. I'm the one holding the gun, and he's the one mocking me.

"Show me your face, or I swear to God, I'll shoot."

Butterfly Man, slowly, moves a hand up to

his face. My heart beats frantically against my chest. Finally, I'll know who my stalker is beyond doubt and speculation. Finally, I'll see my tormentor, my dark savior.

In a flash, he springs and ducks into a narrow passage between two buildings.

"Fuck!" I chase him again, following the endless trail, but I can't find him anymore. My head snaps up and down. My eyes roam every inch around me. He's nowhere to be found, as if I've conjured him from my insanity, and now he's vanished.

I keep running, refusing to believe I've lost him. I end up in a small, enclosed courtyard surrounded by high brick walls, but I can't see the mask anywhere. I turn to the phone, praying, begging for a message, but it taunts me with more silence.

I lost. Another plan backfires and bites me in the ass.

I remove my sunglasses and share my location so Tristan can find me. Then my eyes roll heavenwards. How did Butterfly Man disappear just like that? "Where the fuck are you?!"

"Looking for me?"

With a gasp, I spin around, gun at attention. A man steps out from the shadows near the far wall. No mask. No hoodie.

"Wow, easy." Detective Reid stands before me, his hands raised, his expression surprised rather than menacing.

"Don't take another step," I warn.

"Okay. All right." He stops mid-step. "Can you tell me what's happening here?"

"Enough games. I know it's you. You're the stalker. You've been all this time. Your new name. The flowers, the restaurant, the notes, always fishing for information… The murders."

"What? No, Birdie. I'm definitely not your stalker."

"I said enough lies. I was literally just chasing you, while you had your mask on. You led me down here."

"No, Birdie. I got a text from you, asking me to meet you here so I could show you the new evidence I had."

"What the hell are you talking about?"

"I know who your stalker is. I found a video of him sliding down a note under your hotel room door."

"You're lying."

"I'm not. Let me show you the video—" Reid tries to reach for his phone.

"Don't move!" I tighten my grip on the gun. "Keep your hands where I can see them."

"Birdie, please. You need to see this. It'll prove I'm not your stalker."

"How do you even know about the note he left at the hotel? That was more than a year ago. I've never mentioned it to you."

"You filed a complaint, remember, the one you thought was ignored by the police? That's how we first met on Martha's Vineyard. I've been following up on it. I went to the hotel you mentioned in the report and found the footage. I'm surprised no one has ever asked to see the security tapes. It was literally sitting right there."

Blake did, but he couldn't find anything. "Nice try. You probably doctored whatever video you think you have. You're good at forging those. You managed to alter live security feed, *remember*? When you visited me in my bedroom under the nose of my bodyguards?"

"I've never done that, Birdie, and I didn't doctor anything. The hotel manager gave me access to their archived footage from the night of the incident. The timestamp matches, if you'd just look at the video…" His hand starts to move.

"One move, and I'll shoot. You know I will."

He freezes. "Look, I understand why you don't trust me, but I'm trying to help you."

"Really? Then explain why you changed your name."

His expression shifts, more sinister. "My name is Reid Jacob Ashford. Changing last names for security reasons is more common in our field than you think. For me, I had to change it because of what happened with my partner here in Miami." He pauses. "There was an incident. He got involved in something dirty and left the force. I had to transfer under an alias until it's resolved."

"You followed me to Martha's Vineyard!"

"No, Birdie. Once you see the video, I swear you'll understand everything."

Who is in that video? Who else could Butterfly Man be if not the detective? I don't know what to believe anymore. How can I trust a single word *Reid Jacob Ashford* says? I keep the gun trained on him, my hands shaking. "Tristan will be here any minute. You will throw your phone in his direction, and he'll show it to me."

His jaw clenches, but he nods once. "Fair enough. Can you put your gun down now?"

"No! Just so you know, Tristan is so adamant about killing you. If you so much as think about trying anything, he will shoot."

"Okay." He keeps his hands raised this time. "I'll just wait here."

I keep my eyes on Reid's. He doesn't falter. He just stares back at me with something like…care. How does he do it?

Footsteps echo through the courtyard, quick and purposeful. Tristan appears at the entrance, gun raised, his face a mask of deadly intent. "Step away from her," he commands.

"Tristan, wait. He has something we need

to see first before—" I start, but he's already moving closer, Dixon and Riley in tow.

"Don't tell me you fell for his lies again!" Tristan doesn't take his hateful gaze off the detective. "You led her into a trap, you sick fuck. You're not getting out of here alive."

"No, Tristan!" I position myself between them, my gun still pointed at Reid but my body shielding him from Tristan's. "He says he has evidence. A video."

"Evidence he fabricated. Birdie, get out of the way."

"Please, just…let him show us first."

Reid's voice is steady despite having four weapons pointed at him. "The phone. I need to reach for my phone."

Tristan's finger hovers over the trigger. "One wrong move—"

"I know." Reid's eyes pin on mine. "Birdie, I'm going to move very slowly." He moves his hand inch by inch toward his jacket pocket. Every muscle in my body coils tight. He pulls out his phone with deliberate care and holds it up so I can see it. "I'm going to open the video now. Don't shoot me for moving my thumb." He works the screen and then tosses the phone toward me. It skitters across the cracked concrete.

With trembling fingers, I bend and take the phone.

"Watch the whole thing, Birdie. Look at who has really been torturing you," Reid says.

The timestamp reads from over a year ago—the night at the hotel. I tap play. The grainy security footage begins. A long, empty hotel corridor. Then a figure appears at the edge of the frame. Someone in all black. A hoodie. They're walking toward my room. A black mask covers their face.

My breath catches in my throat as they pause outside my door, sliding something underneath. The note. Then they straighten their back with a flinch, as if they heard someone coming, afraid to get caught.

Quickly, they take off the mask and look behind them. They move down the hallway, checking the right and left passages. That's when the camera catches their profile.

My gun wavers in my grip. The world tilts sideways as recognition crashes over me. "No."

"Birdie?" Tristan's voice sounds distant, muffled by the vertigo wave threatening to take me. "What is it? Who's in the video?"

I can't speak. Can't breathe. I rewind the video to watch again, praying I'm wrong. But there's no mistaking that walk, that build, that face.

Sobs tremor through me, and my knees give.

"Birdie!" Tristan and Reid shout at the same

time, both hurrying toward me.

"Don't move!" one of my other bodyguards bark.

"Leave the detective alone. He's not Butterfly Man," I whisper through the uncontrollable sobs.

Tristan's hands help me up. "Birdie, talk to me." He lowers his gun, concern replacing aggression in his voice. "Who is it?"

The name won't come out. I can't bring myself to believe it even though it makes perfect sense. I hand him the phone. He can see it for himself.

Tristan plays the video until the end. "Son of a bitch."

Reid takes a cautious step forward. "I'm sorry you had to find out this way."

CHAPTER 42

Birdie

I should have seen it coming. I should have read the signs. The clues that are now staring me in the eye, sticking their tongue out at me. The mask didn't hide a stranger. It was a man I once loved.

Too many noises, too many scenes, jam my brain as I put the pieces together. The conversation I've had with Tristan comes first, when he questioned my sanity after Butterfly Man's little night visit.

Give me something to work with here. Any detail that can lead me to find him.

He's tall, strong, unhinged. But in a way, he's… gentle, even familiar.

Familiar? Do you recognize anything about him?

I laugh hysterically. How the fuck could I

not recognize him?

Then Gia's voice rings in my ear, and I burst into tears.

Butterfly Man's actions are driving you to push away the only people who care about you. He wants you isolated, Birdie, and you're letting him win.

The isolation, the control, the mindfucks… They have always been his game. I've lived through it for eight years. How could I be so oblivious? So fucking dumb?

Didn't he come home rushing after you found the note? Didn't he install the security system himself on the very same day? Didn't he literally beg you to come home just so that he could protect you?

I've said it then, and I'll say it now. The stalker situation was an opportunity to slither his way back into my life. To show me I still need him. To convince me that even after all these years, I'm nothing without his protection.

I've always known that blackmail is his backup plan to claim me; be mine or rot in prison.

Husband Dearest's voice stabs my skull. *This isn't over, Birdie. I'm not letting you go. You're mine, you hear me? Mine!*

I scream my lungs out.

"Birdie!" Tristan is the only thing keeping me standing. If he lets go, I'm going to collapse. "Breathe. Just breathe."

My chest feels crushed, like Blake's hands

are around my throat even now. "It's him." I lose control of my tears as if I haven't been training myself to stifle them since I can remember. "It's Blake. My husband is the one who's been sending me the notes. Blake is Butterfly Man, Tristan."

"I know, baby. I know. But he can't hurt you anymore."

"No wonder he couldn't find anything in the hotel surveillance." I laugh at my silliness. "Did you know we had a fight the other day before that night at the hotel? I wanted to leave him. But then… The note happened. I wasn't that scared, but he said things… He convinced me the cameras were tampered on purpose. He made sure that I'd feel scared, so I stayed because I knew he'd protect me."

Bile rises to my throat. "Come to think of it, every other note that came before coincided with one of our fights. Every time he felt I was going to leave him, he played the stalker game."

"He was manipulating you into staying with him with fear," the detective says. "Classic emotional abuse behavior."

"How many times has he held me when I was terrified because of feeling watched, hunted? How many times has he whispered reassurances while orchestrating my torment? For what? All of this pain for what? Money?"

"It's a big motive, Birdie."

My mind reels backward through our marriage. Blake's possessiveness disguised as protectiveness. His need to control every aspect of my life. The way he's isolated me from everyone I've known, from the whole world on that island, claiming he was keeping me safe.

First from what happened here in Miami. Then from the stalker he invented. The stalker he is.

"The murders. Oh God, the murders." Saldana, Gia. But neither Blake nor Shane were going to die. Butterfly Man was stalling, playing his sick game only to take what he wanted. Leverage to blackmail me, to rob me out of all my money.

Aaron… Blake killed him, too. His first kill in my name. "Blake's reaction after Aaron's death flashes in my head. How he'd held me while I cried, murmuring that at least one person who'd hurt me was gone. I'd thought he was trying to comfort me. He'd been gloating."

Then he went back here, just around the same time he disappeared from the Vineyard, to finish the others. To cover his tracks.

"Aaron?" Reid asks. "Who's Aaron?"

"None of your business," Tristan says.

"If it's another murder Abel committed, then it's definitely my business."

"The app." The realization floods through me with nauseating force. "What if Aaron didn't send that message? What if it was Blake who did it? What if after he killed Aaron, he planted the dead man's switch on Aaron's phone?"

"Birdie," Tristan holds my shoulders, "you're spiraling right now. Why would he do that?"

"To turn the whole world against me. To make me think I have nowhere to go. To seek his protection. To make me leave Miami with him. Oh God, Tristan. Remember the shiner he gave me, the one you saw me hiding in the school pantry?"

Tristan's face contorts with rage. "Of course."

"After he hit me, despite the ring on my finger, I wasn't going to stay with him. I've had my share of wife beaters. I wasn't going to repeat the same mistake."

"So he did all that to convince you couldn't stay in Miami. You had to disappear. Different name, different city."

"He knew he couldn't stay here after Aaron. He knew he had to leave. But he couldn't be a cop anymore so he needed another source of money. He'd seen my writings. My first manuscript was getting offers. He knew I'd be his golden goose. The girl he could control into doing anything he wanted. Two birds with one stone. He gets the girl and gets away with murder.

"The new name, Martha's Vineyard, he chose everything, and he made it look like he was looking after me, protecting me." I let out a quivering moan. "All those years, he watched me fall apart. He *made* me fall apart."

Tristan's grip tightens on his gun, his knuckles white with fury. "I'm going to kill him. I'm going to hunt him down and put a bullet between his eyes."

"No, Morra," Reid says firmly. "We need to do this right. Blake is already tied to two murders—Saldana's and Connelly's—and likely others. We have evidence now. Let the police handle this."

"The police?" I wipe the tears from my cheeks. "The same police who ignored my reports for years? The same system that let him get away with terrorizing me, with putting me in a hospital nearly dead, while they dismissed me as some hysterical woman? Blake has people on the inside that manipulate everything for him. He will walk and come back to hunt me."

"Fuck the police," Tristan snarls. "They had their chance. This bastard tortured her for years, just like my father did to my mother, to me, and they did nothing. I'm not letting bastards like Abel slip through the cracks again."

"It's different now," Reid insists. "We have proof. The video, the timeline, the connections." He holds my gaze. "And you have me."

"With all due respect, Detective, you are one person. You've just told me your own partner was dirty, and you were taking the heat for it. The justice system doesn't exactly work for people like us."

"I can't let you commit a crime, Birdie. You or your bodyguard."

"Blake was here, Reid. He led me straight to this place, where you said you received a text from me to meet you. That means he was setting you up. A trap for Tristan to kill you. Is that the person you want to risk everything for?"

Reid's confidence wavers for the first time. He runs a hand through his hair, looking between Tristan's murderous expression and my tear-stained face. "Look, I get it. I do. The system failed you, and Blake manipulated it. But if we do this my way—if I can capture him legally—then it's over. Really over."

"Florida does have the death penalty," I muse.

"But not Massachusetts," Tristan reminds me.

"If we get him for Aaron's murder…"

"Birdie, wake up. The only evidence the detective has is in the murders on the Vineyard, and it's circumstantial at best."

"It's not," Reid retorts. "We questioned his

therapist. She has records of their sessions, and they exhibit dangerous and violent behavior. She also said he was showing compulsive obsessive tendencies toward his wife, and the drugs she prescribed him made it worse. Then the tests proved the psychedelic amphetamines we found in Saldana's blood came from the same source that Abel used."

Tristan scoffs. "Great, you build your whole case based on a dealer's testimony."

"It wasn't just any dealer. It was Gia Connelly."

My head jerks toward Reid. "What?"

"She was spotted multiple times securing drugs, although we didn't find any traces of illegal substances in her blood. After reviewing CCTV cameras, we can confirm she was delivering them to Abel. I'm sorry to add this to the list of betrayals, but Abel and Connelly were having an affair. His semen was found inside her."

"Another girl that would do anything for him. She gave him the drugs, thinking they were for him, but he used them to kill Saldana." I put two and two together. "The gun." I gasp. "Gia saw Blake's gun in my room. She'd asked about it. She must have taken it back to him as a favor. She was the only one who could go in my room without permission or raising suspicion."

Tristan rubs his chin pensively. "But then you told her the truth about him, how he beat you, and she wanted out. That's why he killed her."

"With the gun she stole for him." Pain squeezes my chest. "Oh, Gia."

"What was Abel's gun doing in your room, Birdie?" Reid stares at Tristan. "Is that the same gun you confiscated from Abel but said you'd returned back to him?"

No one answers.

Reid's jaw flexes. "Do you still have it?"

"No," Tristan lies.

"If we run ballistics on that gun and it's a match to the one that killed Connelly, it's a done deal," Reid insists.

I stare at the detective warily. "Hypothetically speaking, if that gun was sent to your precinct, anonymously, would it be admitted without tracing back to any of us?"

He matches my gaze. "Hypothetically speaking, I'll make sure it doesn't."

"Tristan?" I whisper.

"We don't know anything about a murderer's gun. I gave it back to Abel myself."

"Listen, Morra, give me one chance," Reid continues. "Let me bring Abel in the right way first. If it doesn't work—if I can't make it stick—"

"Or if he gets off on a technicality or decides to enter an insanity plea and his therapist's sessions backfires," Tristan adds.

"If he slips through the system again in any way, then… Everyone's gotta do what they gotta do." The detective shrugs and backs away. "Just don't let me catch you."

"I don't trust him," Tristan mumbles as soon as the detective leaves to put out an APB on my husband. "Are you really gonna let him handle Abel?"

The idea is entertaining. A dirty cop captured by his friends, left to rot in prison with enemies he put away. The irony is poetic and cathartic. Except the second Blake is captured, he will talk about the past, all the secrets we've shared. Prison is one step closer to Shane. Together they will try to bring me down with them.

I can't allow it.

"I've been a fool once. I won't be ever again." I secure the gun in the back of my pants. "The detective can't take Blake down, but we will."

"Good girl."

"What did you just say?"

"You heard me," he whispers in my ear, "but I can say it again, when I take you hard and fast on the corpse of Blake Abel."

My pulse pounds, bleeding with hunger, not fear. The intoxicating darkness sends pools of heat between my thighs. "The Enzio to my Bianca."

"I prefer the Mad Dog to your Vixen."

A smile slowly creeps on my lips. Blake wanted to play games with his little bird? The butterfly he's trapped in a jar on display? Time to show him what happens when butterflies develop a taste for blood. "I think I know where to find him."

"Where?"

"The last place I'd want to be. The place we first met."

Tristan's face is puzzled for a second before recognition hits him. "Of course. Your old apartment."

"Where he answered the domestic disturbance call."

"Won't it be rented to someone else by now?"

"A couple of years ago, I bought it." So I won't forget what happened there. A reminder of what should have never happened again. "It pissed him off. That's how I know he'll be there, hiding in plain sight. The last place I'd think he'd want to be." I chuckle. "It wasn't very smart of him to clue me in, though. *The place where we first met.*"

"He never thought you'd outsmart him and figure out it was really him. That works in our favor. The element of surprise." Tristan rallies his men and gives them orders. One will go with me back to the hotel. The other will create a diversion in case the detective decides to follow, and Tristan will find Blake.

"No. I need to be there. I need to see him dead," I say.

"I'll call you to come when it's safe. You'll get your closure, Birdie," Tristan promises. "Here's your phone. I retrieved it from the school. Don't ever pull a stunt like that on me ever again."

I nod, and we all move to our destinations. In the hotel, I place my phone on the table and wait.

Butterfly Man has no idea that his perfect prey has finally learned the truth about her perfect predator.

And she'd do anything to be freed.

CHAPTER 43

Tristan

The city folds around me like a hunting ground. I know its shadows better than Blake Abel ever will. He's sloppy when he runs, arrogant when he hides. Men like him always are. They believe the rules always bend for them because they've bent them before.

The apartment complex where Reagan used to live squats at the end of a forgotten street, all rusted fire escapes and windows sealed with cheap paint. The place that marked the beginning of her end. The first time Abel wrapped his leash around her throat and called it love.

Abel doesn't deserve a clean death. He deserves to feel the weight of his sins grinding down on him while the walls close in. But

Birdie's voice echoes in my head. *I need to be there. I need to see him dead.* And she will. I'll give her that.

I park across the street and scan the area. Third floor, apartment 3B. Windows dark. No movement. The front door will be a trap—if Abel remembers his training. Odds are he's holed up like a coward, a syringe dangling from his arm.

Not worth the risk. Time for another diversion. I call the nearest pizza joint and place a big order for 3B. Payment: cash. No tip.

When the delivery kid shows up, I check my gear and move toward the building. I circle around to the fire escape, climbing the rusted metal like it's second nature.

I reach 3B, crouch and wait.

The doorbell rings. Footsteps. Hesitant. Abel won't open the door as expected. He's paranoid, twitchy. The kid pleads—he'll have to eat the cost if Abel doesn't pay. Abel starts shouting, voice sharp and defensive: he didn't order anything.

That's my cue.

I pull a glass cutter from my thigh pouch— diamond-tipped, military-grade. With practiced ease, I trace a clean circle into the glass, press the suction grip, and lift the pane free. No sound. No resistance. I reach in and flick the latch. It gives with a soft click. Inside, Blake is fighting with the helpless delivery boy. I make a mental note to compensate him later. Now, I slip through the window into the bedroom like a shadow.

The apartment is small, cramped, and smells of stale sweat, liquor, and copper pipes. A place Reagan Fletcher once thought she could turn into a happy home. Her little piece of heaven until it became another nightmare in hell.

The things we'd settle for when we don't know our worth…

Abel scares the boy away with his gun and snaps the door shut. He moves a few steps, but then he freezes. His head jerks toward the bedroom door.

He might be a junkie, but his instincts are intact. Mierda.

I press my back to the wall. The floorboards creak beneath his feet as he inches closer. I count the steps. Three. Four. Then silence.

I hold my breath.

The door swings open just enough for him to peek inside, and that's when I strike. I grab him by the collar and yank him into the room, slamming him against the wall. His gun clatters to the floor. He lunges for it, but I kick it under the bed and drive my forearm into his throat.

"You." He claws at my arm, gasping, eyes wild. "You don't know what you're doing."

"I know exactly what I'm doing."

"You're just her new dog. She sends you to do her dirty work for her. But when she gets tired of you…" He elbows me in the rib. Then his foot does a number on my shin.

We crash to the floor, tangled in sweat and fury. He's stronger than he looks—desperation makes men dangerous. I let him swing, let him burn out his rage, then I twist his arm behind his back and pin him down.

"You think you're the hunter, pulling all the strings," I whisper into his ear, "but the truth is the moment I stepped into her house, you've been the prey."

Abel thrashes under my hold. His shoulder pops, and he bellows, feral and raw. With a surge of rage, he bucks hard, slamming me into the edge of the nightstand. My vision flares white. I lose my grip just long enough for him to twist free.

He comes at me like an animal. Fists, knees, elbows. He catches me in the gut and knocks the air from my lungs. Pain blooms sharp. My knees buckle. He fights like a man with nothing to lose. His weight pins me. His fingers claw toward my throat.

I twist, slam my knee into his side, but he surges forward again, teeth bared in a nasty grin. We're wrestling on the floor. My hand scrabbles against the floor, until I feel it—the cold weight of his Glock beneath the edge of the bed.

Abel sees it, too. His fingers close around my wrist, shoving, twisting, almost tearing the gun free from me. His breath reeks of chemicals and sweat as he snarls in my face, "You don't get it. You can't touch me."

Oh, can't I? I've fought far stronger men than you, you piece of shit. I wrench sideways, slam his shoulder into the wall, and jam the barrel up beneath his chin.

I could finish this in a second. One bullet and it's over, but it has to be clean. A gunshot will draw too much attention. I must make his death look like an accident.

The rage drains from Abel's eyes, replaced by something colder—arrogance. A crooked smile curls his mouth, split and bleeding. "Go on, pull it. I dare you." He tips his head back against the wall, grinning like a lunatic. "You can't, can you? You know about my little app. If I don't check in, Birdie is toast. All her dirty little secrets go wide. Every filthy thing she's done. You put a bullet in me, and you bury her, too. She'll rot in prison before she rots in hell where she fucking belongs."

He thinks he's won, that he's untouchable. I should rip his tongue out and dice it into dog food for talking about Reagan like that.

"You mean the lies you're spinning with

your buddy Shane. I wonder what happens if he's no longer available to cooperate. How the fuck would you prove anything in your pathetic little fabricated story?"

He snarls. "What the fuck did she make you do, Morra?"

Ding.

The sound of his phone chiming from the living room slices the apartment. A message. One he isn't expecting. His eyes flick down to the hallway.

I smirk, pulling him out of the room, switching the gun to the back of his head. Then I push him against the table where his phone lies next to an array of drugs, powder bags, pills and syringes. He's definitely evolved from prescription meds to crack. "Go ahead. Check it out."

He does. Curiosity always kills the arrogant. His thumb swipes the screen. A photo blooms to life. Shane. Face pale, body slumped in a prison cot, blood blooming across his blue shirt. A shiv buried deep.

The color drains from Abel's face.

With the right amount of money, anything is possible. During my very productive visit to Raiford, I've learned that you don't need much to get a scumbag like Shane shanked.

Shane wasn't the only one who got a tablet that day. I was generous with several others. It's rather sad that something as trivial as a device that allows poor inmates to reach their families anytime, charged for a year in advance, can earn you kill favors.

I wasn't gonna use them until it was necessary. Shane sending that message to Abel made it happen. "On the other hand, we have evidence that you are the creep that has been sending Birdie the sick notes."

"What the fuck?"

Ding.

That's the hotel video Ashford has shown us.

He shakes his head, manic laughter bubbling up. "Birdie isn't what you think she is. She's poison. She'll gut you the way she gutted me. You'll see. You'll *all* see."

In a heartbeat, he explodes forward and ducks. The next thing I know he's throwing the table at me. I fall back. Wood splinters. Pill bottles roll. His filthy syringes scatter across the floor. The gun skids out of reach, clattering under the couch.

Abel grabs a shard of wood, swings it and catches me across the jaw. I punch him in the teeth. His head whips to the other side, and then he pulls something from his pants. It glints as he drives it into my arm. A fucking knife.

Pain sears through me as he dives for the

gun. I ignore the burning in my arm and lunge, catching his wrist just as his fingers close around his Glock. The barrel jerks toward me. My own reflection stares back from the hollow muzzle.

He grins through bloody teeth. "Looks like you lose, soldier boy. Birdie is mine. Eight fucking years of my life I've done nothing but lose myself, my mind, my soul, to that bitch. I earned her. She can't just toss me around and replace me with a fucked-up loser like you."

Growling, I slam his hand against the floor, the Glock half an inch from my face. My free hand scrabbles through the wreckage until it closes around the one weapon I'd like to use tonight.

One of his syringes.

I don't hesitate. I stab it into his arm.

Abel's eyes flare wide, the manic grin breaking into shock. He tries to pull the trigger, but his muscles slack, and the gun drops from his grip.

I shove him off me, sucking in air, securing the gun, arm and jaw screaming. "She was never yours. She's always meant to be mine."

Blake Abel twitches on the floor, pupils blown, just like my father during the last moments of his sorry existence. I crouch over him, blood dripping from my mouth, and whisper, "When you clicked on the photo and the video I've sent you, it captured your biometrics and sent them to me. You can kiss your dead man's switch app goodbye. I can now check in and delete the message you have in there." I give him another dose.

"You've made the worst mistake of your life." His eyes droop. "You should read the message before you erase it. You'll know why."

"There's nothing a useless worm like you can say that will ever make me think twice about protecting Reagan."

"You know her real name."

"I know everything."

Something sparkles in his eyes, just for a split second, before they wither away, as if he's finally figured something out, finally, realized the truth. "Oh, I get it now. I've been there, too…so madly in love…obsessed. It's what she does… You two deserve each other."

"Yeah, she deserves someone like me to be her husband, not you, not Shane. Me. Reagan is mine."

"Shane?" An unhinged laugh rattles in his chest. "You think…" His eyes roll back, and froth starts foaming around his lips. "I'm gonna enjoy watching you from hell…when you find out the truth."

"Why don't you watch while I bury my cock deep in her sweet pussy and she screams my name right here next to your filthy corpse? Sure you'll enjoy that more."

A gurgle that might be a groan chokes in his throat. "How about this, Morra? I leave you with a little parting gift, and when we meet in hell, you tell me if that pussy was worth it."

"Just die already."

"I did start the Butterfly Man game…but I didn't finish it. Someone else…left that note on her pillow…not me. But I guess…you already know that." His hands jolt toward my head and bring my ear down to his lips. I yank his hands off me, but not before he manages to whisper his last lie.

"Fuck you, Abel. Enjoy hell." I watch the light leave his eyes.

CHAPTER 44

Birdie

I lean forward into the camera, my hands steady now after an hour of trembling. The interviewer's eyes are kind, expectant, waiting for my final words. The studio-style lights cramming my home office feel warm instead of suffocating for the first time today.

"To anyone out there who is made to believe the lies that you're nothing without them, that no one else will ever love you, no one will ever believe you, that you deserved it—" I pause, feeling the weight of every woman who might be watching, every person still caught in that web. "You are not alone. Your voice matters. Your truth matters. And when you find the courage to speak it, the whole world will shift to make room for your freedom. Don't let anyone—not even someone who claims to love you—silence that voice again."

The interviewer's eyes glisten. "Birdie, thank you so much for sharing your incredible story with us today."

As the cameras stop rolling, I feel something I haven't felt in years—lightness.

Martha practically bounces toward me, her heels clicking against the floor. Behind her, Tristan stands like a sentinel, his eyes scanning the room even now. Always watching, always protecting.

"Birdie, honey, you were phenomenal!" Martha grasps my hands. "The phones started ringing before you were even finished. Seven of your books just hit number one on every list that matters, and," she lowers her voice, eyes glowing, "I got the call twenty minutes ago. Provided that you'll leave them out of your memoir, which by the way is being auctioned for a high seven-figure as we speak, the house will give you your rights back and ten percent over the number you wanted. How crazy is that?" She muffles a squeal.

"What memoir?"

"The one you're going to write very soon, silly." She waves a dismissive hand. "And guess what? Your new series, Butterfly Man, another house is interested, for double the original offer. They doubled it for crying out loud. And with the cinematic rights that are already in negotiation, we're talking eight figures."

I blink, the numbers not quite registering. "Eight figures? For books I haven't even written yet?"

"Yes, baby. It's the least you deserve. You've been through hell and back, and we've all been oblivious. I can't imagine the amount of pain you've had to deal with every day for years. He almost killed you, Birdie, and no one lifted a finger." Tears touch her gaze, but then she grins from ear to ear, brushing into her chirpy self. "Enough of that. May he rot in hell. You have full control now. You're free, Birdie. Financially, legally, completely free."

Free. Another thing that doesn't quite register. Not yet.

Tristan steps closer, and his hand finds the small of my back. The touch grounds me, reminds me I'm not dreaming. "You ready to get out of here?"

I nod, suddenly desperate for air that doesn't smell like hairspray and television lights.

Outside, the Ducati gleams in the afternoon sun next to Tristan's bike. "You had it shipped to Martha's Vineyard, my filthy rich bodyguard."

He laughs. "Ready to take it for a spin?"

My dream ride I wasn't allowed to have.

Without thinking, I put on the helmet. Luckily, I'm already wearing pants. "Race you to the cabin?"

"You bet."

I swing my leg over the bike, feeling the familiar thrum of power beneath me. "Try to keep up."

The wind tears through my hair as we speed down the island roads. Every mile puts more distance between me and the woman who used to apologize for breathing too loudly. Is this what freedom feels like? Is it the taste of fresh air and the roar of a beast that obeys only me?

For now, it is.

We arrive at the old safe house, the secluded cabin where Tristan and I shared a bed for the first time. The beach alcove stretches, waves crashing against rocks that have stood here longer than any of our troubles.

Tristan removes his helmet. "You beat my ass, Birdie."

"C'mon, you let me win. Or is it the arm? Does it still hurt?"

"No, and no. You ride like you've been doing it all your life. You sure you haven't touched a bike since you moved in here?"

"Even before that. Shane taught me how to ride, but I've never had my own bike." I climb off the Ducati and wrap my arms around his neck. "Thank you for this. It means a lot."

"Anything for you."

"I heard about what happened to Shane. Blake wouldn't have done it, so I guess it was you?"

"There is no limit to where I'd go to protect you, Reagan." His lips crush mine with a hunger I feel in my bones. His mouth tastes of devotion so intense it borders on worship.

We move against each other until my back vibrates with the Ducati engine. His hands map every inch of me. The kiss turns reckless, open, consuming.

"Want to ride the Ducati?" I tease.

"I wanna ride you on the Ducati." His hands sneak around my waist and lift me on the leather seat. "Just like you let me be the Mad Dog to your Vixen, let me be the Dusty to your Cammie."

I throb vigorously at how hard I came on Tristan's cock while Blake's dead eyes watched from hell. I clench harder when I realize, for certain, Blake's story ended with no chance of a sequel, and it's all because of Tristan. He killed Blake. He left the apartment spotless and dumped my dead husband's body in a crack house, making his death look like an overdose accident.

My forbidden bodyguard takes off my pants, and I straddle my bike. He pushes inside me from behind with untamed desire. The wind whips my hair as he moves with a force that rattles through the machine and into my veins. Every thrust is a claim, every groan a vow. The roar of the ocean drowns out my cries, but I know he hears them.

"Look at you taking my cock like that. Such a good girl, taking it all for me." He drives deeper, harder, twisting my hair around his fist and pulling it. "My dirty little whore, my filthy queen." He smacks my ass. "God, I can fuck you like this forever, Reagan." The savagery rising in his voice and thrusts drive me insane. He takes me so fast and rough in the end until my body splinters around him, and I lose myself in the sound of my name ripped from his throat and the feeling of his cum inside of me.

Without pulling out, he holds me tight. His lips print little hot wet kisses on my neck. "Te amo, Reagan." His voice is jagged, almost broken. "I love you, and I will never stop."

My body tenses beneath him. "Tristan, I…"

"I know you're not ready to say it back, but I'll say it for the both of us until you are."

I clear my throat as I shift. He takes a hint and breaks our union. I put my pants back on, and he zips his, a frown on his face. "Did I say something wrong?"

My lips part, but the truth won't come out straight. "No, you didn't."

"But?"

I brace myself because what I'm about to say will hurt us both. "I don't think I'll ever say it back, Tristan."

His eyes flare, as if I've just cut his heart out with my bare hands. "Yes, you will. Of course, you will. After everything I've done for you… My cum is literally dripping from your pussy, Birdie. You'll say it when you're ready. You just need time, and I'm a very patient man."

"Detective Ashford does have one sister," I stare Tristan in the eye, "but her name is not Melinda."

Tristan's throat bobs with a swallow. "Did he tell you that? Because he's lying."

"Her name is Nancy, and she's twenty-one, not twenty-three. I know that because I signed a book for her. I also know she's never been in our school because the student list you gave me, the one on my computer, doesn't have any Nancy Ashford on it. That means you only added that made-up name, Melinda Ashford, to your copy of the list, on the spot."

He steps toward me. "Birdie, please."

"The breach at the decoy safe house was staged. Blake was in Florida then, and it definitely wasn't Reid. What, you had one of your men dress up as the stalker to get caught on camera?"

"No."

"It was you, in Miami, isn't it?" I drag myself away, lifting my hand between us to stop him from getting any closer. "You texted me at the school, left me the notes in the cafe and led me to that courtyard where you'd texted Reid earlier from my phone to meet me there. It was you playing the Butterfly Man game that day, not Blake."

He shudders with tears. "I love you."

"You were going to kill an innocent man, Tristan."

"Innocent?" Hatred spits from his voice like venom. "He was taking you away from me. When the stalker game was over, you were gonna choose him over me."

"You didn't know that."

"Yes, I did! You wouldn't have touched me that night if you hadn't believed he was the stalker. Because the truth is *you* would never choose *me*. Don't you remember our deal? You told me if he wasn't the stalker, we'd go our separate ways. You told me to forget all about you and never look back." One tear drops down his cheek. "I couldn't let that happen. I did what I did because it was the only way I could have you."

"Villains burn the world down to save the girl."

"Yes," he sighs in relief, as if we see eye to eye. "A thousand times yes, baby."

"And they kill anyone in the way to have the girl."

He swallows again. "Birdie, *Reagan*, I'm begging you. Don't do this. Tell me what I can do. I'd do anything to make you forgive me, to prove to you that I will never do anything to hurt you ever again. Please."

"I know you won't hurt me, Tristan, but you will hurt others who did nothing wrong in the name of loving me."

"So what, this is it? You brought me all the way here, let me fuck you one last time to say goodbye? Because I'm too fucking dark for you now?"

"You lied to my face. You manipulated *me*. How can I ever trust you?"

"I'm sorry. Do you want me on my knees?" His knees hit the sand. "For you, only for you, I'd beg for the rest of my life if I have to."

My chest cracks with heartache. I'd be a liar if I said I didn't have feelings for Tristan. His darkness, his groveling… It's taking every ounce of willpower not to succumb to his toxic love, the only kind I've known, the one I crave despite knowing how excruciatingly painful it always ends.

"Please, Reagan. I've been waiting for you all my life. Everything that I've done, every line I've crossed, was just to be with you. Don't take that away from me. I can't live without you."

I throw my arms around him, embracing him with all my strength. My thumb caresses the scar above his lip, and I kiss it ever so gently. "I'm so sorry, Tristan. I didn't break free from Blake's prison to throw myself in another, no matter how beautiful the bars."

CHAPTER 45

Birdie

Home feels foreign when I open the door. Blake is gone. Gia is gone, and today, Tristan and his crew will leave, too. I've already said my goodbyes to Marcus, Brandon, Dixon, Riley and even Morrison.

All except for Tristan.

I couldn't risk it. I couldn't bring myself to look at his face, to feel his arms around me one last time, to let his scent wreck me and say to hell with it. There's a part of me that will always long for getting lost into his hazel eyes. That part has to stay buried and forgotten.

Through the window, I watch Tristan outside with the other bodyguards and their equipment. His gaze lifts and finds mine. For a heartbeat, neither of us moves. A million words. One silent goodbye.

As he closes the gate to the house, another cracks open in my soul, setting all the tears I've locked up for years free. Everyone who has ever hurt me is gone. No one is here to stop me from feeling everything I'm allowed to feel, from being my true self.

My phone rings. It's the detective. I sniffle and wipe my face. "Hi Jacob, or should I call you Reid from now on?"

"You can call me RJ." I can hear the smile in his voice.

"I like the sound of that."

"How are you, Birdie?"

I wish I could tell him to start calling me Reagan, but I haven't let him in on all parts of my past yet. He'd asked about Aaron and Miami, but had I answered, it would have led to Jacksonville, too. Those stories don't belong between us. Some secrets should stay buried no matter what.

"All over the place is one way to say it. Happy, sad, relieved, scared…alone. That's the scariest part. I'm thirty-four, and I've never been alone before."

"Are your bodyguards still in the house?"

"No," I sigh. "They finished their job. On to the next gig."

"It's a big house you have there in the middle of nowhere. Are you sure it's safe to stay there all by yourself?"

"I still have the alarm system, not that I've ever needed it. There was no vigilante stalker, taking down the people who have wronged me. It was just my psychopath husband scaring me into taking all my money."

He pauses, like he doesn't know how to respond.

"Did I make you uncomfortable? It takes some time to get used to my classic, nonhumorous verbal vomit humor." Tristan picked it up easily.

"It'll be my honor if you make me more uncomfortable tonight…at dinner. You pick the place this time, and I won't bring flowers or books with NSFW drawings."

I chuckle, but then reality hits. "Are you sure you still want to do this, RJ? You almost died because of me." Blake still got the blame for Miami. I haven't told RJ about Tristan. I owe my former bodyguard that much.

"I've never been sure of anything more in my life."

Something warm and fuzzy blankets me. "Dancing. I want to go dancing tonight."

"Then it's a date."

I hang up and start writing. The words pour out of me. I haven't felt inspired like that in a while. Later, I shower and get ready for dinner. In the dressing room, I slide hangers one by one, inspecting every dress I'd hidden away years ago. Blake never let me wear bold designs unless it was for him—his private little theater where my body was the costume. Eventually, I'd given up on wearing them in public, so I tossed them far in the back.

My fingers pause on one I'd nearly forgotten. Hot pink, plunge neckline, a high slit that leaves nothing to the imagination. My favorite.

I tug it forward, but the fabric catches on something at the back panel of the wardrobe. Frowning, I push the other dresses aside and reach in. My hand presses against the wood, and instead of the solid resistance, it shifts. Gives.

"What the fuck?"

Heart pounding, I push it open and cross over. The narrow passage leads into the room next door. Blake's room. Tristan's after him.

Have I just walked out of a secret door in my own closet? I turn on the lamp next to the bed and stand in the middle of the room, dumbfounded. Did Blake build this? A way to spy on me? To sneak into my room when he was no longer allowed into my bed? Is that how he got in there the night he violated me with his own gun?

"You sick bastard." I try to breathe, but the air is stale, as if it's been locked for years, yet a chill crawls up my spine. Suddenly, the feeling of being watched is back.

A draft stirs the air, brushing against my skin. I spin on my heels, searching the room for ghosts. "Is someone here?"

Of course, silence answers me.

I run my hands through my wet hair. "Blake is dead, Reagan. What the hell are you doing?" That's when I see it.

On the meticulously made bed, placed like an offering on an altar, lies a piece of paper.

My pulse skitters as I take a step closer, every nerve in me screaming not to.

I slap a hand over my mouth when a butterfly flies out of the piece of paper. "No. No."

This isn't real. I fell asleep when I was writing, and I'm having a nightmare. But when my quivering fingers unfold the dark note, I realize what I see is so very real.

> *Nothing is what it seems*
> *XOXO, little butterfly*

Under it, there's a pasted photo that shows Blake and RJ together, laughing like old friends. They both have their Miami PD shields on.

The room spins. The note falls on the bed. Blake and RJ knew each other. They worked together.

Changing last names for security reasons is more common in our field than you think. For me, I had to change it because of what happened with my partner here in Miami. There was an incident. He got involved in something dirty and left the force. I had to transfer under an alias until it's resolved.

I gulp. RJ and Blake didn't just work together. Blake was his partner. The dirty cop who left the force.

I've figured out who the stalker is. He's not working alone.

What if Tristan was right? What if… My date with RJ flashes in my head.

There was this girl that I met so many years ago. She…stole my heart without so much of a word. But I didn't let myself believe my feelings for her were true. This kind of love couldn't be real. So I let her go, just like that. Watched her fall for someone else, and I didn't lift a finger to earn her love.

After years of pain, despair and loneliness, I learned my lesson and decided that if I ever came across something remotely close to how I felt about that girl, I wouldn't let her go, no matter what it takes.

"Oh no, no, no, please no." Did I get this right? Is RJ—

A sound behind me curdles the blood in my veins. I don't turn, terrified, not of the unknown, but of what I know I'll see.

"Missed me, little butterfly?"

I run for the door, but a force hurls me and knocks me flat on my back. The butterfly mask catches the lamplight, that horrible beautiful

face that has haunted my dreams.
    The last thing I see before everything goes black.

To be continued…

Thanks for reading book 2 in The Storyteller's Bodyguard series
Preorder book 3, the finale, Z for Butterfly Man
Please leave a review

Special Edition Hardback of this book is available on https://njadelbooks.com

For more stalker books read
The Italian Obsession
Furore and Tirone duet

P.S. in this book, there are quotes from my favorite movie, The Fight Club. It also has references to imaginary books/characters AND real ones I've written.

Interested to find out who they are, read them here:
Enzio and Bianca: The Italian Marriage
Dom: The Italian Dom
Tino: The Italian Obsession
Mad Dog and Vixen: Whisper of Shadow and Bone
Dusty and Cammie: Dusty and Cameron duet

Also by N.J. Adel

Dark Mafia Romance
Forbidden Cruel Italians

The Italian Marriage
The Italian Obsession
The Italian Dom
The Italian Son

Steamy Forbidden Contemporary Romance
Off-Limits Italians

The Italian Heartthrob
The Italian Happy Ever After

The Night Skulls MC series
Furore
Tirone
Dusty
Cameron
Night Skulls Mayhem

Standalone MC Romance
Savage Crown

N.J. ADEL

Romantasy

Veils of Desire and Darkness

Curse of Blood and Moon
Whisper of Shadow and Bone
Ballad of Fire and Fae
Court of Heaven and Hell

Psychological Thriller Romance
The Storyteller's Bodyguard
You Will Be Mine
XOXO Little Butterfly
Z for Butterfly Man

About the Author

N. J. Adel, the author of Forbidden Cruel Italians, Night Skulls MC and Veils of Desire and Darkness series is a cross genre romance author. From chocolate to books and book boyfriends, she likes it DARK and SPICY. Mafia bosses, psycho anti-heroes, bikers, rock stars, dirty Hollywood heartthrobs, supes, smexy guards and men who serve. She loves it all.

She is a loather of cats and thinks they are Satan's pets. She used to teach English by day and write fun smut by night with her German Shepherd, Leo. After Leo passed away, she only writes dark and twisted books.

www.ingramcontent.com/pod-product-compliance
Lightning Source LLC
Chambersburg PA
CBHW022258310726
48973CB00001B/119